ARNE

A SKÖLL RANCH SHIFTER ROMANCE
BOOK TWO

A SAMSON

Copyright © 2024 by Avery Samson

All rights reserved.

No part of this book may be reproduced or transmitted in any form or by any means, electronic or mechanical, including photocopying, recording or by any information storage and retrieval system without the written permission of the author, except for the use of brief quotations in a book review.

Without in any way limiting the author's exclusive rights under copyright, any use of this publication to "train" generative artificial intelligence (AI) technologies to generate text is expressly prohibited. The author reserves all rights to license uses of this work for generative AI training and development of machine learning language models.

This book is a work of fiction. Names, characters, places, and incidents either are products of the author's imagination or are used fictitiously. Any resemblance to actual persons, living or dead, events, or locales is entirely coincidental.

Editor: My Brother's Editor

Cover Designer: Rachel McCarthy

Cover Photo: Emma Jane Photography

Arne
Derived from Old Norse for eagle.

Ulvmand Family
Sten
Freja
Roar
Dane
Tani
Arne
Erik
Thyra
Aksel

AUTHOR'S NOTE

This is the continuing story of the Ulvmand family, a family of shifters. In book one, I tell in depth how they became shifters in the ancient world. In case you haven't read book one, I've included this story at the end of this book.

You can find it in the table of contents listed as "Origin Story." It can be read at any time without spoiling the story. If you read book one, it's copied verbatim at the end. There's no need to read it again. Unless you want to. Then knock yourself out.

Avery

CONTENTS

Seven in the morning wasn't considered early in Arne's line of work, but just once he wouldn't mind sleeping in. Especially when it was cold enough outside to see the breath leaving his horse's nostrils in mighty snorts. However, it was the middle of the workweek, and the sooner he got to work, the sooner he would be done.

November always brought with it the threat of poachers. He still had a couple of months before he had to worry about calving, but that didn't mean they needed the problem of unlicensed hunters running around the cattle with guns.

Cody, the game warden, had his hands full trying to govern the rest of the county, so Arne was on his own to patrol the family ranch. Not that he was looking for poachers today. He was hunting the hole in the fence the cattle were using to move to a different pasture.

It seemed like he spent half of his time fixing fences on the eighteen thousand acres in Southeastern Oklahoma where his family has called home since his great-grandfather moved from Denmark after a brief layover in Minnesota.

His mother and father still lived in the big house that his grandparents built down the road. It had been added on to over the years to accommodate their growing family. Arne was square in the middle of five kids including his two older brothers, Roar and Dane, a younger brother, Erik, and sister, Thyra.

Dane lived with his wife, Tani, in the only other house on the ranch. He was in charge of crop farming, which meant he spent half of his time repairing his equipment in the large shop behind their parents' house.

Roar had chosen to follow a different path, becoming the controller for the local university several towns over. His younger brother, Erik, was still in college on a football scholarship which just left Thyra at home. She was a junior in high school this year.

Arne rubbed his hands together entering the tack room. He had decided to take his gelding to check the fence lines this morning. It wasn't as fast as using one of the ATVs, but he would be able to cover more acreage.

Sliding his saddle and pad off the rack, he walked back into the chilly fall wind to finish tacking up. Once he had the horse ready, he swung up and pointed the animal toward the south. He figured he could get in several miles before heading back for lunch.

After two hours, he had only found a few places requiring repairs. Having brought some supplies like pliers and wire stays with him, he was able to do a quick fix to all of them. The cattle looked healthy. He fed them all yesterday and would be back tomorrow to do it all over again.

He and his horse, Elmo, rounded the point on top of the

hill with nowhere left to check but the bottoms. He would just use marking tape to mark anywhere that required more repair so he could return with his side-by-side full of fencing supplies to fix it after lunch.

"Alright, buddy, do we feel lucky?" he asked, reining the horse in at the top of the hill. "Well, do we?" The horse snorted before throwing his head. "I think you're the only one that ever appreciates my jokes. Okay, lead on."

He pointed Elmo over the side and gave the horse his head. They walked down parts of the hill and slid down others. Finally, they were almost at the bottom.

They had just made it to level ground again when he felt the air change as something went by him in a blur. Had he been expecting trouble, he probably could have stayed on the big sorrel when the horse reared up feeling the same disturbance. Instead, he went off the back and landed hard on the ground.

"Whoa," he yelled at the horse when he caught his breath. It hadn't gone too far having been trained to stand still in the pasture until Arne came back to him. Its whole body quivered, however, as it watched something in the trees.

Arne sat up and squinted at where the horse was looking. Lying not a hundred feet away was a young deer with a bolt from a crossbow in it. He crouched behind one of the trees hunting for where the bolt had come from. Suddenly, he saw someone stand from the brush and run.

"Oh hell no," he growled before taking off after them. "You'd better fucking run," he shouted. He'd be damned before letting someone shoot at him while poaching one of his deer, then get away. Crashing through the underbrush, he caught a glimpse of someone running ahead of him.

Arne had been fast enough in high school to be chosen

as the anchor on most of the relay teams, and a few years of age hadn't slowed him down much. Breaking through the trees into the open bottom, he gained quickly on whoever was in front of him.

When he had bridged the distance to just an arm's length, he reached out, grabbed a hold of the back of their coat, and brought them both to the ground. They landed hard, but he kept a grip on the poacher as they kicked to get free.

A small boot landed a blow to his chest before he could pin the legs down. When he finally got a hold of the other guy's knees, he found a fist aimed at his head. Trying to stop this poacher had turned into a wrestling match worthy of the WWE.

Arne finally managed to wrap his arms around the guy's chest. "Son of a bitch, hold still," he snarled as an elbow made contact with his nose. Straddling the poacher, Arne rolled over until he was on his back with the other person in a headlock. He tightened his grip around their neck and placed a couple of punches to the side of their head until he felt them go slack on top of him.

Flipping the stranger over on his stomach, Arne fished out a piece of tie rope to secure his arms behind his back. Walking back to his horse, he pulled out another tie rope and bound the poacher's legs.

"Damn, horse. I think he broke my nose." He wiped the blood flowing from his nose with the back of his glove. Grabbing the poacher by the back of his coveralls, he lifted him off the ground and flopped him in front of the saddle. With his horse still jumpy, it took more skill than usually necessary to secure him with his billet straps.

"Give me a second to field dress that deer. No reason for it to go to waste." He walked over to the deer and made quick work out of it. Dragging it back across to his horse, he tied it to the back of his saddle.

"Now, where in the hell am I supposed to sit?"

Elmo stomped his foot on the ground.

"I guess we should make sure our poacher is still breathing first." Holding the reins, he walked to the other side of the horse. "Hey, buddy. You still alive?"

It was hard to tell how they were doing inside all the layers of clothes. Arne reached up and pulled off the balaclava the poacher was wearing. Long dirty-blond hair fell out of it. He stared at it as it cascaded down the side of his horse's front leg.

He slowly squatted next to the horse. Gently, he held up their head. "Shit, Elmo. I've knocked out a woman. Now what are we supposed to do?" The horse bent his head until he could nudge Arne with it. "Wait here," he ordered.

He walked back to where he saw her rise from the bramble. Poking around in the bushes, he didn't find anything but some extra bolts.

"Where did you come from?" he mumbled. Taking a slow look around, he didn't see an ATV or other way she got here. It was a long hike from the edge of their property. Rarely did someone just poaching a deer venture quite this far in. They usually stuck to the edges of the property where it was easier to disappear after they got their game.

He walked halfway back to where he tackled her to collect the crossbow. She had tossed it during the chase to get away. There were no identifying markings on it. He slung it over his shoulder and walked back.

"This makes no sense, Elmo. She has to come from somewhere, but damn if I can figure out where."

Jinn felt disoriented when she woke up. The fog in her head made it hard to remember what had happened. She had been trying to kill them something to eat when a small deer crossed her sights. They were so hungry anything would have worked at that point. She had carefully aimed her crossbow at it and pulled the trigger. Then the rest came rushing back.

She had failed to notice the man on his horse enter her line of sight until she turned loose of the bolt. Panicking that she hit him, she rose up from her hiding spot to check on him only to be caught by his piercing blue gaze. She had only frozen for a moment but it had been enough to give him an advantage. She put up a good fight when he caught her, but based on her aching face, he had fought back. Laying perfectly still, she tried to listen in the hope of scoping out her situation.

"I know you're awake, you're holding your breath."

Her heart started to hammer hearing the voice across the room. Slowly she opened her eyes. She was lying on a couch in what appeared to be a mobile home. Her eyes roamed over a lounge chair, large television, and a scuffed coffee table before coming to land on the man standing in a small open kitchen.

Jinn immediately started to fight whatever he had tied her up with. She landed on the floor between the couch and coffee table with a painful thud.

Rounding the kitchen bar, he walked to the couch and wrestled her back onto it. She tried to fight him, but there was little she could do while bound. She couldn't help but smile a little looking at the black forming just below his eyes and the butterfly bandages holding his nose closed. At least she got in a blow or two before being overwhelmed.

She fought with her bonds a few more minutes before giving up with an angry growl.

"By all means, keep fighting," he said, sitting on the coffee table. "I have all day. Whenever you want to tell me what you were doing, I'm happy to untie you. I can't wait to hear this." She glared at him. He would get nothing out of her unless it was the sharp end of a knife.

"I tell you what," he continued. "If you promise not to kick me." He lifted his shirt to show her the bruises forming on his ribs. "Or bite me." He pointed to his arm that had a large gauze bandage covering it. She didn't even remember doing that. Good, maybe he would die of sepsis. "Or elbow me in the face." That answered the question of the bruising under his eyes and the taped nose. "I'll untie you."

She narrowed her eyes at him. It couldn't be that easy; he was luring her into a trap. It was always a trap. They lured you in with their charm before stripping everything from you. She wouldn't fall for it this time. Never again.

"On second thought, maybe not."

She sighed in resignation. It was no use, you escaped one and the next one was always waiting. He stood and walked back to the table.

"Are you hungry? You're barely more than skin and bones, although you fight like a fucking cougar. His icy gaze met hers again. "I made some mac and cheese. It's not much, but I could hear your stomach growl the entire way back."

She had to get away from him. Someone was counting on her to come back. She knew that the food he offered wouldn't be free. He would demand something in return, something that she swore she would never allow to happen again.

He walked back to the coffee table and sunk down

holding a bowl of something that smelled amazing. It had her mouth watering in a matter of seconds.

Carefully, he scooped some into a spoon and blew on it. When he deemed it cool enough, he held it up to her mouth. She wasn't eating anything he made. Clamping her lips tight, she snarled back at him. With an infuriatingly indifferent shrug, he popped the spoon into his own mouth. Her stomach let out a loud growl of protest.

Would it really hurt to have just a little bit? He scooped up another bite, cooled it, and held it out to her. This time she opened her mouth. He carefully slid the spoonful onto her tongue. It would have been impossible to hold in the moan that escaped her throat when the flavors exploded in her mouth.

"See, I'm not too shabby of a cook." He placed the bowl on the table in front of her. Slowly, he reached toward her.

She couldn't control the flinch when he began to untie her wrist. Somewhere in the back of her mind, she knew she should quickly untie her ankles and run before he could entrap her here, but fierce hunger, brought on by days without food, overran her common sense. The second her hands were free, she snatched up the bowl.

"You might want to slow down," the man suggested.

She knew she should. So much creamy decadence on an aching stomach could only end up one way. Her stomach started to churn; she needed to find a bathroom fast. The man was suddenly gone as she tried to rise from the couch. Her bound ankles made it impossible to walk.

Right as she felt the macaroni making its way back up, a bucket was shoved under her head. Strong hands gathered up her hair as she heaved. She was so exhausted by the time it was over, she forgot about using the opportunity to get free. He took her arm, helping her back onto the couch. Calmly, he walked back into the kitchen.

"You must really be starving," he said when he returned. "Here, these should settle better in your stomach. We'll work up to more."

Taking the bucket, he handed her a sleeve of plain crackers. He also handed her a bag of peas which she looked at curiously. Was she supposed to eat the frozen peas with the crackers? He nodded to the bruises on the side of her face. Gently, he moved the peas to cover them.

"I'm Arne. Had I known you were a woman, I would never have hit you. I'm sorry."

She studied him as she munched on the crackers. He was being too nice to her. It was becoming worrisome that she couldn't see what game he was playing.

"You're pretty good with a bow," he added, sitting back down in a chair. "Next time though, I would appreciate it if you'd make sure I'm not between you and the deer." He smiled at her as if he was trying his best to put her at ease.

"It was a shock when I pulled off your balaclava to find a mass of golden-colored hair. I'm not sure my ego can handle getting my ass kicked by a woman." He grinned for a second before his face fell. "I've never hit a woman before, though. I'm sorry about that."

He was lying. They all lied. She had learned that over and over.

"Where is it?" she asked.

"So you *can* speak."

"Where. Is. It?" She had to find that deer. She began desperately trying to untie her ankles. They needed that deer to survive. It would give them enough food for a month. Her frustration grew when she couldn't get her legs free. Jumping up, she tripped over the coffee table.

Knowing she would hit the ground thanks to her stupidity, she threw out her hands and closed her eyes.

Right as she felt the floor racing up to meet her, a strong pair of arms wrapped around her waist pulling her back on her feet. Spinning her around, Arne sat her down in the chair. He kneeled in front of her to untie her legs.

"Slow down, sweetheart. You're going to hurt yourself." He shook his head as he worked the knot out, freeing her legs. "The deer is hanging outside. I'll take you home, and you can come back to get it." No doubt expecting to be kicked in the face as she sprang to her feet. He wrapped his arms around her legs. This time she fell over him taking them both to the ground.

"Please, don't kick me," he said, lying on his back with his legs wrapped around hers.

"Just let me go," she said, struggling. She felt him slowly relax his grip and scrambled away to crouch against the wall. He was between her and the door. She would keep her back to the wall and wait for her opportunity. If only she still had her knife on her, but he had helped himself to that also. What else would she have to give up to get away?

"What has you so spooked?" Arne asked. "I promise I won't hurt you. I haven't yet, and I've had plenty of opportunities." She thought about that as she watched him slowly stand up. True, he had had plenty of chances to do his worst. He had knocked her out and tied her up after all. But for some reason, he had only wanted to feed her. "Let me give you a ride home." He backed against the far wall so she could reach the door.

"I need the deer," she said in a whisper.

"Okay. I can take you and the deer, but you'll have to tell me where you live."

She nodded, rising to her feet. "We'll have to take your horse. Back to where I was."

His eyes narrowed, and his head cocked slightly to the left, but he remained silent. He considered her for a moment before he shrugged. Gathering up the bowls, he set them in the sink to be washed later. She followed him outside to where he had left the horse tied up. He lowered the deer to the ground.

"This is Elmo," he said.

She desperately wanted to take a moment to stroke the horse's nose, but she needed to stay focused. Arne tied the deer in front of his saddle and swung up. He offered a hand to help her swing up behind him. She debated her situation one last time before taking his hand. She was out of choices, and they desperately needed the food.

TWO

Arne had always liked living here. The nearest town was small, the summers were amazingly hot, and it rained a lot, but overall it was a peaceful world to live in. They grew up riding horses, and Arne had always enjoyed riding out through the pastures.

But there was something about the woman riding behind him that made it so much better. When she slid her arms around his waist, he shivered. Not in a figurative way, but an actual tremor raced through his body.

He had spent years teasing Dane about doing the same thing every time his brother was near Tani. But Dane had known her since elementary school.

Arne didn't even know what this woman's name was. Other than the fact she fought like a rabid bobcat, he knew nothing about her. He had fully intended to call Cody to come haul her off, but his conscience couldn't let the skinny, scared woman be arrested. He would just return her to her home with a stern warning.

"If you don't give me something to call you, I'm going to just start throwing names out. I'm starting with Rapunzel."

"That's a horrible name," she said after a few minutes.

"Yeah, you strike me as more of Merida. You know, from the movie Brave."

"I saw that, on the television." Her voice sounded way too excited about a cartoon princess movie. "You like princess movies?" Now he could feel her smirking at him.

"I have a little sister. If my younger brother, Erik, wasn't around, guess who was next on the list to sit with her at the movies? Erik hid a lot, and I can guarantee you neither Dane nor Roar would be caught dead sitting through a princess movie. Thyra got hung up on Brave." They rode for a while in silence. Arne had almost given up when he heard her speak softly.

"Jinn."

"What?"

"My name is Jinn."

"Like short for Jennifer or something?"

"No, J-I-N-N. As in Arabic for a genie."

"I like it. It's different," he said.

"More different than Arne?"

"Arne is just weird. Jinn is a badass name." They rode a few more minutes in silence.

"Where does Arne come from?"

"It's Norse for eagle. It's not a bad name, but everyone mispronounces it constantly. Don't even get me started on the many different ways it can be misspelled. Hold on." Jinn tightened her grip on Arne as they started down the hill. Arriving at the bottom where he had wrestled her into submission, he pulled the horse to a stop. She slid off the back of the horse in one fluid leap.

"Thank you," she said. She began untying the deer from the billets.

"Wait. I'm just going to follow you anyway. Let me get

that deer the rest of the way to your truck." He slid off of Elmo and pushed her hands away from the saddle. She growled at him. "I promise I'm not a threat. I just want to make sure you get back okay."

She studied him with narrowed eyes just long enough to make him shift his weight from one foot to another.

"There's no way you can carry this by yourself," he added.

Finally after a slow perusal down his body and back, she shrugged. "I think you're more of a threat than either one of us realize yet." Turning around, Jinn pushed through the undergrowth. Taking that as an invitation, Arne pulled the horse behind them through the undergrowth.

"So where are you parked?" he asked.

She looked over her shoulder at him. He could tell she was debating how much to tell him. Never had he known a woman so distrusting of him. She was a lot like the skittish deer she had shot. He waited patiently while she deliberated about him. Finally, she squared her shoulders meeting his gaze.

"I walked. From the other side of that hill." She pointed toward the south.

"Alright then," he answered, looking in the direction she pointed. "Why walk when you can ride, I always say."

Climbing back on the horse, he reached for her hand again, swinging her back up behind him when she took it. He did that weird shiver thing again when she wrapped her arms around him. They rode for another fifteen minutes as she issued short directions to Arne, until they came upon the old shack where she was staying.

"Why did we stop here?" he asked.

Without answering, Jinn slid off the back of the horse. She was reaching for the ties holding the deer on the front of the saddle, when there was a fierce roar behind her. Elmo reared again, knocking her to the ground. He managed not to get tossed on the ground this time. Jumping off, he made it to her side just as another woman ran at him, swinging her fists.

"What the fuck," he growled fending off her weak blows. He caught her wrist, holding her back before Jinn could regain her feet.

"No," Jinn screamed, prying at his fingers. "Don't touch her."

As if stung by some invisible force, he immediately turned the girl loose, taking a step back.

"*What* is going on?" he asked loudly.

Jinn pulled the girl behind her. She flinched as if she expected him to hit her. When nothing happened, she opened her eyes; her golden gaze meeting his glacial one.

"Start explaining," he said, realizing he had to treat them like skittish colts.

Ignoring him, she turned to pull the half-eaten package of crackers out of her coat. "It's okay," she told the girl.

She grabbed the crackers and began shoving a handful into her mouth.

"Slow down," Jinn gently admonished her. "They'll just come back up. Here, I brought you some water too." She produced the rest of her unfinished water bottle. "Go inside, I'll be there in a second."

The girl looked warily at him until Jinn gave her a careful push.

"Go on."

They watched as she disappeared back into the tiny room.

"Just give us until tomorrow, then we'll be gone. Please,

Arne." Jinn walked slowly toward him until she could lay her hand on his chest.

Seductively, she began to run her hand downward. He caught her wrist stopping her progression. Her eyes met his in desperation. He felt even more confused than before. Everything about this woman confused him. She dropped to her knees, rocks cutting into her knees.

"What are you doing?" he growled.

"Please," she whispered, her eyes shone with the tears threatening to spill down her cheeks. "I'll do anything you want, just let us leave." She tugged on his hand, but he held her wrist tightly.

His gaze ventured to the shack as he tried to put together what was happening. When he looked back down at her, he found tears streaming down her face.

"Please, I'll suck it good. Just don't hurt her."

"So, you think you have to give me a blow job so I won't molest what has to be a teenager?" he asked. He felt the disbelief crawl up from his belly. What had he done to make her think this?

"Here," he said, turning her loose. Walking to his horse, he untied the deer and pulled it off his saddle. Throwing the deer in front of her, he swung back up onto Elmo. "Stay as long as you want." Spurring his horse, he rode off up the hill without looking back.

ARNE SLAMMED the door to his house hard enough to rattle the windows. It had taken him almost an hour to ride back to his parents' house, put the horse up, and drive home. He was still furious.

Hanging his coat up by the door, he stomped into the

kitchen to grab a beer from the refrigerator. What in the fuck had he done to make her think he would exchange safety for sex? Sure, he had tackled her, knocked her out, and tied her up. It wasn't the most stellar start, but at no time had he done anything except try to help her after that.

He slumped down on the couch, turning on the television. Flipping through the channels, his mind still boiled with indignation. And what did she think he was going to do to that other woman? Woman, that was a generous term. She couldn't have been any older than his sister. Wash off all of the grime, and he bet she was even younger than that.

Did they come into contact with a lot of men who would happily rape a girl before letting them move on? The thought made his stomach turn. The thought of his sister trading sex for one more night in a tiny cement cell with no heat or water was unfathomable.

"Fuck!" he yelled into the empty house.

There was no way his conscience would allow him to let them stay in that unsafe squalor while he slept in his warm bed with a full stomach. He had been raised better than that.

Turning off the television, he walked to the front door. After pulling his boots and coat back on, he grabbed the keys to his truck. Jerking the door open, he ran straight into his brother, Dane.

"What in the hell?" Dane said, trying to hang onto the top of an infant car seat. When the immediate crisis had been averted, Dane turned to look at his younger brother.

"Sorry, man," Arne said.

"You wake this baby, you just think you're sorry," Dane growled. "Where are you going in such a fucking hurry?"

"Just needed to run an errand. What are you doing here?"

"It's Tani's night out with her work friends." Arne mentally rolled his eyes. Dane came over every other week at the same time to hang out while his wife ate with her friends at one of the only two restaurants in town.

In the beginning, their evenings together usually resulted in him bouncing Aksel in his arms while Dane slept on the couch. Now they took turns holding the baby like a football while watching a game. Arne moved so Dane could walk into his house.

"What errand?" Dane asked as Arne hung up his coat again. Tossing his keys on the small table by the door, he pushed off his boots before walking into the kitchen. When he returned with two bottles of beer, Arne had Aksel out of the car seat cooing to him on the couch. "Do I need to help you with any fence repairs tomorrow?"

"I'm still checking it. I'll let you know," Arne answered. Settling the baby between them on the couch, he picked up the remote. He managed to ignore his brother's appraising look for as long as he could. "What?" he finally asked.

The problem with living most of his life with a brother who was only a few years older than him was, that brother could read him like a book. He really didn't need to try and explain what was happening with Jinn before he could even understand it himself.

"What the hell happened to your face? What have you been up to."

"Came off my horse and I'm not up to anything," Arne answered, trying hard to focus on a game show. Dane let out his trademark harrumph. Arne rolled his eyes. That had stopped working on him somewhere around fifteen.

Dane didn't need to know all of his business any more

than he wanted every detail about his and Tani's life. He had heard enough of their "business" when he and Dane still lived together to last a lifetime.

By the time Dane left for his own home, it was late. Arne waited until he could no longer see his brother's tail-lights before grabbing his keys off of the entry table again. Walking quickly to his truck, he brought the big engine to life with a roar. He knew it would take him close to ten minutes to reach the old mine shack.

The building, if you could call it that, had been used to store dynamite for the old mining office when that side of the ranch was still a rock quarry. It consisted of one tiny room with no windows and a heavy metal door.

The water nearby had been shut off when the crusher was abandoned in the sixties, as had the electricity. It had been built out of cement block and was a testament to the builders that it was still standing. The roof leaked like a sieve, and the last Arne remembered, there was a family of raccoons living in it.

The four Ulvmand brothers had spent many hours in this old room when they were kids growing up. It had become a sort of clubhouse for them. They had stashed their comic books there, then their contraband Playboys later. He hadn't been inside in probably seven years. Once Dane left for college, he nor Erik went down there anymore.

Pulling up outside the door of the shack, he hopped out of the truck. Knocking on the door, he waited for Jinn to open it. When his knocks went unanswered, he pushed open the door. It just took a second to see there was no one inside.

They couldn't be far away, however, since there were a handful of personal items near a pallet made out of old brush and a blanket. With one more look around, Arne stepped back outside trying to see any movement in the trees around him.

"Jinn?" he called out. "It's just me, Arne." He listened, but no one answered. "Jinn, you can't stay out here tonight. It's supposed to freeze." Still nothing. Reaching into his truck, he turned off the ignition and killed the lights. "Fine, we'll just all freeze out here together."

Leaning against the hood of his truck, he settled in to wait her out. He could feel her watching him from nearby. After ten more minutes, his patience began to run thin.

"Think of the girl with you. She's not going to last out here all night." He wasn't beyond playing dirty if he had to.

"It would be better than going with you," Jinn's voice said from just slightly to his left. He smiled to himself but didn't dare to move for fear of spooking her even worse.

"How can you say that? All I'm offering is a place to sleep where you'll both be warm and safe. Nothing more." The silence engulfed him again as he waited for her to respond. "You'll both catch pneumonia out here." Finally he saw movement out of the corner of his eye. Slowly, Jinn stood up from behind the bush they were cowering in.

"You swear to me you won't touch her?" she asked.

What had these women gone through? He had an overwhelming urge to find out and protect them from whatever it was ever happening again. He turned to face her.

"I swear on my mother's honor, I won't touch either of you," he answered.

Jinn reached down, taking the girl's hand. Moving in the dim light of a small lantern Arne held in his hand, she turned the girl loose.

"Go pack our things," she said. When the girl disappeared back inside the tiny hut, Jinn walked over to him with her head held high. "You can do whatever you want to me," she said so only Arne could hear her. "But you touch one hair on Kip's head, and I swear I'll kill you."

He assumed he should be surprised, but at this point, he was beyond letting anything this woman said shock him.

"I know they're just words, but I promise, all I want to do is help," he answered.

She nodded without conviction before walking to the shack. Arne could feel anger bubbling up inside of him at whoever had taught her that men were to be feared.

When they reappeared carrying two backpacks, he instinctively reached out to get them. He froze when Kip flinched away from him. Jinn calmly handed him her bag before easing Kip's off of her shoulders. Slowly, Arne lifted them into the back of his truck.

"Sorry, I just have a single cab truck. Are you okay sitting next to me?" he asked Jinn.

With a nod, she climbed into the middle seat, pulling Kip up behind her to sit against the door. Arne closed the door and walked around to the driver's side. Sliding in, he felt a shiver rack his body when his thigh touched hers.

He saw her give him an odd look as he started the engine. It couldn't mean anything, could it? He barely knew the woman. He knew virtually nothing about her life. For all he knew, she already had a man in her life. Although, based on her response to him, if she did, he wasn't a good man.

"Is Kip short for anything?" he asked, trying to put them at ease.

They would be back at his house in less than ten minutes, and he wasn't looking forward to how long it would take to talk them inside.

"Kipling," Jinn answered, staring out the front windshield.

"That's a pretty cool name. It ranks right up there with Jinn." He caught the corner of Jinn's mouth twitch up slightly. "I should come up with something better than Arne. My first name isn't much better. Alfred. I'm literally A.A. Ulvmand. Stupid."

He knew he was rambling, but he couldn't think of any other way to put them at ease. He had always been able to talk his way into or out of anything.

"I like Arne," Kip said quietly.

He looked over at her, his eyebrows almost lost in his hair in surprise.

"It means eagle in Norse," Jinn said.

It wasn't lost on him that they had a death grip on each other's hands. Fuck, he hated this. It shouldn't have to be terrifying to accept a little help when you need it.

"We read about the Vikings," Kip answered, quickly taking a glance at him before turning to look back out the windshield.

"Yeah, my family is originally from Denmark. I don't look much like a Viking, though. My older brother, Roar, does. He's this big, burly guy with a red beard. It makes the fact he's an accountant hilarious.

"My sister, Thyra, looks a little like one, too. She wears a long braid and acts like a warrior half the time. I think you're probably close to her age, Kip. She's sixteen. She got her driver's license this summer. If we see her come toward us, we're hitting the bar ditch." He laughed.

"I'm fourteen," the girl said after a few minutes.

"Kip," Jinn warned. "Remember what I told you?"

The girl turned to stare out the side window. Not wanting to rock the boat any further, Arne drove in silence back to his house. Pulling up in front, he put the truck in park and turned off the engine. He grabbed their packs and waited for them to join him at the door. He could see Jinn say something to Kip before she opened the door. With trepidation he could feel, they followed him inside.

"It's not much, but then you already know that, Jinn. Let me show you around then I'll make something to eat." He kicked off his boots and hung up his coat watching them do the same.

"So the living room and kitchen," he said, waving an arm in their direction. "Feel free to eat anything you find in the kitchen. The laundry is in the back of the pantry, there's detergent under the cabinet if you want to wash your clothes." He pulled open a door at the back of the kitchen pointing to the washer.

"My bedroom is at the end of the hall, the spare one is here." He opened up another door showing them the spare room. It had a set of twin beds with a nightstand between and a dresser on one wall. He moved farther down the hall, so they could see inside without him crowding them.

"The bathroom is across from the bedroom. There're fresh towels in the cabinet. Just make yourselves at home."

Neither woman said a word.

"Okay, I'll just lay out some extra clothes in case you want them." Turning toward his bedroom, he heard the bathroom door slam shut and the lock engaged. He blew out a breath. All he could do was offer them a safe place to stay. He couldn't make them trust him.

THREE

Jinn looked around the bathroom of the mobile home. Crossing to the door, she checked it once again to make sure it was locked before turning to Kip. "Let's start with showers, then maybe I can wash up our clothes. Arne said he would leave us something to wear. You get in while I go find him."

Kip stood still looking at her with big eyes.

"Kip, shower."

With a nod, she turned toward the faucets. Waiting until Kip had stepped in, Jinn stuck her head out cautiously. Just because he hadn't done anything yet, didn't mean he wouldn't.

With equal parts trepidation and curiosity, she made her way down the hall to the back room. Slowly pushing open the door, she stepped into Arne's bedroom.

It was obvious a man lived here based on the large bed. She had guessed Arne to be well over six feet so it made sense he would need such a massive place to sleep. Next to it was a matching nightstand covered with a stack of books, a lamp, and a handful of chargers.

Crossing to his dresser, she discovered a framed photo of a large family. Picking it up, she recognized one of the blonde kids as a younger Arne. Replacing it on the dresser, she stooped over to look at a strange-looking contraption. It had bits of metal put together to form something she didn't recognize. More scraps of metal were lying on the dresser waiting to be added.

Quietly pulling out the first drawer of the dresser, Jinn found a mound of unfolded underwear. Definitely a man. The next drawer had an equally unorganized mound of socks. She smiled, sliding it closed.

She had made it as far as the bedroom door when she turned to look back at the nightstand. Her curiosity got the best of her as she crossed back through the room. Reaching down, she pulled open the top drawer.

Now it was really obvious that a man lived here. The drawer contained a few girly magazines, a bottle of lube, a couple graphic novels, and a handful of loose change. The next drawer down was full of odds and ends including an old knife, some jewelry, an iPod, some headphones, and a birthday card.

The remaining drawers looked much the same. The one thing missing were condoms. Before she could put much thought into that glaring anomaly, a deep voice startled her.

"I put a couple different choices for clothes on the bed in the other bedroom," Arne said.

Jinn stood perfectly still as her heart hammered in her throat. He had caught her snooping through his things. How could she be so stupid? She would deserve the beating he gave her.

"We can do a load of your laundry if you want, while you eat," he added.

She slid slowly to her knees, waiting to be punished. It seemed she was always waiting. She was so tired of waiting. Arne watched her for a few more seconds before straightening from where he had been leaning against the doorjamb.

"Well, I'm going to finish supper. Come out whenever you're done."

Arne disappeared back down the hallway. Jinn remained on her knees in disbelief until she heard the water in the bathroom shut off. Knowing Kip would be frightened when she discovered she was still alone, Jinn jumped up and rushed down the hall. Grabbing the clothes out of the spare bedroom, she slipped back into the bathroom.

"Hey, you clean up good," she said, laying the sweats and T-shirt on the bathroom counter.

Kip pulled on the large clothes. She had to roll the pants to keep them up. A towel was wrapped around her wet hair. "I smell like a man now, but it is a definite improvement over what I did smell like," Kip admitted.

They had survived a little over a week now on their own. Jinn agreed, anything would smell better than what she smelled like right now. How Arne had stood to sit so close to her in his truck she didn't know.

"I'll run through the shower, then Arne said we can wash our clothes. He's making us something to eat. Just give me a few minutes."

Kip nodded as Jinn started the water again. She turned the water on as hot as she could stand it before climbing into the shower. For a full five minutes, she simply stood under the steaming water with her eyes closed letting the water wash away the last week.

Even before she had grabbed Kip and ran, she never had

the luxury of a daily hot shower. She intended to enjoy it as long as she could. It would be worth whatever Arne made her do in payment.

Opening her eyes, she found a bottle of shampoo. Sniffing it, she had to agree with Kip. It was definitely the intoxicating aroma that had come from Arne when she was riding behind him. Inhaling deeply, she imagined what it would be like to wake up surrounded by that smell every morning.

It was a dangerous thought. She knew nothing good could come from being around a man. She didn't know where safety and happiness lay, but she was hell-bent to try to find out. For Kip's sake, at least.

She shampooed her long hair twice working the soap through each strand until the water ran clean. Finding his body soap, she repeated the scrubbing on the rest of her body. Only when she literally made her skin squeak did she shut the water off.

Climbing out, she panicked not finding Kip in the bathroom. Where would the girl have gone? Had Arne grabbed her while Jinn was distracted? Wrapping the towel around her body, she barreled out of the room.

Her panic grew when they weren't in the living room. She was spinning around to search the rest of the house when the sound of laughter wafted out of the kitchen. Running around the bar, she slid to a stop.

Kip and Arne were leaning over the washing machine. Kip was looking inside excitedly while Arne measured laundry soap into a little cup. He handed the cup to Kip showing her where it went into the machine. Kip added the soap, closed the little drawer and grinned up at him.

"Perfect. Now push this button. It will wash everything

on warm, which hopefully will get out the dirt but not shrink anything."

Kip pushed the button in before turning back to Arne.

"Great. Push this button to start it."

She did and jumped back when the machine started to hum. Arne laughed.

"It's supposed to make that noise. If you watch in the window, it will start to move."

Kip sank to her bottom in front of the washer.

Arne turned to walk back into the kitchen. He stopped abruptly finding Jinn standing in the middle of the room, water dripping on the floor. She watched as his eyes roamed down her body before snapping back up to her face. His face turned slightly pink before he smiled.

"Are you okay?" he asked, standing perfectly still.

"Yes," she answered. But she wasn't. Not really. She was standing mostly naked in a strange man's kitchen, and he had yet to make a grab at her. What man would pass up sex, pass up beating her for her snooping, and blush at letting his eyes roam for a brief moment? He was certainly not like any man she knew.

"Umm, Kip wandered into the kitchen with an armful of clothes. I was just teaching her how to run the washing machine," he said, waving vaguely behind him.

Kip was sitting near his feet still mesmerized by the machine.

"I'm sorry. I should have..." he stuttered to a stop before running his hands through his hair in frustration. "Fuck, Jinn, I don't know what I should have done. She was curious."

"Kip," Jinn growled, holding out her hand.

Kip flinched but rose up next to Arne before squeezing past him to go to Jinn. Pulling the girl behind her, she returned to the bathroom. Closing the door, she turned to Kip.

"You need to stay with me. We don't know what he's capable of. Remember what I've taught you."

"What if he's capable of being good?"

Jinn scowled at Kip.

"I know," the girl said, rolling her eyes. "You can never trust a man. But, Jinn, what if he's just good and is doing all of this to help us."

What if? No, those questions only led to crushing pain. They would stay here tonight, then be on their way at first light tomorrow.

She finished towel drying her hair then pulled on the black sweatpants and matching Oklahoma State University baseball T-shirt. She had to roll the waist forever to not fall over the extra material. They were soft and warm. The shirt hung to mid-thigh and smelled like Arne.

She wished she could stay in them forever. With a sigh, she hung her towel over the bar. Tomorrow she would leave it all behind for a chance at freedom.

ARNE WAS FRUSTRATED by not really understanding what he kept doing wrong. He had never been the outsider in any situation. He was the brother everyone loved hanging out with, the one with the personality in spades, the one with the reputation of being a playboy throughout his years in high school.

So how was he supposed to handle suddenly being the one that women ran from? Well, one woman anyway. But even one was too many. How did he convince her that he would never hurt either one of them?

With a sigh, he flipped the remaining pancakes onto a plate. It was all he could come up with this late that stood the best chance of staying down. He would have loved to call his mother for advice, but how would he explain bringing two women who were obviously running from something bad, back to his house for the night? Hell, he couldn't even explain it to himself.

He opened the oven to slide the plate of pancakes in to keep them warm. Normally, he would just holler that food was up, but he didn't dare this time. With his luck, they would dive out of a window in their panic to get away from him.

He was finishing the hash browns when Jinn and Kip came into the living room. Arne couldn't decide what he liked more, Jinn in just a towel or in his old baseball workout clothes. Both were now permanently branded on his brain. With a smile, he motioned to the two seats on the other side of the bar.

"I hope you like pancakes," he said, pulling the plate out of the oven. He placed it and another plate with summer sausage on the bar in front of them. Scraping the potatoes into a bowl, he added it to the bar.

"What would you like to drink? I have milk, orange juice, water, soda." He opened the refrigerator, waiting for a response. When he heard none, he looked over his shoulder. "Beer?"

"Milk," Kip said with a giggle.

"Milk is fine. Thank you," Jinn added.

"Good choice," he said. "Fortunately, I went to the store yesterday, so it's fresh." Taking the cap off the jug, he filled both of their glasses. He scowled, finding them both still sitting quietly while they stared at the food. "Eat before it gets cold."

"Aren't you going to eat first?" Jinn asked, lifting her eyes to his.

Had he truly appreciated how incredible her eyes were? They were the color of caramel, but there were gold flecks running through them.

"I've already eaten. My brother, Dane, came over earlier. His wife, Tani, has some sort of work social thing every other week. He and his son hang out here for the evening. Between you and me, I think he just needs babysitting help." When she just sat staring at him, he motioned to the food on the bar. "Please."

Slowly Jinn picked up her fork and reached for a pancake.

"Oh, I'm stupid." Turning back to the refrigerator, he pulled out the butter and syrup. "Can't eat pancakes without this."

Kip watched Jinn closely as she spread butter and syrup on her pancake. She then did the same to hers. Taking a bite, Kip let out a loud moan making Arne laugh.

"I'm glad someone likes my cooking. Dane used to gripe about it all the time."

Soon Kip had filled her plate with a pile of everything offered. She ate like she hadn't eaten in a month. Based on the size of both her and Jinn, Arne wondered if they had. Kip plowed through her food like Jinn had earlier, and he worried it would come right back up. Jinn seemed to have learned her lesson the first time, taking small measured bites.

"That'd be the washer," Arne said when the buzzer went off. Standing up from where he had been leaning against the counter watching Kip start on her second round, he headed toward the laundry area.

"No," Kip yelled, bounding off of her chair. "Let me do it."

Sliding around the end of the bar, she shoved Arne out of the way, beating him into the small room. He laughed and held up his hands as she plowed him into the refrigerator. Looking over at Jinn with concern, he sighed in relief when he saw her fighting a laugh. Maybe, just maybe, he could win her over after all.

"Okay, put everything in the dryer," he said, giving Kip instructions from the doorway. He knew Jinn was keeping a close eye on him, looking for anything that would send up a red flag. It was his goal not to send up a single one.

"I never knew doing laundry was so exciting," he said over his shoulder at her. "Add one of the sheets from that little box," he added, turning back to Kip. "Can everything dry on normal?"

"That's fine," Jinn said, taking another bite of sausage.

He looked back to find Kip had already punched the button that said "normal" on it. She pushed the start button before turning back to Arne with a hopeful look on her face.

"You're a quick study. That much skill demands ice cream," he said with a grin at the girl.

Her eyes grew wide making his heart begin to pound. What had he done wrong this time?

"I've never had ice cream," Kip whispered. She looked at Jinn with so much hope in her eyes, it broke his heart. He saw Jinn nod at him.

"Never had ice cream?" he exclaimed. "That has to be corrected right now."

He pulled open the freezer and leaned in to survey the ice cream choices. Kip leaned in next to him, her eyes even wider. He looked up at her in mock concern. "You're not going to barf later from so much sugar, are you?"

She shook her head vehemently at him before they both looked back into the freezer. "I think, since this is your first ice cream experience, I should scoop you out a little of all of it. If you're going to hurl later, at least make it monumental, I always say."

Arne pulled out the first carton, handing it to Kip to set on the counter. There were four different flavors, he was a single guy after all, so he lined them all up on the counter. Grabbing three bowls and the ice cream scoop, he started digging. He laughed as Kip's eyes continued to grow even wider with each scoop. When her bowl was ready, he added a spoon before handing it to her.

"Go sit on the couch, and we'll find something to watch while we eat."

Grabbing her bowl, she headed toward the living room. Jinn watched her until she had settled on the couch. Kip took a tentative bite of her ice cream. When the girl let out another Oscar-worthy moan, Jinn turned back to him. She really did have incredible eyes.

"I won't even bring up what happens when you add chocolate syrup and pecans to the top. What would you like?" He read off the flavors, and she chose a small bowl of rocky road. Handing her the bowl, he motioned for her to join Kip on the couch.

By the time he joined them in the living room, they had managed to curl up at the farthest end of the couch from where his chair was. They were wrapped in the blanket he kept on the back of the couch. Kip was still hugging the empty ice cream bowl, staring at the television.

Jinn had, with instructions he had called to her from the kitchen, found a show he knew his sister watched. He made it through most of the episode before he found himself drifting off in the chair.

"I've got to get some sleep," he said, pushing himself up. "I've got work in the morning."

Turning off the television, Jinn and Kip stood quickly. He noticed Kip grab Jinn's hand as they moved to follow him.

"Your clothes will be dry in the morning. There are extra blankets in the closet." They continued to follow behind him to the hallway. Stopping at the spare bedroom, he turned around. "Yeah, so let me know if you need anything else. I'll be out early." He didn't understand why they just stood in front of him staring at the floor. With an exasperated huff, he turned, walked into his bedroom and closed the door.

Shit, he hoped he didn't wake up in the middle of the night with a knife sticking out of his chest. The problem with being the fun-loving brother is you're also the impulsive brother. Would Dane bring home some obviously deeply damaged woman he found in the underbrush with a crossbow? No, of course he wouldn't because his brother didn't have a death wish.

Sticking his head back out of his room, he found the hallway clear. He quickly walked to the bathroom. He took a quick shower, brushed his teeth and slid on a pair of pajama pants. His house was great, but his bedroom faced the north and got cold at night.

Listening at the spare bedroom door, he slipped back down the hall when he heard nothing. He flopped onto his bed. If he lived through the night, he could question his choices tomorrow. He was too tired tonight to give a damn.

FOUR

Kip scooted to the edge of the twin bed as close to the window as she could. Jinn had fitted the dining room chair in the corner of the room under the doorknob, hoping to block anyone from surprising them in the night.

Looking around the room, she deemed it as safe as she could get it. Leaving the closet light on, she turned off the overhead light before crawling in bed with Kip.

There were two beds in the room, but Jinn didn't want to risk sleeping through an attack on Kip. Though she was beginning to question her belief that it would be Arne. He hadn't locked Kip in the room and dragged her to his bedroom to work out his frustrations. He hadn't even drank until he was so drunk he could barely walk to his bed either.

She heard him trying to walk quietly down the hallway, but he surprised her when he closed the bathroom door instead of forcing theirs open. He surprised her even more when he went back to his bedroom after finishing in the bathroom.

Was she wrong? Were there good men in this world? No, once she let those doubts start drifting into her mind they were trapped. They needed to leave here as soon as possible. She would just get a few hours of sleep in the warm bed, then they would be on the move. Kip snuggled up against her back as her breathing started to even out. Yeah, just a few hours. She was so tired. What could it hurt?

Jinn was jerked awake by a scream. Throwing the covers back, she sat up, turning to face Kip. The girl was having a nightmare. She had often woken her up in the basement screaming in the throes of a particularly vicious one.

Jinn shook her shoulders, trying to get her to wake up before Arne heard. In the past, she had been dragged out by her hair following one of Kip's dreams and beaten for waking up the house. The one time he had threatened to beat Kip, Jinn had begged him from her knees to beat her instead. It had been a particularly bad beating, but at least Kip had been spared.

"Kip, wake up," she said, fear lacing through her words. "Please, Kip." It was too late. She hugged the frightened girl to her when she heard a thud followed by stomping coming toward them down the hallway. Her arms tightened when the doorknob turned.

"Oww, fuck," she heard Arne say when the door didn't give way. He had obviously banged into it thinking it would open. Fortunately her makeshift lock had held. "God, that hurts." She could hear his muffled voice from the hallway, but strangely, it didn't seem to hold any anger. "Jinn, is everything okay? I heard a scream."

With shaking knees, she turned Kip loose and eased off of the bed.

"No!" Kip said, grabbing at her hand.

"Shh, I have to open the door. He'll just be angrier if he has to break it down."

Kip looked at her with terror. She had sat up in the bed, pulling the covers up to her eyes. Her head was shaking back and forth furiously as tears slipped down her face. Seeing how badly Jinn had been beaten because of the nightmares was almost as bad for Kip.

"Jinn!" he said a little more forcefully.

Taking a breath, Jinn threw her shoulders back and opened the door. The sight that greeted her took her breath away. Arne didn't grab her hair to pull her out of the room. He stood rubbing his tired eyes in nothing but a pair of flannel plaid pants that barely rested on his hips.

"I heard screaming," he repeated, lowering his hands.

She already knew he was the most handsome man she had ever seen before, but like this, he was simply beautiful. She stood frozen as she took a slow perusal of his body.

His blond hair was a mess flopping in his eyes, and he wore a necklace with curious little silver beads around his neck. Her eyes coasted over the tattoos of strange symbols she didn't understand on his muscled chest until they crossed over his rippled abs, his happy trail, his barely covered cock, and all the way to his bare feet. Hearing him clear his throat, her face blazed red as she fell to her knees.

"Goddammit! Stop doing that." He reached down, taking her by her biceps. He pulled her back to her feet before turning her loose. Looking around her, he saw Kip hiding in the covers. "Kip, are you okay?"

"Yes," Kip whispered.

"I'm sorry," Jinn said, at last pulling herself together. "She has nightmares. It won't happen again."

Arne looked down at her then at Kip. Instead of anger, she saw concern etched in his eyes.

"I promise," he said, splitting a look between the two of them. "You're safe here. Do you need anything? Water?"

"No. Please," she said, easing him back out of the room. "I can..." She reached for his pants. "I can help you get back to sleep. Please don't be angry."

Arne stepped back, grabbing the wrist she had managed to sink in the waistband of his pants.

"Jinn!" he said, the frustration thick in his voice. "Look at me."

She slowly picked her head up until her gaze found his.

"Make as much noise as you want, eat everything in my kitchen. Fuck, shoot at me with a crossbow. There is nothing you can do to make me hit you or bend you over. I'm sorry I knocked you out, but you have got to believe me, I thought you were a man." He pulled her hand away from his pants before turning it loose.

"Now, just go back to your room. Try to get some sleep." With a snort, he stomped back into his bedroom and closed the door.

When she walked back into the room, Kip was curled in the corner sobbing. Jinn kneeled down, prying the girl's hands away from her face. Kip had her eyes clamped shut as she rocked back and forth. Slowly, she opened her eyes, searching Jinn's face.

Jinn knew the new onslaught of tears that followed was because of what she found missing this time. There were no new bruises on her face, just the one from that morning. Jinn wrapped Kip back in the covers and hugged her close as the sobs turned into slow rhythmic breathing.

She was so confused by the man down the hall, she no longer knew what to think. Except for this morning, for which he had apologized repeatedly, he had yet to raise a hand to her. He had even turned down her offers of sex twice.

There was something about him that kept drawing her closer. It was dangerous. They needed to run before it was too late. It was the last thought Jinn had as she slowly drifted off. She hadn't even noticed that she never secured the door with the chair the second time.

The next morning, Jinn woke to sunshine streaming through curtains. She stretched lazily before reality hit her. Sitting up quickly, she searched the strange room for Kip. She wasn't there.

Jumping out of bed, she ran down the hallway, screaming her name. She slid to a stop when she found a smiling Kip sitting on the couch in the living room. Her heart pounding, she stared in disbelief as Kip grinned at her holding up a plate of something.

"He calls them blueberry muffins. He let me help make them!" Kip had a plate of buttered muffins she was eating on the couch. The television was on, and she was wrapped up in the blanket they had shared last evening. "He left some for you in the kitchen. They're so good, J."

Jinn looked at the clock on the wall by the front door. Nine o'clock? How had she slept so late? They needed to have been miles from here by now.

"Kip, why didn't you wake me up?"

"He said you were tired, and I should let you sleep," she answered with a shrug. Turning back to the television, she took another bite of the muffin.

"Kip, we need to leave."

The girl just looked back at her with cool eyes.

"Arne said he would teach me how to make my own hamburger if we stayed tonight. Please, Jinn," she pleaded. "It has cheese on it. Cheese!"

Jinn's heart was breaking. Kip should be rolling her eyes at things like eating another hamburger, not pleading for one. She should be attending school, flirting with boys, and hanging out with her friends.

Instead, she had lived on a dirty pallet in a basement for most of her young life. Jinn had managed to teach her basic math and how to read using discarded magazines she found around the house.

"Please."

"Yes. Yes, okay. One more night." She couldn't stand to see the beseeching look in her eyes. Just one more night wouldn't hurt, would it?

ARNE SPENT the rest of the morning deep in thought as he repaired fence. It seemed like every time it rained, this particular fence line fell over no matter how he fixed it. He had majored in animal science in college before returning home to take over responsibility for the family's cattle herd. If it pertained to cows, he handled it.

He also spent his fair share of time sitting behind the wheel of a tractor helping Dane with the farming. In exchange, Dane spent a large amount of his time helping Arne with the cattle work.

"What crawled up your ass? Only one person in this family can be the grouch, and I called dibs on it a long time ago." Arne jumped at the sound of his brother breaking into his reverie. It took him a minute to process what Dane had just asked.

"I'm not a grouch, I could never usurp your crown. Can I not just have a day of quiet introspection?"

"You can't," Dane responded with a smirk. "Roar,

maybe. You, never. Your mouth opens and shit just flies out of it continually." Dane pounded the last T-post back into the ground before tossing the driver into the back of the side-by-side. "Arne?"

"It's nothing. I'm just tired."

Dane was not quite four years older than Arne and seemed to feel he was responsible for his well-being. They had both played baseball in high school as well as college. They had only overlapped one year, but Arne had loved being on the same team as his older brother.

While Dane had fallen in love with his wife in elementary school, never wavering from his devotion, Arne had gotten the reputation as a player with the women. It wasn't an accurate assessment, but he never bothered to correct the image.

"Then, if we're done, I'd like to meet my wife in town for some lunch." Dane and Tani had a new baby at home that kept them up most of the night. Though Dane wasn't the biological father of their son, he was his father in every other way a man could be.

Lately, he tried really hard to be done with his work early so he could spell Tani for a couple of hours before they fell into bed exhausted. She had begun teaching science again at the local high school not long after Aksel was born.

He finished securing the wire to the final post and tossed his pliers into the back before climbing in beside Dane. They drove back to the shop in silence. He ignored his brother's pointed side-eyes. It was still better Dane knew nothing about Jinn and Kip. He would lose his shit.

"Thanks, Dane," Arne said, climbing out of the vehicle. "I'll see you later. Give Tani a hug for me."

"Will do," Dane answered.

Carrying his stuff to his truck, Arne felt the exhaustion climbing up him from being up half the night.

"Hey, Arne."

"Yeah?"

"If something is bothering you, you know you can tell me, right? Whatever it is, I can help."

"I know. But everything's fine. Now go chase your wife around her desk."

With a wave, Dane pulled out of the gate.

Heading back to his home he wondered if he would find anyone still there. He thought the bribe he had baited Kip with was pretty effective, but that might not have been enough to make Jinn hang around. Whatever they were running from, he wanted to know about it before helping them disappear. If it was that bad, he would buy them a ticket to wherever they wanted to go.

Arriving home, he turned off the truck. He sat staring at the front of his house as if it would give him a clue as to what he would find inside. With a sigh, he finally climbed out. Pulling the key out of his pocket, he slid it into the lock and opened the door. He froze just inside taking in the scene playing out in front of him.

Both women were in the kitchen cooking in more of his clothes. He should have pulled more out for them before he left, but he had been too busy trying to teach a teenager how to make breakfast. The stereo by the television was at an impressive volume as they sang along to what was play-ing. Dancing around, they both spun at the same time to find him standing in the doorway.

Freezing at seeing him, the grins on their faces vanished in an instant. Kip ran over to shut off the stereo before flying back over to rejoin Jinn. He took in both women staring back at him. In the daylight, he could see they both had the same long wavy golden hair and matching amber eyes. Something about Jinn, though, had his heart pounding.

"I'm sorry, don't let me interrupt." He wiggled out of his coat and hung it by the back door. Wrestling off his mud boots, he set them on a rug, then unzipped his coveralls. The women watched him closely as if they were waiting for something. "It smells amazing in here. What are you cooking?" The question finally must have knocked them out of their trance.

"We're not sure. You had everything on one of these cards in this little tin," Kip said with a grin.

"Mystery lunch, I love it."

They both watched him with such trepidation; it made him even more tired than he already was. Trying to always say the right thing to keep from scaring them off was exhausting. At least they were still here. Not only were they here, but they seemed to have made themselves reasonably comfortable.

"How long do I have before it's ready?"

"Umm, half an hour?" Jinn asked, consulting the timer on the stove.

"Good, I'll be back." Without waiting to drag out the next thing from Jinn's mouth, he walked down the hall to the bathroom. He washed the grime from the morning off of his hands then ran his wet hands through his hair to try and get it to stay out of his face. His mother was always nagging at him to get it cut, but he liked it messy. That way no one ever expected him to be perfectly put together.

Opening the bathroom door, he made his way to his bedroom. Someone had been busy. His bed was neatly made, there were no clothes on the floor, and everything was dust-free. Pulling out the top drawer of his dresser, he found everything neatly organized. He did not understand her fascination with his room. With an even more disturbing thought, he crossed over to his nightstand. Sure enough, it was all in its proper place.

Turning back around, he saw that all of the pieces of scrap metal sitting on his dresser had been organized by size. He had been piecing together found objects into art since he was a kid. Usually when something was done, he just tossed it into the recycling trailer at their shop to be sold for scrap. Over the years, his mother had managed to rescue a few of his better pieces out of the trailer to adorn her garden. He hadn't even figured out what the current piece was supposed to be yet.

"Jinn!" he yelled. He heard her hurrying down the hall a moment later. He also heard the door to the spare bedroom close with a resounding click. "Did you clean my room?" he asked when Jinn rushed into the room.

She stood trembling for a moment before starting to sink to her knees.

"No," he growled.

She just caught herself on the edge of the bed and straightened back up. He breathed out a frustrated puff.

"I'm not angry," he said for what felt like the two hundredth time. "But you don't have to work while you're staying here."

She remained silent, staring at the bed.

"At least say something. Tell me to fuck off if you want, it's still not going to piss me off."

"What's that?" she whispered, pointing shyly at the dresser.

He felt his frustration siphon away as he followed her hand. At least she hadn't asked what he did with the stuff in the top drawer of his nightstand.

"Here, grab all of the pieces and follow me." He picked up the already assembled piece and carried it to the living room. Jinn joined him shortly, balancing the loose pieces in her shirt. Placing it all on the coffee table, he sorted the extra metal into sizes again. "Kip!" He reminded himself to speak softer when Jinn jumped next to him. "Come out here, please."

The bedroom door creaked open, and Kip eased out.

"Kip, can you see to the oven? I want to show Jinn something."

With a nod, the girl ran for the kitchen.

"Sit down," he said, patting the couch next to him.

When she sank down to the edge of the cushion, he picked up one of the spare parts.

"So this is a hobby I picked up years ago. I pick up strange pieces of metal and turn them into weird pieces of art. See?" He held up the extra piece, turning it in different directions to see where it fit. "When you find where you want it, you can use this epoxy to attach it. If the piece has bigger objects on it, you have to solder them together, but for this little one, we can glue it."

Setting the piece down, he picked up another one, handing it to Jinn. Standing, he left her staring at it in concentration to help Kip in the kitchen. If he didn't eat and get back to work, someone would show up to see what happened to him.

By the time they set the table, Jinn had let out several small squeaks of satisfaction. Reluctantly leaving the couch, she joined them as Arne was setting the dish of what looked like his mother's tuna casserole in the middle of the table.

"How's the art going?" he asked, scooping a large helping onto Kip's plate.

"I like it. It"—she looked up considering—"makes me think. Sometimes I think a piece will look perfect in one place only to find out it's all wrong there."

"It's like a puzzle."

"Yes!" she said excitedly, looking at him.

He grinned back at her. "Now you know why I got so addicted to working on them. I'm the kid born right in the middle of my siblings. When I started getting lost in the shuffle, my mom enrolled me in an art class. I think she thought it would help draw me out of my shell."

"It might have worked a little too well," Jinn answered. Her eyes grew big when she realized exactly what she had just said to him.

"Ohh, I see how it is. I have a smart-ass in my midst," he teased.

Kip giggled covering her mouth. Jinn gave him a tentative smile as if feeling him out.

"My brothers say the same thing."

This time she gave him an even brighter smile. It was so beautiful, it made his chest ache.

"Is the food good?" Kip asked, staring at him anxiously.

He pulled his eyes away from Jinn to smile at Kip.

"It's amazing," he said, popping a spoonful into his mouth. When they just sat watching him eat, he stopped chewing. "Why aren't y'all eating? You poisoned me, didn't you?"

They both looked down at their plates.

"We never eat until he tells us."

Arne's eyebrows scrunched together in confusion. Who was Jinn talking about?

"Well you don't have to wait in this house," he said. "Eat while it's hot. I got to tell you, Kip. This is as good as the one my mom makes, and that's saying something. I mean, it's fucking fantastic."

That slow smile crept back onto Jinn's face again as she scooped up a spoonful. She swallowed before nodding at Kip to eat.

"Good, huh?"

"It really is fucking fantastic."

Kip's head whipped up to look at Jinn in shock before she burst into laughter. Arne joined her shortly before Jinn finally gave in. Arne thought it was the best sound in the world.

FIVE

J inn decided Arne was the hardest man she had ever tried to read. He didn't follow any of the rules she knew. Even frustrated with her, he didn't strike out. More shocking than that, he had turned down sex. Twice. He also made her laugh, a sound she hadn't heard come out of her in such a long time.

He did scold when he became frustrated as he had earlier when he found she had cleaned his room. However, it hadn't escaped her notice that his cheeks blushed slightly when he glanced at his nightstand. So maybe he was only embarrassed instead of frustrated.

With a snort, she tried to find a place on the thing she was working on for a rusted spring. He had left her to finish the project. She didn't want to know what would happen if it wasn't done by the time he returned home. It had been moved to the small dining room table when her back began to ache from bending over the coffee table.

Looking up in the hope that Kip could help her, she found the girl curled up under the blanket on the couch sound asleep. She set the spring down and picked up another piece.

Her frustration turned into panic when she heard Arne's truck pull up outside. She had been so focused on the sculpture she had failed to note the light softening outside the window.

Standing when she heard his key turning in the lock to the front door, she grabbed up the extra pieces, closing her fist around them. Maybe if she hid them behind her back, he wouldn't notice that she hadn't finished. As if in slow motion, she watched the door open.

"I'm home," he called out, stepping inside. He smiled at her when he spotted her standing next to the table. "How was your afternoon?" he asked, taking off his coat to hang by the door. Bending down, he untied his work boots. "Don't everyone answer at once." Was he teasing them? She looked over at Kip who had sat up on the couch rubbing the sleep out of her eyes.

"Oh, hey, that looks great." Walking to the table, he studied the sculpture sitting next to her.

Her heart had been hammering in her chest the moment she heard his truck, but when he stepped closer to her still studying the statue, it began to race for a completely different reason.

"I'm sorry, I didn't finish."

Slowly she brought her hands around to the front of her body. She opened them to reveal the handful of remaining parts. He looked up from where he had bent closer to the piece. He flashed her a brilliant smile. It made her heart pound even harder.

"That's cool. Sometimes it takes me months to finish one, and I don't always use all of the extra pieces. I just add them to the pile for next time," he said. Raising back up to his full height, he looked over at the couch. "Hey, Kip. Let me run through the shower, then we'll start the burgers."

Jinn let out a small breath. He didn't seem to care at all that she had failed.

"I'll be right back," he added, turning toward the hallway.

"He's good, Jinn," Kip whispered when they heard the water turn on.

How Kip could still have such hope in the goodness of the human race was beyond her. Jinn had simply seen too much to have the same hope. She wanted to trust Arne. She wanted him to be good so badly it made her ache. Perhaps she had gotten Kip out before she had become too jaded like Jinn now was. "We could–"

"No!" Jinn hissed before Kip could finish her thought. She didn't want to hear that they could stay. She didn't want to believe that she could remain in this house with Arne until she grew old. That wasn't how life worked, not her life anyway.

She didn't know how she would make it through the rest of her life, but she knew it couldn't include the man standing naked in the shower. The thought of the water cascading over the hard planes of his body made the ache build again. No! She would ignore it, and tonight, they would make their escape.

She stood considering the piece of metal sitting on the table that could only be considered in the remotest part of the mind as art. But why was he acting so calm when it was evident she angered him at every turn? Why was he trying to keep them here?

She hated the feeling of not knowing what to expect. It was less terrifying when the rules were plain. Hearing the bathroom door open, she walked toward the hallway. It was always better to know where you stood.

"Stay here," she told Kip.

Trying to dredge up the last of her courage, she walked down the hall. Opening the bedroom door, she slipped inside before closing it. She found a surprised Arne standing in front of the dresser in nothing but a towel. He opened his mouth as if to speak but reconsidered and closed it again. After a moment of deliberation, he tried again.

"Jinn—" he began before she cut him off.

"Why?"

His eyebrows shot up in shocked confusion.

"Why are you doing this?" She took a step toward him. "You bring us here, feed us, let us sleep in your bed. What do you want?"

"Why do I have to want something?" he said, taking a step backward.

"Because nothing is free," she answered bravely.

His eyes narrowed on her. Good, at least she would know where his patience reached. She would know what to expect afterward.

"Maybe my helping you is." His voice remained calm.

"No, it can't be. If you don't want sex, then what do you want?" She knew she was pushing him right to the edge. She had learned at an early age to tell when a man was on the verge of lashing out.

"I never said I don't want sex," he answered. Somehow, he had backed up to the wall on the other side of the bed. She kept advancing on him giving him no option but to fight. "I like sex just fine, but I would never force you against your will. I wouldn't force any woman."

"Then what will you do?" Jinn was positive this was the

moment he hit her. If he would just bloody her up, she would have proof for Kip, and in some way herself, that they had to run. Arne would become just like all the rest, given time.

"Why would I do anything? What the fuck happened to you?"

Somehow, they had switched positions. He had one hand flat against the wall behind her as he looked down, his eyes blazing. The other one had tightened into a fist. He had her trapped. She closed her eyes waiting for the first blow. Nothing happened. Feeling the air in the room change, she opened her eyes. Arne had taken a step away from her, his eyes searching her face for something. Could Kip be right?

Before she could think about that anymore, there was a roar followed by the sound of something being hit with a heavy object. Arne slid to his knees before his eyes closed, and he fell the rest of the way to the floor. Standing behind him was Kip with the metal sculpture in her hand. Jinn stared at her in horror as fear cleared from the girl's eyes.

"Kipling! What did you do?" Crashing to her knees, she felt his neck. "He's still alive."

"He was going to hurt you," Kip whispered, dropping the heavy piece of metal on the floor.

"No, Kip. He wasn't." Feeling the back of his head, Jinn's hand came away covered in blood.

"There was yelling."

"I was yelling; he wasn't."

Kip looked at her in confusion.

"Go get a towel. Quickly."

Kip jumped up and ran to the kitchen. Jinn tugged on Arne until she finally had him stretched out flat on the floor. Taking the towel from Kip when she returned, she pulled him up until he lay in her lap so she could hold the towel tight to the back of his head. It was a good thing she was pretty good at patching up injuries. Gently pulling the towel away after several minutes, she found he had almost stopped bleeding.

Brushing his hair off his forehead, Jinn sat wondering what else she should do. If she was smart, she would leave him here, grab their stuff and run. She looked over at Kip who had taken his hand in hers. She was rocking back and forth as she cried.

Kip had been right. He was good. She couldn't explain how she knew, but the moment he stepped back she had just known. By not grabbing their stuff and running, she knew she was taking a leap of faith that she was right. That Arne really was one of the good ones. It was dangerous, but she had to try. For the first time since she could remember, she felt a little less tired.

Arne woke up in a haze, his head pounding so hard he could swear his brain was trying to fight its way out of his skull. He closed his eyes hard against the blinding overhead light. Slowly they fluttered back open. The overhead light had been turned off with the only light left filtering in from the hallway.

Kip knelt in front of him, her eyes wide in fear. Feeling the shiver run through him, he knew it could only mean one thing. He must be leaning against Jinn.

"I'm sorry," Kip whispered. "I thought..."

"You thought I was about to hurt Jinn," he moaned. His head was swimming, and he wasn't completely positive he wasn't about to vomit. Leaning forward, he felt Jinn move against him to reach his head as he put it between his knees.

"It's okay, Kip. You were just trying to protect your sister." Even talking made his head swim.

This whole thing had turned into a shitfest of the highest order. He had just wanted to help. Both women sat blessedly quiet for several beats. Finally he felt Jinn adjust her position behind him before speaking.

"Why would you think she's my sister?" Jinn asked.

Strangely, whatever happened while he was out seemed to stifle some of the fear in her words. She seemed calmer, her words came out a little stronger.

"Because only a sibling would try to crack a man's skull open with no thoughts of the consequences." He lifted his head to look at Kip only to put it back quickly when he felt the nausea rising. It took one gag before a trash can was thrust between his legs. Emptying what was left of his lunch into it, he grabbed on to the bed next to him. "Help me get on the bed. Hopefully without flashing anyone."

"Kip, can you go grab a bottle of water from the kitchen?" Jinn asked.

When she rushed down the hall, she wrapped her arms around him. It took several tries before she got him off the floor. She rolled him onto the bed and pulled the sheet over him.

"Thanks," he said.

At least he didn't scar the teenage girl for life if he had lost his towel. It was smart of Jinn to send her on an errand. Kip rushed back into the room, setting the water on his nightstand. She also handed Jinn a fresh towel. He hissed at the pain that shot through his head when she changed out the bloody one for the fresh one.

"You can't fall asleep," he heard Jinn say when his eyes

drifted closed. He suspected he wouldn't have a choice. He had had a handful of concussions over the years, most from either playing baseball or being thrown off of a horse. There was no doubt this was a doozy.

If he hadn't died from his brain bleeding by the morning, he knew he would be of little use for the next couple of days. He couldn't risk trying to explain to hospital staff why two women had tried to cave his head in during a half-naked argument in his bedroom. That would be nothing compared to the questions his family would have. No, he would just have to tough it out.

"What the hell are you doing?" he moaned when his head felt like it had been set on fire. Jinn was pulling on his scalp in the back right where he had apparently been hit.

"I'm trying to decide if I need to stitch this up."

"You're not sticking a needle in my head," he growled.

"Hold still, and let me look at it," she growled back from behind him. "Stop acting like a child."

Stop acting like a child? Who was this mouthy woman torturing him, and what had she done with Jinn? He felt the small smile tug at the corner of his mouth. He liked this version much better.

THE NEXT MORNING, Arne woke to sunlight flooding in through his window. His head was still pounding like a mother, but at least the room had stopped spinning. Taking inventory of his body, he realized something warm was resting on his thigh.

Raising his head, he found Jinn asleep at his side, her hand wrapped around his thigh. He felt the shiver rack his body. Was it not enough to be fighting a raging headache and morning wood first thing, he also had to have this ridiculous visceral reaction every time she touched him? How did Dane deal with it for so many years around Tani?

"How's your head?" she asked, sitting up. "I was afraid to leave you. So was Kip."

Cautiously picking his head up, he found the girl curled up in a blanket at his feet. And just like that, the morning wood was gone.

"How many fingers am I holding up?" Jinn asked, kneeling next to him. She had her face in front of his studying his eyes.

Groaning, he laid his head back down. "What time is it?" he asked, batting her hand from in front of his face. She laid across him, reaching for his phone. And now the wood was back.

"Seven-fifteen," she answered, laying his phone back down.

Shit.

"I have to get to work," he said, pushing himself up slowly.

Kip didn't move, but Jinn pressed a hand to his chest. A massive quake worked through his muscles as if the universe was trying to tell him something. Feeling it, Jinn yanked her hand back.

"You're hurt," she said.

"I have to show up, or they'll send someone to check on me." With an effort, he pulled his feet out from under Kip and swung them over the edge of the bed. He waited for the pain to subside in his head before heaving himself upright.

After a few moments, he carefully walked toward the bathroom. Closing the door, he looked in the mirror. He still had blood caked in his hair which was blindingly obvious with hair as blonde as his. Using a washcloth, he removed as much as he could, careful not to scrub at the cut in back.

After he was reasonably sure he was as together as he was going to get for the day, he stepped out of the bathroom. Still wearing the towel from last night, he stepped back into his bedroom to dress. He found Kip had scooted up in the bed and was now snoring happily wrapped in his comforter. Jinn, however, was gone.

Grabbing the first work clothes he found in the dresser, he walked back to the bathroom to dress. His house had been taken over by women. The idea shouldn't make him smile, but it did. Finally making it out of the bathroom, he headed for the front door. Jinn was in the kitchen fussing over the stove.

"You need to eat," she said, stirring something vigorously on the stove. "Please," she added.

When she looked at him with pleading eyes, he couldn't tell her no. Pulling his phone out, he texted Dane that he was running late and would be there as soon as he could. He sat down gingerly on the barstool to watch her.

"Do you want milk?"

"No, just water." He was afraid anything else would just bounce right back up. He didn't know how he was going to hold down the mound of eggs Jinn was piling on his plate.

"Jinn, I can't eat all of that, sweetheart." He watched her physically flinch at what he could only assume was the endearment he used. Just one more thing he needed to remember. "You put half on your plate."

She nodded, quickly doing as he asked. Sitting down next to him, she anxiously pushed the eggs around her plate instead of eating them.

"We'll go today," she said quietly.

With a sigh, he put his fork down on his plate. "No,

don't leave. As a matter of fact, I insist you stay here so we can discuss what all of this is about when I get home later. If you run, I will hunt you down and drag you back kicking and screaming if I have to." He knew he was scaring her, but he was about done with being in the dark about what was going on.

"Understand me?" he asked, picking her chin up so she had to look at him.

She gave a small nod.

"Good. I have to get to work." He stood and walked to the door. "I'm serious, Jinn. Be here when I get back."

Shrugging into his jacket and boots, he grabbed his truck keys and walked out the door. He leaned back against it as he tried to get his head to stop the shooting pains. It was a good thing it was overcast today. Even with his sunglasses on, it was damn bright outside.

He managed to drive the five miles to his parents' house somehow without wrecking. If he could just make it through today, he could collapse later. Pulling behind the house, Arne parked next to the large feed room. The building was large enough to hold everything they needed except for the bulk food stored in overhead bins outside.

Unlocking the door, he froze at finding the space where he normally parked the feed truck empty. It was always parked inside since it held a large automatic cake feeder that leaked if it rained hard. The back, behind the feeder, also held the bagged mineral he put out in each pasture, various supplies to solve whatever problem he found, and an occasional protein tub.

He looked around as if he could make the truck materialize just by conjuring it. Everything else seemed to be in place. The back wall had various types of minerals lined up on pallets according to what time of year and what deficiencies his cattle had. To the side was bull feed in bags also on pallets. Cabinets full of medicine and supplies and even a refrigerator for medicines like penicillin sat in the corner.

Scratching his head in confusion, he walked over to a door to look in the tack room. It didn't have a door even remotely large enough to drive a truck through. Maybe the hit to his head was worse than he thought.

"So you decided to show up for work finally," he heard Dane say loudly behind him.

When did Dane become so loud? Pulling the door closed to the tack room, he turned around.

"Where's the truck?" he asked. Dane motioned with his head for Arne to follow him. Closing the door to the feed room, he followed behind his brother to the equipment shop.

The five acres that included his parent's house contained several outbuildings. He mostly just used the combination feed and tack room and one of the large hay barns, but Dane spent his time in the equipment barn or chemical barn when he wasn't out in the fields.

They also had several large gas tanks and two sets of working pens, including two pens just for sick or injured animals with loafing sheds. The back pens included a covered working hydraulic chute which allowed Arne to doctor cattle by himself when no one was available to help.

Arne plopped down on one of the old rolling chairs Dane kept in the tool area of the shop. Sitting under the large cover was the tractor Dane was servicing. It was too big to fit inside the shop, so Dane had to make do with working on it under the overhead cover that extended out from the main shop. After he was done with it, he would pull it off the hill so he could power wash it clean before storing it for the winter. He always spent most of the winter servicing and repairing equipment before spring sent him back into full gear.

"Dad decided after your weird behavior yesterday and not showing up first thing this morning that he had better feed today. He left me to figure out what bullshit you've gotten yourself into now."

That was his older brother—never minced words if he could prevent it. How he had ever gotten Tani to give him a second look was beyond Arne. Dane walked around the tractor, stopping in front of him. Bending down, he studied his face for a beat. "Look at me."

"What are you doing?" he said, trying to push Dane away.

Dane sank down on his knees so he was even with Arne. "What's the capital of Texas?"

What? Arne sat thinking about it for a moment before finally answering.

"Austin."

"Repeat these numbers backward: three, seven, nine."

What was wrong with him? After a few minutes of concentration, he really couldn't remember the original numbers.

"Okay," Dane said, holding his finger up at shoulder height. "Touch my finger, then touch your nose as quick as you can until I tell you to stop."

"You're giving me a concussion test?"

"You look like you've been in a fight, so I prefer to think you got hit on the head and are suffering a concussion. It's a better thought than you deciding to go hardcore into the drug scene."

Arne batted Dane's finger away. Standing, Dane took a step back.

"So which is it?"

"I hit my head last night. It's not a big deal. I just got a slow start this morning because of it. I'm here, aren't I?"

Dane narrowed his eyes at him obviously not buying it, but he let it drop. "I'll trade out with Dad when he comes to refill."

"Not like that, you won't. He can handle today while I keep an eye on you."

"Dane, you're not in charge."

Dane stopped changing one of the filters to look at him.

"You're not," Arne added, realizing too late that he sounded like a petulant child. When Dane continued to stare at him, he looked out at the rest of the barns. His head really was pounding.

"I have always been in charge of you, and I will still beat your ass down if you're doing something stupid," his older brother growled before turning back to the tractor.

Arne sat in the chair, holding his head as Dane worked on the tractor in silence.

"So that weird-ass shiver thing you used to do around Tani," he said, breaking the silence. "Did you ever do that when some other woman touched you?"

Dane turned to look at him with a scowl.

"Have you met someone?"

Damn it, he should have known better. Dane was too damn perceptive. Roar would have been a better option to ask about this.

"I'm just talking," he said. "It's called conversation. You should try it sometime. It might make you seem more human."

Dane rolled his eyes before turning back to his tractor. Roar it is then. Pulling out his phone, Arne typed out a text to his oldest brother asking the same question. A few minutes later, Dane's phone rang.

"Hey. I asked him. No, he got all defensive. I would say that's a yes."

Arne sat glaring at Dane's back as he continued his obvious conversation with Roar. Asshats.

"Yeah, he's acting weirder than normal. I'll try." Dane hung up, crossing back over to the chair. Reaching down, he pulled Arne out of the chair and dragged him to the house. Arne let out a moan, but Dane simply ignored him. "The answer to your question is no, it just happened with Tani. Now what the fuck is going on?"

CHAPTER

SIX

J inn looked around the small home with sadness. Today had to be the day they moved on. There was no other choice. She had only agreed to stay one more night so Kip could learn how to cook hamburgers. But before she could, she had tried to kill Arne with the metal artwork. It was better for everyone if they simply moved on.

She dug through her pack, looking for any money still tucked inside. They had already spent some of it on food. Panic ripped through her body when it wasn't in the pouch she usually left it in. She emptied the pack until her fist closed around the last of their money. Unfolding it, she counted it carefully. There was only a twenty-dollar bill and a handful of ones left. She doubted that would get them very far. She needed to find more.

The idea of going through Arne's bedroom again in hope of finding a few more dollars entered her mind. She didn't want to steal from him, though. He had been too good to them.

Maybe she could just take a few things from his pantry so they would have something to eat for a while. Once they got settled and she had a job, she could send him the money to replace what they took. She walked to the pantry and threw open the door.

"What are you doing?" Kip asked.

Jinn startled. Last she knew, Kip was in their room with one of Arne's books.

"Are you making lunch? I'm starving."

"You scared me," she answered. It seemed like Kip was always starving now. How would she ever be able to provide for her? "I'm just looking at what's in here." She took out a jar of peanut butter, a couple cans of easy-open tuna, and a box of crackers.

"It looks like you're about to make the worst tiny sandwiches ever." Kip watched as she added spray cheese to the growing pile. "You're packing up his food, aren't you? I thought we were staying here. For now anyway." Kip was a lot more astute than Jinn gave her credit for. But then, she had already had to survive so much in her short life.

"You know we can't," Jinn answered. "We're still too close to him. What if he looks for us? What would he do to Arne if he found us here?"

Kip slumped against the kitchen counter. Jinn hated the look of absolute misery on her face.

"I'm sorry, but we have no choice. We have to move on. We're not safe, and Arne's not either as long as we're here."

"Okay," Kip said. "Do you think he'll be mad if I take the book I'm reading?"

"I don't think so," she said, adding a bag of powdered donuts to the counter. Pausing, she glanced at Kip. It broke her heart to see how crestfallen she looked. "Besides, when we get settled, we can send it back. Then it'll be just like you borrowed it. We'll send money to replace the food too."

She said the words as much for her benefit as Kip's. She

didn't like the idea of leaving either. Arne had made them feel safe for the first time in a long time. He gave them everything they needed and asked for nothing in return. Kip had been right all along; he was a truly good man. The first one she had ever met.

"Okay, I'll go get my stuff together." Kip turned to walk to the bedroom. Before she could take a step, they heard a key being inserted into the front door lock.

"Go," Jinn hissed. She ducked behind the counter as Kip raced for the bedroom. The door to their room closed softly as the front door was pulled open.

"Hey," Arne called. "I'm back. I was sent home to rest. According to Mom, if my skull was broken, I would have died last night. She deemed me well enough to nap." He stood in the living room taking in the pile of food on the kitchen counter.

Jinn watched him from around the kitchen. His face fell to match the one Kip had.

"Is there any way I can convince you to make me a sandwich out of some of that before you take it?"

"We were just—" Jinn started as she looked at the growing pile of food.

"Slipping away while I was at work is what it looks like."

"No," she said. Her cheeks felt hot as she blushed at being caught in a lie. She learned long ago it was better to deny everything than to take responsibility. If she got in trouble regardless, why did it matter? Her gaze traced the floor tile. It was also best to avoid eye contact when you've provoked a man, better to look downcast.

"Then you won't mind an early lunch."

She could feel his cool gaze on her. It made the color of

her cheeks grow an even deeper shade of red. She heard his sigh of frustration.

"I'll make us a sandwich."

"No," she said when he moved toward the kitchen. "I'll do it. You sit down and rest." Grabbing the peanut butter off the counter, she busied herself preparing lunch. "Kip," she called when everything was plated.

"Arne," Kip said, her grin reaching across her entire face.

Jinn froze in her tracks. The girl was already getting too attached to him. She watched as Kip sat next to him on the couch and began to babble about her book. Arne was too kind to brush her off, but the look of pain on his face told her he would like to.

"Headache?" she asked, handing Kip her plate. The girl fell silent immediately. A headache was always a bad thing. Too much noise would lead to punishment.

"It's not too bad," he said.

She knew he picked up on Kip's fear. He looked miserable.

"I just need to catch up on some sleep, is all. Thanks," he added when she set his plate on the coffee table. "I'll just finish this, take some aspirin, and head to the bedroom." He took a bite of the sandwich while she watched him closely. "Eat, please. Tell me about the rest of your book."

Jinn began to pick at her sandwich if only to make him happy. She would never get used to eating when he did. Kip went back to chattering between mouthfuls. Arne agreed in all the right places in the conversation and commented when necessary. Her opinion of him grew with each passing moment. He was a man so rare she doubted she'd ever find another one like him.

"I think I'm going to head to the bedroom. Thank you

for lunch." Arne stood and turned to Jinn. "If you're still here when I wake up, I'd really like to talk about this. I can help you make a plan. Help you get to somewhere you feel safe." He stepped toward the bedroom so his back was to her.

"If not, well, there's a new jar of peanut butter in the bottom cabinet." Taking out his wallet, he tossed his cash on the table. "Take whatever you need."

"Jinn?" Kip said when he disappeared into the bedroom.

"Kip," she said, holding up a palm to stop the next comment. "Just...can you go read for a while? I need time to think."

Kip nodded and headed to their bedroom. Jinn walked into the kitchen to clean up. What was she supposed to do? She knew they needed to clear out soon. If he found them here, he would kill Arne. She couldn't live with herself if that happened.

But some help figuring out what their next move should be would be good. She looked at the money lying on the table. Where would they even go, and how would they get there?

With a heavy sigh, she began wiping down the counters. One more night. If they could just stay one more night, she would have the answers. She couldn't leave Arne injured anyway. What if something happened after they left? No, it was best that they stick around just a little longer. Just one more night.

ARNE FELT like he was swimming through the depths of the ocean trying to reach the surface as he struggled awake. His head was still pounding, but that wasn't what woke him up.

He lay in the bed with his eyes screwed shut as he listened for what had brought him out of his fog. All he heard was murmuring from the living room. So Jinn had decided to stay a little longer after all. But that couldn't be what he heard. She barely spoke above a whisper most of the time.

"Arne!" Dane shouted from the living room.

"Shit, that can't be good," he mumbled.

Swinging his feet off the bed, he sat on the edge as his vision swam. Once everything settled, he hauled himself to his feet. He heard his name yelled again as he walked down the hallway. The scene that met him in the living room made him pause.

Dane was standing near the front door with his hands raised at shoulder level. Jinn was at the table with the barrel of his shotgun pointed at Dane's chest. Kip hovered behind her like a skittish rabbit ready to bolt at any moment. He was just wondering how long this had been going on when he heard Dane growl his name again.

"Easy, he won't hurt you." He crossed to Jinn and carefully eased the gun from her hands. "Where did you find this? Let me guess, you've been digging around under my bed." He broke the barrel open and pulled the shells out. "I'll just go put this back."

"Stop," Dane snarled. He hadn't moved from the door, but his hands were now crossed over his chest. "You have three seconds to explain what's going on here."

"Or what?"

"Or I cave the rest of your thick skull in. What the hell is going on here?"

"Can I at least get something to drink first?"

"No. Start talking." The room grew silent as the brothers glared at each other. Finally, Dane turned to Kip. "Can you get him some water out of the fridge? Also some aspirin by the look of him."

Her eyes grew big right before she scurried off to the kitchen.

"She's skittish."

"Like a fawn," Arne agreed. "But once she gets to know you, she can be very chatty."

"Mmm," Dane hummed. "What's that supposed to mean, gets to know you?"

Kip returned quickly from the kitchen carrying three bottles of water. She handed one each to Arne and Jinn. Then, leaning as far away as possible, she extended a bottle to Dane. His scowl turned soft as he took it from her hand. "Thank you," he said.

She blushed and rushed off toward the bathroom.

"That was Kip," Arne said. "This is Jinn. I found them living in the old dynamite shack by the quarry."

"So you moved them in?"

"I almost shot him. With my crossbow," Jinn added.

"Jesus," Dane mumbled. The crevice between his eyebrows grew deeper.

"I thought she was a poacher, so I tackled her. She fought back, so I knocked her out," Arne said.

"Arne," Dane growled.

"I honestly thought she was some guy. Anyway, I didn't want to just leave her or turn her in, so I brought her back here. It gets so cold in that shack in the winter. So, I moved them in..." Arne's voice trickled to a stop when he noticed Dane cock his head to the side.

He had always saved that look for when Arne had been

at his dumbest. With a small shake of his head, Dane's gaze moved to Jinn.

"Why were you living in the shack?" When she remained stubbornly silent, his eyes moved back to Arne. Arne shrugged. To be honest, he still had no idea himself as to why they were there.

"We ran away," Kip said from her hiding space behind the couch. She must have crept there from the hallway when they weren't paying attention.

"Ran away from whom?" Dane asked, leaning over to see Kip as she peeked around the corner of the couch. He smiled at her.

"You look like Arne."

"Because I'm his older brother. We also have a younger brother that looks like us named Erik. Our older brother, Roar, doesn't look like us, though. He looks more like our mother's family and our sister, Thyra. You look about her age. How old are you?"

"I'm fourteen."

"Thyra is sixteen. I bet she'd love to meet you."

"Is she locked in the basement?"

Dane's startled gaze met Arne before he answered. "No. She has her own room upstairs. As a matter of fact, she has most of the upstairs since the rest of us left."

"Was she sad when you left her? I would be sad if Jinn ever left. I would still be in the basement. It's cold down there too."

"Kip, be quiet," Jinn barked.

Kip slunk back behind the couch.

"You were kept in a basement?" Dane asked.

She nodded.

"By whom? For how long?"

"By a very bad man for a long time," Jinn said. "It's why

we need to keep moving. We have to get as far away as possible so he doesn't find us."

Arne felt Jinn's body almost vibrating as her anxiety ramped up like a caged animal. He reached out and took her hand. A tremor worked through his body at her touch. Dane studied him closely, his eyes narrowing at Arne's reaction. It was almost impossible to hide anything from him.

"Well," Dane said, pushing off the couch. "You're safe here for now. No one knows you're here, and we'll make sure to keep it that way until we can help get you where you want to go. You don't have to worry, none of us have basements." He walked to the front door. "Arne, can I talk to you a second?"

"Sure." Arne stood, and they walked outside.

"Have you lost your mind? How much more do you know about them?" Dane asked the second the door closed.

"Not much. As you saw, they're terrified about something or someone. I would guess it's whoever locked them in a basement. But neither one is very forthcoming with the details. I thought Jinn might open more over time, but it's only been a couple of days."

"A couple of days? Damn, Arne, what were you thinking?" Dane's eyes narrowed. "Did she have something to do with the knot on your head? That wasn't an accident, was it?"

"We were arguing. Kip was just trying to protect her."

Dane grunted in response. He moved down the steps to his truck.

"Tomorrow, you need to come clean about all this mess. We can help them escape, but it'll take the family to do it. You can't hide this from everyone. They already suspect something is going on with you."

"Yeah, I know. Tomorrow." He waved as Dane drove away. With a sigh, he turned to face the door.

The aspirin had done nothing to cure the pounding in his head. He was positive what he was about to do wasn't going to help either, but it was time he got some answers. They owed him that at least. If he was going to harbor two fugitives, he needed to know what they were fleeing from. He could protect them, but not if he didn't know what was coming.

"Jinn. Kip," he said, pushing through the door. "It's time to talk."

Arne walked back inside fully expecting to find both women locked firmly in their room for the night. It was their automatic response to anything that scared them.

Instead, he found Jinn sitting patiently on the couch waiting for him. He sat down at the other end and turned to face her. She stared at the small electric fireplace against the wall; its leaping flames seemed to have her mesmerized. He was about to say something, anything, when her gaze turned to his.

"This isn't the first time we've run," she said. "It's just the first time we've made it this far."

He sat perfectly still as her gaze searched his face. He wished he could reassure her that nothing she said would change how he felt. He knew deep in his heart that he was sworn to protect them regardless of the cost.

"It's not a pretty story," she continued.

"I don't expect it to be." He took her hand in his, a shiver working through his body at her touch. "I promise, though, I can handle whatever you're willing to tell me."

"You won't want us here after you've heard everything. All I'm asking is that you let us slip away. Kip and I will find our own way, and you'll be away from this nightmare. Just give us that."

"Jinn—" Arne started, but she held up her hand to stop him from saying more. Then she began to tell her story.

SHE REMEMBERED HEARING ONCE when she was small from one of the people in town how her mother had been the most beautiful rodeo queen to ever come out of the county. But that was before she took up with that no account Pierce boy. She was never the same after that. When she found out she was pregnant at the age of seventeen, she quit school to move in with him.

Jinn couldn't remember ever hearing the sound of laughter in their home. More often than not, the sounds that reached her room were always shouting. Sometimes she heard doors slamming or someone hitting the floor. She never checked; she'd learned early it was better just to stay in your room.

When she was seven, her parents brought her sister home from the hospital. From the beginning, Kip was a fussy baby. Jinn would hurry home from the bus stop after school every day to help her mother with her little sister. Until the day she turned ten and she ran into the house only to find a tearful three-year-old Kip in her playpen and her mother nowhere to be found.

Jinn fed her, bathed her, and dressed her in a clean outfit. Then she sat on the floor to play with Kip as they waited for a mother who never returned. Her father stomped into the house that evening only to leave again. Jinn heard him muttering about their good-for-nothing whore of a mother as the front door slammed.

That was both the last time she saw her mother and the first time she was left by herself all night to tend to her sister. She missed school the next day to stay with Kip. By the third day of being absent, the school called her father. He begrudgingly found marginal childcare for Kip so Jinn wouldn't miss any more. That still left her as the sole care-taker of a toddler every evening while her father was out doing who knew what.

By the time she turned twelve, her father's partying had moved to their house. Every night, she would tuck Kip into bed and return to the living room to serve as hostess to his drunken friends.

"How old are you, girl?" one such friend asked one night.

She ignored him and picked up more beer bottles for the trash.

"Don't be like that. I just asked you a question."

She walked into the kitchen to grab another dish towel to wipe up the floor. Turning around, she found herself pinned to the counter by the man.

"She's almost thirteen," a voice said behind the man. He instantly skittered away, leaving her to face someone new. "Isn't that right, sweetheart?" The new man wasn't like the last one. He was large and foreboding. Her heart raced in her chest as he peered down at her. "I asked you a question. I expect you to answer."

"Yes," she whispered. A smile tugged at the edges of his mouth. Instead of it giving her comfort however, it made the blood in her veins freeze. Every instinct she had told her to get away from this man. Nothing good would come from him.

"That's better," he said. "I'll be seeing you again. In a month." He turned on his heels and stalked from the room.

She didn't want to ever see him again. Why was he even here? He didn't look like any of her father's usual friends. His clothes were better, and he spoke like he had more education than the rest of them.

"Dad?" she said later while she finished cleaning the living room. He was stretched out in an old lounge chair in a stupor. "Who was the big man here tonight? He was wearing a shiny watch." She flinched when he jumped to his feet.

"What did you do, girl?"

"Nothing." She felt the moment her lip split open from the back of his hand hitting it. "I promise," she begged as she hit the ground. She waited for him to hit her again.

"You better make sure you're real nice to him. You hear me?" he raged.

"I will."

She held the old dish towel to her face to catch the blood. Her eyes stayed focused on the cracked linoleum floor in front of her. He stood staring at her a few more minutes before stomping down the hallway. She heard the door to his bedroom close with a slam.

Slowly, she pulled herself off the floor. Trying to see through the tears silently streaming from her eyes, she finished cleaning before sneaking into the room she shared with Kip. It would be the last time she cried.

Her father found it much easier to take out his frustration on her after that. She learned to accept it with a stiff upper lip as long as he left Kip alone.

She celebrated her thirteenth birthday a month later

with a healing black eye and a cupcake her teacher brought her. Dividing it in half, she shared it on the bedroom floor with Kip while her sister sang a six-year-old's rendition of "Happy Birthday."

Jinn turning thirteen fell on a Friday, so that evening she tucked Kip into bed before heading to the living room. A party was in full force. With a silent sigh, she began picking up trash as her father and his friends drank the night away. She had just carried a handful of bottles to the kitchen when she felt the air change.

"There's the birthday girl." She turned around to find the large man she met earlier leaning against the doorframe. "I told you I'd see you again."

"Yes," was all she could think to say.

"Let's go," he said with a motion of his head.

She stood frozen in place, trying to work out what he was talking about. Nothing could convince her to go anywhere with him. Maybe something had broken in the living room, and she needed to clean it up. He pointed to the back door.

"No," she said. He reached out and snatched her by the arm faster than she thought possible for such a large man. His charming smirk morphed into a sneer.

"Don't ever tell me no," he hissed in her ear.

"Just go with him," her father said from the doorway. "Don't cause problems, and he'll be good to you."

Two men stepped in through the back door. They took her arms and began dragging her into the yard.

"No!" she screamed.

It did her no good; there was no one here who would help her. "Kip!" she screamed right before she was tossed in the back seat of a large SUV.

She didn't go easily though. She fought the men with

everything she had. Her teeth sunk into flesh; her fists met solid muscle. She wrestled for freedom until the large man got into the front seat, turned around, and slapped her in the face.

"Either calm down, or I let him strap you to the roof rack. Your choice," he said.

She felt the fight drain from her body.

"That's better."

She watched out the window as her house passed her for the last time. A small prayer was silently lifted for the little sister she was leaving behind. Would Kip think she had abandoned her just like their mother had?

They drove farther and farther away until they reached the wealthier side of a town she didn't recognize. She was blindfolded before being pulled from the seat. Half walking, half dragged, they moved her inside a building and down a set of stairs. Her blindfold was removed once she was in front of the door to a small room. One of the guards shoved her inside before slamming a door closed.

Jinn looked around the room. It had an old metal bed in one corner with a worn blanket on it. A small bathroom was tucked in the corner with a toilet, sink, and small open shower stall. A faded blue towel lay across the sink. The one thing she didn't see, however, was a window. The walls were a gray cinder block without even a speck of natural light permeating through the blocks.

She tugged on the door several times, but it was locked tight. She tried yelling in the hopes someone would hear her. All she managed to do was give herself a sore throat. Finally, as she was sitting on the bed trying to decide what to do next, the door was unlocked. It swung open to reveal the large man who had taken her.

"This is where you'll live until I decide where you'll serve best. The better you act, the more we'll let you have in your room. Books, blankets, extra food can all be negotiated," he said.

"Why am I here?"

"Because your father likes to have a good time. That led to a lot of debt he owes me for. He sold you to clear that debt."

Her mouth hung open in shock. He had sold her to another man. "What about my sister?"

"Your sister is not my concern. Not now at least." With a smirk she would learn to hate, he stepped out of the room. The door was closed and locked again. No matter how much she pounded on it, no one came.

ARNE'S HEAD spun with questions when Jinn stopped speaking. He knew, though, that pushing her further would only guarantee that she told him nothing more. The story didn't end there, but it was enough for tonight. Her gaze flicked to his momentarily before drifting back toward the fireplace. He needed to say something.

"I wish I had the ability to always say the right thing," he said. "But words seem hollow. Right now I'm trapped between wanting to burn the world down to right every wrong you've been dealt and wanting to pull you onto my lap to protect you from it."

Her face turned to his. "I don't need you to burn the world down," she said. "But the second option sounds perfect."

As soon as she spoke the last word, he was dragging her

across the couch and onto his lap. His arms wrapped around her as she snuggled against his chest.

"All I can say is I'm sorry, and as long as you're here, I'll do whatever it takes to keep you safe," he said. His lips pressed gently against the top of her head. "You don't have to be afraid of me."

She sat silently, her body curled against his chest. They sat perfectly still simply enjoying the strength of the other until the bedroom door opened. Jinn quickly slid off his lap to the other side of the couch.

"Are you in trouble?" Kip asked as she crept into the living room.

"With Dane? I'm usually in trouble where he's concerned." Arne smiled at her, but it fell when he saw how worried she was. "No. You just surprised him is all. He's fine."

"I like him," she added.

"It pains me to admit it, but I do too." He tried a wink in her direction this time. It seemed to do the trick as a bright smile lit up her face. "Are you hungry?"

She nodded enthusiastically. He didn't know if he could eat after hearing Jinn's story, but he stood anyway and walked to the kitchen.

"How about I teach you how to make waffles for supper."

"Yum!" Her smile turned into a toothy grin.

"Alright then, let's get out the waffle iron."

"Don't go to too much trouble," Jinn said.

"Nothing's too much trouble when it comes to my girls," he answered. Throwing an arm around Kip's shoulders, he gave her a side hug. "Right?"

She nodded.

"Got it?"

His words were aimed at Jinn. Slowly, she nodded.

"Good." He turned and set the waffle iron on the counter. "Now to begin, grasshopper."

Kip laughed, and he thought it was the best sound he had ever heard.

EIGHT

"Are you sure you're okay?" Arne asked.

Jinn hadn't realized how tight her grip on his arm was until just then. She nodded as she loosened her grip.

"I promise the only thing the people in this house are worried about is keeping you both safe. Just like me."

She met his cerulean gaze.

"We can go, though, if you're not ready."

"No," she answered. "We're ready."

Arne opened the door of his truck and slid out. He held his hand out for her to take. Slowly, she eased to the ground. Kip followed behind her. Her sister seemed to be less apprehensive about what they'd find waiting inside the large home than her.

Jinn took a minute to take in the two-story home. It was made out of an unusual rock with a deep red metal roof. Flowers were obviously well cared for in the flower beds that wrapped around it. An old swing set sat in the side yard looking well worn from years of use.

Sitting on the front porch was a large floppy puppy. Kip

ran into the yard to greet it. The dog covered her in sloppy kisses before wandering over to bump Arne's hand.

"This is Dane's dog, Otto. He's a recent addition."

"He's also a lot of trouble," Tani said, stepping out of the house. "You must be Jinn." She stepped toward her with her hand outstretched. Jinn squared her shoulders and stepped forward to greet her. "This is Aksel," Tani added, nodding to the baby on her hip.

"This is Kip," Jinn said.

"Kip, it's so nice to have you here."

Kip shook her hand exactly how Jinn had taught her.

"Everyone is inside anxiously awaiting to meet you. They decided I was the least overwhelming to start," Tani said. They turned toward the door when Freja eased outside. "This is Jinn and Kip."

"It's very nice to meet you," Freja said. "I'm Arne's mom, Freja."

Both women nodded.

"Dinner is almost ready. The men are inside. Arne, you might introduce your guest around while we set the food on the table."

"Come on, Kip," Tani said, holding a hand out to her.

Kip slid her hand in Tani's hand.

"Thyra is dying to meet you. She got stuck icing a cake."

Jinn watched as the two women disappeared inside with Kip in tow. She already liked Arne's family, what she's seen so far anyway. It wasn't the women she had to worry about, though.

"Are you sure you want to do this?" Arne asked. She found herself clinging to him again. "What are you worried about?"

"Your brothers."

"They're all large and boisterous in a grumbly sort of

way. I'm definitely the best looking in case you're wondering."

She laughed. "Naturally."

"Dad's the same. They're all very protective, and no matter what they say, Mom wears the pants in this family."

Jinn laughed again. "Okay, you win. Let's go inside."

With his hand on her back, he opened the door and ushered her in. They hung their jackets in the mudroom before stepping into the kitchen. Jinn's smile grew when she found Kip animatedly conversing with another beautiful young woman.

"This is my sister, Thyra."

"Oh my gosh, hi," Thyra said, throwing her arms around Jinn for a hug. "Sorry, I was told not to be too grabby, but Kip and I were having the best conversation and I couldn't wait to meet you. Kip and I were comparing favorite books. I can't wait to introduce her to my library upstairs."

"Moving on," Arne said, taking Jinn's hand. "And they say I talk too much." He pulled her behind him into the living room.

She froze when she found four giant men standing near the fireplace. Only one of them did she know, but they all looked very similar.

"These are my brothers. You already know Dane. This is Roar and Erik," he said, pulling the huge blond into his arms for a quick hug. "I didn't know you were coming down."

"Umm, Dane said you kidnapped two women. Of course, I came down to see this," Erik answered.

"Erik," Roar mumbled. "Sorry," he said quietly. "Mom threatened us within an inch of our lives if we said anything or did anything that was in any way intimidating.

Hi, I'm Roar. I'm the oldest, smartest, and best looking of this crew."

"And the most full of bullshit obviously," Erik added, rolling his eyes.

"What is the rule about cursing around the women?" Sten asked. "Welcome, I'm these idiots' father. We're very glad you decided to join us tonight."

"Y'all are starting to freak me out," Arne said. "They're never this well-behaved," he added to Jinn.

"Dude, you know how Mom can get," Erik responded.

"No. How can Mom get?" Freja asked, stepping into the living room.

"More lovely with each passing day," he answered.

"Dinner's on the table," Freja said with a smirk.

"Kiss ass," Dane snarled as they watched her disappear back into the kitchen.

"You're just jealous I'm her favorite. I'm the special one."

"Yeah, you're special all right," Roar said. He shoved Erik toward the dining room.

Jinn couldn't fight the smile that was turning the corners of her mouth up. She never had brothers, but she wished just a little she had if they were all like this. They acted very differently from the men she had always been around. Although, there were a few nice ones who taught at her school years ago.

Was it possible that the men her father hung with were actually the exception? She took Arne's hand again and let him pull her into the dining room.

"Have you ever seen this much food?" Kip whispered as she moved to her side.

"It takes a lot of food to feed all these men," Freja answered. "Kip, why don't you sit between Jinn and Thyra.

Arne, you're next to Jinn. That leaves Roar, Erik, Dane, and Tani on the other side."

Everyone shuffled around the table until they found their seats. Jinn settled next to Arne across from Tani.

She bowed her head when Sten gave grace and then watched in fascination as the food was passed around the table. No one waited for Sten to finish his plate first.

"You can eat. No one at this table ranks over anyone else," Arne whispered in her ear.

Slowly, she took a bite of meat. Flavors burst in her mouth making her hurry to take another bite.

"This is very good," she said.

"Thank you. I should have extra if you'd like some to take back to Arne's," Freja answered.

"Speaking of, I'd like a little more information about what exactly is happening at your house," Sten said.

"Can't we wait until after dinner?" Freja asked.

"No, I think this is as good a time as any."

All eyes turned to Arne. He looked at Jinn with a silent question in his gaze. She nodded. Though she would prefer not to tell anyone about who they were, she knew his family deserved some answers.

"You know, he is over twenty-one, right? He's allowed to have houseguests," Roar said.

"I say the more guests, the better," Erik added.

"Tani did live with me for a while," Dane said.

"It's okay," she said with a smile. That was the moment she fell in love with Arne's brothers. They had sided with her even against their father. "There are some things that you need to know." She nodded again at Arne. Some things needed to be said, but that didn't mean she wanted to say them.

"Jinn and Kip are escaping, from everything I've heard so far, a very bad domestic situation," Arne began.

A collective growl rose around the table; the food was all but forgotten for a moment.

"I found them hiding in the old dynamite shack. I couldn't leave them there with no food, water, or heat, so I brought them to my place."

"Of course not, it's been near freezing already at night," Sten agreed.

"I've talked them into staying until we can put together a plan to get them to safety. Jinn thinks that someone will come looking for them soon."

"There's no chance they'll give up?" Roar asked.

She looked at Kip who shook her head. Her gaze traveled around the table to take in the family. Everyone was watching her. They waited for an answer.

"No. I don't think so. He used to talk about how much money we cost him. We were exchanged for a gambling debt our father owed him. That's what I understand anyway."

"What's his name? Maybe we can negotiate something," Dane said.

Jinn felt Kip grow anxious beside her. Talking about him was like poking a hornet's nest that neither one of them wanted a part of. If he found them this time, he would kill them. He said as much to her the last time they tried to run. Kip had been locked in the basement while she was stripped naked and beaten. When he was done, he dragged her downstairs and threw her at Kip's feet.

"Hey, you want to head upstairs and figure out what books you want to borrow?" Thyra asked.

Jinn's gaze met hers in gratefulness. She had obviously picked up on Kip's fear.

"You'll call us when dessert is ready, right?"

"Of course," Freja answered.

"Come on, I think I have the perfect series in mind." Thyra stood and eased Kip from her seat.

Jinn smiled when Kip's fearful gaze met hers. She nodded in encouragement.

"You just have to answer one question. Do you like a little romance with your fantasy?" Gently, she led Kip up the stairs and out of sight. Jinn listened to their voices until they faded away.

"We never learned his name," she said, turning back to Dane. "We were told to call him sir. Everyone who worked for him was referred to by a nickname. When he had a party, the guests wore masks."

"Jesus," Erik whispered.

"Do you think you could find the house again?" Dane asked.

"No," Arne answered before she could get a word out. "They're not going anywhere near it ever again."

"But if she could identify it, then—" Roar began.

"I said no," Arne said, cutting him off. "It's not up for discussion."

"I can answer for myself," Jinn said, placing her hand on Arne's arm. She felt the tremor that racked through his body the moment they touched. "It was dark when we ran. I never saw the outside, so I don't know if I could say for sure."

"Arne's right anyway," Sten added. "We can't take a chance on endangering Jinn by asking her to do that." He turned to Arne and speared him with his icy gaze. "They're under your protection now, Arne. What ideas do you and Jinn have to keep them safe?"

"There's really just two options," Arne said. "Either we

find somewhere for them to disappear far enough away that he never finds them."

"That option means they'll be watching over their shoulder for the rest of their lives, waiting for someone to pounce," Freja pointed out.

"I agree. The other option is they stay here until we can find a resolution that guarantees they never have to worry about him again."

"Arne," Jinn said, shaking her head. "We can't stay. He'll kill you if he finds us here."

"Arne can take care of himself," Sten said. "We can also take care of you and Kip if you'll let us."

The room grew silent, everyone waiting to see what she said. She wanted so desperately to stay here.

"You don't have to decide tonight. Sleep on it, and let Arne know in the morning. Either way, we'll help you."

"How about we move to the living room for cake?" Freja asked, breaking the silence.

Jinn jumped to her feet to clear the table.

"Sweetie, you're our guest. The boys can help me get this."

"Please, Mrs. Ulvmand. I would like to help as our thank you for making such an amazing meal," she answered, head bowed.

"That would be lovely, but only if you call me Freja."

Jinn dared a glance up only to find Freja smiling at her. She gave a brief smile back before carrying several plates to the kitchen. Arne followed her with the remaining bowl of salad.

"Are you okay?" he asked.

"Yes," she said. "Your family is unlike anyone I've ever met. I hope we behaved correctly."

He took the plates from her hands and set them on the

counter. Taking her hands, he stooped until he was gazing at her face. "All you have to be here is yourself. They'll love you simply because you are you. Understand?"

She shook her head, and he chuckled.

"You will."

"I'm glad I almost shot you," she said, throwing her arms around his waist. He pulled her in tight against his chest.

"It seems weird to admit it," he said. "But so am I." They stood just holding on to each other until the kitchen door swung open, and Erik walked in carrying a bowl. Jinn immediately moved away from Arne.

"Hey, do I get one of those?" Erik teased. "I am the best-looking of the brothers, after all."

"Get out," Arne said, shoving him back through the door.

They heard a thump, and then Dane yelled at him. Looking at each other, they both started to laugh. Jinn thought the sound of Arne's laughter was the best sound she had ever heard.

J inn lay awake staring at the ceiling. Kip was lying in the other bed on her stomach. She hadn't stopped reading since they got back from dinner. They had agreed that it was safe to each have a bed, though they still locked the door at night.

She wished she had nothing more to worry about than dragons in a faraway land. Instead, she had their fate to determine.

The smart thing was to run, but the way Arne's dad seemed so certain they could protect them made her want to stay. The men sitting around that dining room table looked like an army of Vikings. Would they really go to battle to save her and her sister?

"I don't know what to do," she mumbled.

"About what?" Kip asked, looking up from her book.

"About all of this," she answered, motioning around vaguely with her hands. "About everything. What do we do?"

"I vote we stay here. Arne said we could. He's obviously into you, and he's nice on the eyes. A little old, but still."

"He's not old and is just being nice," she argued.

"That's not what Thyra said. She said that he shivers when you touch him because you're his chosen mate. They're like wolves or something. I tried it with Erik, but he didn't so much as move." Jinn shook her head at her sister's fantasies. A pack of wolves was ridiculous. Sometimes she wondered where Kip's real life ended and her books began.

"You're being crazy. I do need to ask him a few more questions, though. I'll be right back." She threw back the covers and stood.

"Take your time," her sister said as her hand rested on the doorknob.

Jinn knew if she turned around, she'd be met with a smirk. Kip was both too young and too old at the same time. She left the room for Arne's room. Quietly, she opened his door.

"Arne?" she called.

He sat up immediately. "What? What happened?"

She could just see him sitting up in bed from the night-light in the hallway. His hair was already disheveled from sleep. He rubbed his face, trying to wake up.

"Jinn?"

"I'm sorry I woke you."

"No, that's no problem. What's wrong?"

"I just had some more questions."

"Yeah, okay." He pushed up until he was sitting with his back resting against the headboard. He tapped the comforter by his knees for her to sit.

Slowly, she walked into the room. She hadn't counted on him being shirtless. Her eyes took in the muscles of his chest, the ripples of his stomach, and the smattering of hair that spread across them.

She had so many questions that swirled through her

mind. Where would they go? How would they get there? How did they make sure he wouldn't come here if they stayed? But only one seemed to matter at that moment. Slowly, her fingers reached out until they grazed his breast-bone. She watched in fascination as a tremor raced across the hard planes of his body.

Her fingers slowly traced a line down his chest to the ridges in his stomach. The muscles relaxed as she progressed. When she reached the covers, she pulled them away. Waiting just a moment, she touched her knuckles to his abs. His body reacted to her touch much the same as it did before. Only, she noticed his lungs contract in a slight inhale.

"Why do you do that?" she whispered.

"I don't know. It started from the moment I touched your face on the horse," he answered.

"Kip said Thyra told her it has something to do with finding your mate."

"Thyra has a big mouth and an active imagination."

"What does it feel like?" she asked.

He looked away as if searching for an answer. When his gaze swung back to hers, she felt all the breath leave her lungs. Even in the half-dark, she could see his crystal-blue eyes as they met hers.

"Like my heart skips a beat," he said. "It feels like I can't breathe, but my lungs are overflowing with air. There's a need in that moment to do whatever I have to to protect you."

"Maybe your sister's imagination isn't quite so far off the mark." She smiled at him. "But if that's the case, why did you refuse me?"

He brushes his thumb lightly over her cheek. It's a gesture so sweet it almost makes her cry. "Because I don't want to be just another man who uses you. You have to want to stay because you choose to, not because I've trapped you." His hand drops away. "Why don't you ask your questions tomorrow."

"Alright." She got off the bed and walked to the door.

"Try to remember," he said, pulling her up short, "that you're here because you're safe and wanted."

Without another word, she walked to her room. Kip was already asleep; her book was carefully laid on the nightstand between them. She climbed into bed and pulled the covers up. Silently, she brushed a tear from her cheek. Her eyes closed, her last thoughts on what he had said. As she fell asleep, she knew what her answer was.

ARNE FLOPPED onto his side in the bed. An hour after Jinn left his room, he was still struggling to fall asleep. Perhaps it was because he could still feel his skin burning everywhere her fingers had traced. More likely it was the raging erection he was fighting caused by those fingers. Keeping his promise to be nothing more than their rescuer and protector was proving harder and harder.

He tried closing his eyes again, but it was no use. Every nerve in his body was screaming for relief. The problem was he didn't want one of the women to open his door with a problem and find him rubbing one out. There was also that chance he'd moan Jinn's name when he finally came. She would be gone faster than he could count.

There was always the relaxation technique one of his college trainers taught him when he was anxious about a test. Slowly, he breathed in through his nose and out through his mouth. He visualized one of the places he loved most, the banks of his favorite fishing hole. His mind led him across the pasture to the edge, carrying his gear. He worked through baiting his hook, casting into the water, and teasing the line to lure in a fish.

He imagined the warm sun on his back. Not the earth-scorching one of summer that burned your skin, but the gentle warmth of spring. The pasture was lush with life, both plant and wildlife. The water was flowing slowly down the river heading toward the ocean as its final resting place. He had nowhere he had to be other than right here.

He's not alone, though. Looking over, he finds Jinn smiling back at him. She has her own line in the water. Her eyes dance with happiness as she laughs. The sunlight picks up every color of gold in her hair. Anyone else, he would have been unhappy to have his time in this beautiful place interrupted. But Jinn simply seems to complete his fantasy. For him, it is the perfect day.

His alarm jerks him awake several hours later. Grabbing his phone, he shuts off the alarm before it wakes the rest of the house. The thought of having a full house is an odd one. At one time, it was him and Dane sharing a house. Then he didn't give a rat's ass if Dane was disturbed. Now, he finds himself tiptoeing into the bathroom as quietly as possible.

"Hey, what are you doing awake?" he asked, walking into the kitchen. "Did I wake you?"

"I wanted to catch you before you go to work," Jinn said. She turned back to the stove. "You also need breakfast."

"You don't need to cook me breakfast. I usually just heat up something in the microwave."

"Nevertheless, here you go."

He sat at the bar as she scooped eggs, sausage, and toast onto his plate. "Thank you," he said.

"You're welcome," she answered.

He could feel her watching him eat. There was something else on her mind, but he knew it was best to just wait. She would tell him in her own time.

"I thought maybe if I start doing more around here, we can stay a little longer?"

He took his time swallowing his mouthful of eggs before picking up his glass of orange juice. Taking a large drink, he contemplated what to say. Finally, he set the glass down and met her anxious gaze.

"You don't have to earn the right to be here. You just have to choose to stay," he said.

"Then we choose to stay." Her face is defiant as she gazes at him.

"Good," he said with a grin. He couldn't think of anything better than having Jinn here. "I guess we should start making some plans then."

"Like what?"

"Well, Kip needs to be enrolled in school at some point. You'll both need more clothes. Things like that. We also need to decide when it's safe to venture out in public," he said. "Let's talk about it more tonight." Finishing his breakfast, he moved to the front door to pull on his outerwear.

"What are you doing today?"

"I have to feed in the morning," he said, bending to tie his boots. "Depending on what I find, it might take part of the afternoon too." He stood and took in Jinn. She was standing just outside the kitchen. Her hands were gripping each other tightly in front of her. "Do you want to come?"

"Yes," she said quickly before her face fell. "But I can't leave Kip by herself."

"I'm sure Mom won't mind her hanging out over there."

Jinn's face lit up again. "We'll get dressed. We won't be a second."

"Take your time," he said, dropping onto the couch.

Ten minutes later, they burst into the living room ready to go. Both women had on the hunting gear from the first time he met them. They carried their boots to the door before pulling them on. Both pairs looked too big for their wearers. He made a mental note to check with his mom for smaller ones.

"Ready," Kip said. She looked as excited to stay with his parents for the day as Jinn did to go with him.

"Then let's go," he said.

The women scrambled out the door and into his truck. He locked the front door before following them. They drove the twenty minutes to the main house. Arne parked in front and shut off the engine. He led them into the mudroom.

"Mom!"

"There's no need to shout," she responded from the kitchen.

"Can Kip spend the day with you?"

"Of course," she said, stepping into the mudroom.

"Can you also find them some smaller boots while I fill the feed truck?"

"Absolutely." She smiled at Jinn. "Just leave those there, and we'll go see what we can find. Kip, you probably won't need shoes this morning. We'll work on something for you later."

"I'll be right back," Arne said.

He left his mother fussing over Jinn. He walked to the feed barn, pulled out the truck, and filled it with cubes from the overhead bin. Jinn was at the gate waiting in a relatively new-looking pair of boots when he pulled back over to the house.

"Look," she said after climbing into the truck. She held up one of her feet so he could admire the boots.

"That looks much better."

"We took what we could find when we left. It was better than nothing."

They pulled through the back gate into the first pasture in silence.

"How did you get away?" he finally asked.

Jinn wondered how much longer she could survive this life. If it wasn't for Kip in the basement with her, she would have found a way to end it long ago. But her sister depended on her to save her. For that reason alone, she would stay alive at least a little while longer.

The last time they tried to get away, she hadn't done any planning. It was just a chance opportunity she couldn't pass up. That was what got them caught.

Once again, Kip had been locked in the basement alone for days while she was fed to a particularly sadistic group of partygoers. She had returned to the basement broken and bloody. That was when she knew they needed a plan.

It was a couple of weeks later when she noticed she had caught the eye of one of the guards. He started by bringing them extra treats on their dinner trays. Then he stayed a little longer than he should to talk to her.

At first, her instinct was to push him as far away as she could. Then she realized he was exactly the opportunity she had been hoping for. Kip was getting more beautiful every day. It wouldn't be long before she was dragged upstairs for a party. Jinn had to act fast.

"I don't like him, Jinn," Kip complained.

"I know you don't. I don't like him either, but we need to pretend just a little while longer. Do you think you can hit him on the head with this pipe?" She had spent several nights working on securing a pipe from the bathroom. It had taken her a week to find the valve in the wall and uncouple it. "I'll lure him in here, but I need you to do what I ask."

"I'll do it," Kip said resolutely.

"Tonight then."

"Tonight."

They had to wait several more hours until it was time for dinner. Jinn had picked this night because there was a child's birthday party in full swing. That meant only one guard would be watching them. All she had to do was entice him into the room and pray Kip had the courage to hit him with the pipe.

Finally, they heard a key in the lock. Jinn nodded at Kip who sat across the room on the extra bed. She slid her hand under the covers where the pipe lay. Jinn leaned back on their bed which was directly across from the door. With her back against the wall, she could swing her legs open with her feet on the bed. The man took several steps inside before his gaze landed between her legs.

"Hey, what do you have for me tonight?" she asked, lazily swinging her legs open and closed. He didn't seem to even notice the other person in the room, the one with the metal pipe in her hands.

"I can think of something you might like," he said.

He moved toward her still carrying the trays. Right before he reached the bed, Kip swung the pipe like a baseball bat. It made a sickening crunch as it made contact with the back of his head. Jinn watched his eyes roll as he fell to the ground.

"Close the door until we're ready," Jinn hissed.

Kip was shaking, but she hurried to do as instructed.

"Help me get him in the bed. We'll cover him so he looks like it's us sleeping."

It took everything they had to hoist the deadweight into the bed. When Jinn was satisfied he might pass as two sleeping people at a glance, she cleaned up the food on the floor. She then soaked up the blood on the floor with an old T-shirt.

"Come on." She wrapped her hand around Kip's wrist.

Together, they eased into the hallway and up the stairs. There were doors on either side lining the basement, but she didn't have time to worry about who might be behind them right then. That would be for another day if they made it out alive.

No one was in the back entryway when they stepped out of the door to the basement. She could hear party guests singing "Happy Birthday" in the front dining room. That gave them a few minutes to run. She quickly helped Kip into some of the hunting gear kept in the large closet along one wall before pulling on some herself. At the last minute, she grabbed a crossbow and a quiver of bolts.

She used the keys she found in the man's pocket to let them out the back door. There was no alarm since there were so many people milling around the house. Carefully, they stuck to the darkest part of the yard until they reached the tall metal fence that ran along the perimeter.

"What do we do now?" Kip asked.

The fence was at least eight feet tall with spikes on the top.

"We climb," she answered. Taking off her coat, she threw it on top of the spikes. "I'll lift you. You'll have to pull me up from the top using the strap from the crossbow. Think you can do it?"

Kip nodded.

She cupped her hands to give Kip a step and pushed her to the top of the fence. Balancing on top, her sister caught the crossbow when Jinn threw it at her. Carefully, she lowered herself over the fence without releasing the weapon. She hung there until Jinn made it to the top of the fence.

"Now, we run," Jinn said, dropping down on the other side.

She wasn't sure where they were going. They needed to stay away from the roads, she knew that. The woods around the house looked like the safest bet, so she began to crash her way through. Kip stayed right behind her.

The first night they made it as far as they could. At dawn, Jinn built a very rough lean-to out of branches for them to rest under. The day was spent listening for the men who would soon find them and take them back.

When night fell with no one catching them, they continued on. A week after escaping, they stumbled along an old cinder block shed in the middle of a pasture near the river.

At first, Jinn wasn't sure about staying inside where escape would be almost impossible, but she knew they needed rest and their food stores were non-existent. They had managed to survive on what she could steal from empty houses along the way.

They built a bed using the old girly magazines stored in some old boxes, branches, and a moldy blanket. She slept better that night than she had in years. The only noises were from the other animals living there. They were finally alone.

That was until she decided to try and shoot a deer.

TEN

Arne rolled the pickup to a stop in the pasture. Her story was so heartbreaking that he wanted to gather her in his lap and never let her go again. But that's not what she had in mind. With a gasp, she bounded to his side of the truck with her face pressed against the glass. It took a minute to see what she was so excited about.

"Is that a calf?" she whispered.

"Looks like a brand new one," he answered. "It's still a little early to begin calving yet though."

"Someone has been sneaking around," she replied with a grin.

Mischief danced in her deep caramel gaze when it met his. It took everything he had not to kiss her. She looked truly happy.

"Let's try to ease a little closer and give her momma something to eat." Slowly he drove the truck as close as he dared and dropped some feed on the ground. He backed up until the cow walked to the pile of food.

Jinn watched out the window happily as the calf struggled to its feet and moved to nurse from its mother. Arne, however, couldn't tear his gaze away from her. When she grabbed his hand in excitement at seeing the new calf so close, he knew they both felt the shiver that raced down his body.

"Are you ready to move on?" he asked after a few minutes. "We still have a lot to feed."

"Yes." She sat back in the seat. "Wait, is it a boy or girl?"

"Mmm, looks like a heifer."

She stared at him blankly.

"Girl," he added with a laugh.

"So I'll name her...Daisy."

"You're going to name them all?"

"Of course."

"You know that's a lot of names you have to come up with."

"Oh." She cocked an eyebrow at him. "Challenge accepted."

He laughed as he drove away in search of more cattle. They didn't find any more calves, much to Jinn's disappointment. She did enjoy counting what they did find, operating the lever that dropped feed, and helping spread mineral supplement in the bunks. Everything they did seemed like a new and exciting adventure in her eyes.

For the first time, he didn't mind the early start this morning since he got to spend it with her.

By lunch, he could hear her stomach start to growl. He pulled into the next pasture and drove down by a large pond. He turned off the truck and pulled a cooler out from in front of the feeder. Jinn joined him on the back of the truck bed. He handed her a sandwich he made that morning.

"It's so pretty out here," she said. "So peaceful."

"It is that. Sometimes to the point of madness."

"What do you mean?" she asked, glancing at him between bites.

"I mean that I do a lot of this alone. It's a very solitary life. Dane likes to live this way, though he's much happier with Tani than he was alone. I don't know, I just wonder if I'm cut out to be this isolated."

"Well, I'm here for now," she answered, bumping her shoulder against him.

"For now," he echoed.

There was a low rumbling bellow before either one could say another word. A large bull walked around the front of the truck only to stop just out of arm's length. Jinn scampered around him on the bed.

"Here, let me get some feed." He stood and pulled back the door on the top of the feeder. Pulling out a handful of cubes, he handed them to her.

"What do I do?" she asked.

"Just hold one out."

He took a cube and held it out to the bull. Slowly the animal inched closer until he could take it from his hand. Jinn held out a piece the way he had. The bull licked the piece from her hand. She laughed before offering the next piece.

"He's slobbering all over me," she said.

"A little slobber never hurt anyone."

"It's gross." She laughed as she held out another piece. The bull took it, and she wiped the excess mess on Arne's shirt.

"Hey, I didn't say I wanted any."

She wiped more of it on his shirt. He batted at her, but she persisted until he was on his back. They were both laughing when she straddled his lap working to get every bit of the slobber off her and onto him.

"Stop," he said, wrestling with her.

She stopped just long enough to turn her stormy gaze on him. Then her lips were pressed against his.

He only had a moment to take in everything he could about her. How soft her lips were against his, how warm. The way he could feel his hands wrap around her small waist hidden inside all the layers. How his body came to life when her heat pressed against him. Then she was gone. Her silhouette rose above him as she sat up. She sat as if waiting for him to react.

"Jinn," he said, his voice deepened from the lust coursing through his body. "Don't make me fall for you if you're only going to leave."

She watched him lying underneath her for another minute before she whispered, "What if I stay?"

He sat up and pressed his hand behind her neck. She let him guide her back against his lips. His tongue traced the line that separated them until she opened. Then he imprinted her taste in his mind.

They broke away only to find a better angle. He felt her sigh against his lips as he deepened their kiss. She tilted her head when he insisted on tracing his tongue down her neck to her shoulder. There wasn't much more he could reach without some time peeling clothes from her. There were several reasons that wasn't a good idea.

"As much as I'm enjoying this, we should probably get finished feeding," he said as he leaned away from her.

"Yeah," she agreed. "My knees are cold on this bed, and I bet the big guy would like more than a handful of feed."

"We still have a couple more hours to go."

Neither of them moved. They sat staring at each other

until Arne couldn't take it anymore. He pulled her to his lips once more. A moan slipped out from between her lips as his hands fought under her coat to find soft skin. They nipped at each other hungrily until finally, he pushed back again.

"I think I'd really, really like to stay," she said.

"I think I'd really, really like you to stay too," he answered with a grin.

Carefully, he helped her from the back of the truck. She settled inside against him as he continued through the pasture. He liked her next to him. He was even getting used to the way his body responded every time she touched him.

"Can I ask you something?" she said, sitting back so she could turn toward him. "Is this a relationship?"

"I think this is the beginning of one," he answered after a few seconds. "They usually involve dating instead of just sharing a house, though."

He watched her in his peripheral vision stare out the windshield. *Where could this conversation be going?* he wondered.

"Okay, then you need to tell me if I'm doing something wrong."

"I think that works both ways."

"What do we do on these dates?"

"You've never been on a date? How old are you?" It wasn't something he had thought about until now. Please tell him he wasn't sharing spit with an underaged woman.

"Twenty." She laughed. "I've been with a lot of men, but no one ever took me somewhere. I used to hear my classmates talk about their older siblings dating, but they didn't know any more than I did."

"Okay, well, I've gone on a lot of dates, but I've never been with any of them," he said. "How about we see if Kip can stay this evening with Mom, and we'll have our first date. At the house, of course," he added hastily when a look of panic crossed over her face.

"In that case, I accept your invitation."

"Perfect. Let's get this done so we can get ready." He winked at her, and she grinned. This was going to be interesting.

They finally finished feeding in the late afternoon. He would have been done sooner, but Jinn had insisted they stop several times to investigate something. They wandered along the river, looked in the old shed, and watched a badger hole just to see if anything showed up.

Pulling back to the main house, they found a game of softball happening in the field next to it.

"Hey, am I the only one who works around here?" he asked, climbing out of the truck.

"Arne!" Kip squealed. "I'm learning how to play softball." She rushed to him, grabbed his wrist, and tugged him back toward the game. "They say you're the fastest. I want to see how fast you can chase a ball."

"Here's your glove," Roar said, slapping his baseball glove against his chest. "Watch her, she catches on fast."

Arne took his place in the outfield. Roar was squatting behind the rock they called home plate. His dad tossed a ball and Dane waited near a feed sack that substituted for first base. Thyra yelled encouragement from second.

"Can I play?" Jinn yelled.

"Of course," Roar said, digging another glove out of a box.

"What do I do?"

"Catch the balls that come to you and throw them to Dane," Thyra instructed.

Jinn was shown to another feed sack that served as third base and waited. Thyra returned to second and nodded at Sten. He tossed the ball in a slow arch to Kip. She swung with everything she had and hit the ball straight at Arne. He caught it easily and winged it back to Dane.

"Did you see that, Arne?" Kip said, jumping up and down.

"I did. You're a natural." He noticed even Dane smiling at her excitement.

They continued to play until Freja called them in for dinner.

"Did you see me?" Kip asked the moment she entered the kitchen.

"I did," Freja answered. "I watched for a while out the window. You were amazing." Kip threw her arms around his mother.

"I've had the best day." Releasing Freja, she turned to Arne. "I learned to bake a pie, we worked in the garden, and then Thyra taught me to play softball." Her smile was at least a mile wide. "And Dane even taught me how to drive a tractor."

He looked around the table as they found their seats, everyone had a smile on their face.

"I might have to put her to work come harvest season," Dane teased. Even he couldn't suppress his amusement.

"Hey," Tani announced, walking through the door with Aksel in tow. "What did I miss?"

It was just the prompt Kip needed to start telling about her day all over again. Jinn squeezed Arne's hand under the table. He winked at her.

"Speaking of," Arne said when Kip finally took a breath. "Would it be alright if Kip stayed a little longer? I have a date this evening." He grinned at Jinn as the table grew quiet.

"Of course," Freja finally said. "Kip is welcome here anytime."

"Yay," Kip answered before falling into conversation with Thyra over their evening plans.

Neither girl caught the concerned looks from the rest of his family, but Arne did. He knew they were worried about the situation. Hell, he was too. He was worried someone would come looking for them. He was worried he'd fall hard and then lose Jinn. There was a whole ton of worry slowly building up inside him, but all he knew to do was take each day as it came.

Dinner had ended, and he was carrying dishes to the kitchen when Dane motioned for him to follow outside. They stepped into the backyard where they wouldn't be overheard.

"Are you sure you know what you're doing?" Dane asked.

"Dane, you've known me for twenty-three years now. When have I ever known what I was doing?" he answered.

"Fair." Dane considered him for a moment before adding, "We just don't want to see you hurt. No one is certain this is the safest place for them. We have no idea where they came from. Dad has been sniffing around, but it's hard to do without throwing up flags."

"I know, but it's just a harmless night of a movie and popcorn, or maybe a game over ice cream. Nothing more, I promise. Will be back later for Kip."

"Okay," Dane finally relented. "Just use your brain, Arne. You tend to think with your heart. This time, it might just get you hurt." Dane slapped him on the back and started back toward the house. "I don't want to wake up one morning to find my little brother was killed by some unknown men," he said over his shoulder.

"How's that different from what happened with Tani?"

"It's not, that's why I'm worried. I know what we went through for her. I'll be right by your side if you need me. Just don't do anything stupid without one of us around." He walked inside the house without another word.

Jinn stepped outside. "Are you alright?"

"Yeah, I just think he still thinks of me as some kid who can't take care of himself."

"He says what he thinks you need to hear because he loves you. I do the same thing with Kip."

"I know. Are you ready?" he asked, changing the subject.

He could deal with his brother another time. Right now all he was thinking about was enjoying the rest of their evening.

"Let me just go make sure Kip is fine and say goodbye."

"I'll wait out here for you." He leaned against the fence to wait while she moved back inside. Dane was right about something; they didn't know if anyone was still looking for them. If so, he needed to have a plan if they showed up on his doorstep. Tomorrow he would go over a plan just in case that happened.

"Ready?" Jinn asked, stepping back outside.

"More than you can imagine," he answered with a smile.

ELEVEN

Arne woke early the next morning to get a headstart on the day. He wasn't feeding the cattle today but instead planned to spend half the day up to his ankles in the mud trying to fix a water pipe in the pens. Just another day in the glamorous life of a cowboy.

He crept as silently as possible into the bathroom. It didn't matter, Jinn was still in the kitchen when he walked into the living room.

They had spent the evening playing board games across the table from each other. He did kiss her goodnight after picking up Kip from his mother's, but that was as far as it went.

It was still a nice night. Jinn had caught on to most of the games quickly and even managed to beat him soundly at dominos. He tried explaining to her that dominos were mostly played now at senior centers. She didn't care; she liked the challenge of it. He would have to introduce her to chess next time.

"I told you I don't need breakfast in the morning. You're welcome to sleep in," he said.

"I'm not sleeping in while you go to work," she answered, squaring her shoulders. "I'll come help you." She stepped out from behind the bar fully clothed.

"You're going to get wet."

"Okay." She set his plate on the bar and walked toward the hallway. "I'll wake Kip."

He shrugged and dug into his eggs. He wasn't about to argue with her when her mind was made up. Voices argued in the bedroom. It didn't sound like Kip was on board with the plan at all. She came stomping out of the bedroom a few minutes later with a sleepy scowl on her face.

"Don't look at me; this is your sister's idea."

"Whatever," she sulked.

She might be spending too much time with his sister. Taking his toast, she chomped into it violently as she crossed to the coat rack. She slid on her coat and turned to face him.

"Well, are we going?"

"Yes, ma'am." He had to stifle a smile as he set his plate in the sink.

"Kip," Jinn warned. They all jumped when there was a rap on the front door. "Come." The women scrambled back down the hallway as Arne crossed to the door.

"Arne, it's me," he heard Dane call from just outside the door.

"You have a key," he said, opening the door. "Why didn't you just let yourself inside?"

"I don't want to be almost shot a second time."

"Fair. What's up?" There was a time when they went to work together. Now, with a new baby to help get ready, it's a wonder Dane made it to work at all. He didn't have time to deal with Arne too.

"I wanted to let you know what I heard in town this

morning. Tani's car is acting up, so I took her to work. I swung by Donna's to pick up breakfast. Oh, here you go." He handed a bag to Kip who had strolled back into the living room the second she recognized Dane's voice. Arne was pretty sure she had a schoolgirl crush on him.

"Anyway, Donna said a couple of big guys were in yesterday asking about two runaways. Said one kidnapped the other. She said no one said anything, but I thought you should know."

"So they finally made it here," Arne said. His gaze drifted to Jinn. Her eyes were wide as she stared at Kip. "Hey, you're okay. We won't let anything happen. They'll probably drift on to the next town." She gave him the briefest nod. "We were just heading to Mom and Dad's."

"Good idea. Come on, Kip. You can ride with me," Dane said.

The teenager happily followed him out the door.

"Arne, what are we going to do?" Jinn hissed when Kip was out of earshot.

"We go to work as usual. You'll be safe at Mom's; so will Kip. I promise." He stared down into scared eyes.

Finally, as if it took a monumental effort, and he supposed it did, she nodded again. Now, he just had to keep his word.

"I'll take Dane and go to town later to see what I can find out. We just have to stay one step ahead." He took her hand and led her outside. "It's all going to be fine." Now, if he could just believe that himself.

The morning passed quickly. Jinn helped him dig the line out while wearing his mother's rubber boots. He found the problem valve right where he thought it was. She sat on the side of the hole and watched as he replaced it. They turned the water back on only to find a broken float in one of the troughs. He let her work on fixing it until he couldn't stand to watch her shiver with her hands in the cold water for another second.

"Son," his father greeted him as he walked toward the pens. "Good morning, Jinn."

"Good morning," she answered.

"I think you and Dane should have lunch in town. Royal called to say a couple of men were asking around town about two women. You need to see what you can find out about them."

"That's what we planned on. Dane said Donna told him they were sniffing around this morning at the diner."

"Jinn and Kip will be fine here. Your mother has Kip working through one of Thyra's old math workbooks. I guess Tani is bringing some school books over after work this evening. Jinn can help me throw hay later."

Arne looked up at where Jinn still sat on the side of the water trough. She smiled and nodded.

"We'll be just fine, won't we, Jinn?"

"Yes. Absolutely." She stood, dusted off her pants, and followed him to the house.

"Okay then. I'll get Dane."

Arne watched until she disappeared inside before walking to the equipment shed. This time of year, Dane was guaranteed to have his head stuck in some piece of equipment. It was the only downtime he had until he started right back into farming. Their busy seasons were the opposite of each other, which made getting extra help easier.

"Ready for lunch?" he asked, walking into the equipment barn.

"I could eat." Dane wiped the grease off of his hands with a rag and tossed it on a table overflowing with tools. "We going to town to nose around a little?"

"That's the plan."

"Come on. We can take my truck."

Arne followed his brother to the truck parked right outside the door. They slid inside and started the drive to town.

"So how's it going?" Dane asked after they turned onto the pavement.

"Fine. I guess we're already calving, which is early. The water in the pens might actually be fixed this time—"

"I meant with your living arrangements," Dane growled.

"Oh. Good, I guess?" Arne answered. Truth be told, he had no idea. "It's like having roommates, except I get to kiss one occasionally. Is that what you felt like when Tani lived with us before you got married?"

"Not really. All I could think about was getting in her pants."

"Yeah." Arne stared out the window.

It's not like his brothers didn't discuss sex or their lack of it, but somehow this felt different. Dane had found his soulmate. He had known she was his since the first time he saw her as a boy. Arne was different. Jinn had almost dropped right into his lap. He wasn't positive either one of them believed they were each other's soulmates.

"I just don't want to add to her struggles, you know?" he added. "She's already been through so much."

"What does she say about it?"

"I don't know. I don't know if she knows. She told me she's never been in a relationship before."

"Then be the one she can't live without."

"Jesus, you're beginning to sound like Roar," Arne said with a laugh.

Dane punched him in the arm.

"Oww."

They pulled up in front of Donna's diner. Dane turned off the truck and climbed out. Arne followed him inside.

"Hey, Arne," Donna greeted him. "Haven't seen you in a while."

"I've been crazy busy." They found an empty table by the windows. "Couldn't go without your chicken fried steak too long though. Or that last piece of pie?"

She laughed and pulled a pie plate out from under the glass cover. Walking to the table, she placed the last piece of chocolate pie at his elbow. "You know I always have a piece for you, sweetheart," she said. "What's been keeping you so busy?"

"Can you believe I already have a calf on the ground? Not to mention the stupid fence I keep repairing."

She laughed when Dane rolled his eyes. "What can I get you boys?"

"We'll both do the special," Dane said.

"Gotcha. I'll be back with your drinks."

"Hey, Donna," Arne said before she could return to the kitchen. "What can you tell me about the men who were sniffing around for some missing women?"

She slid into an empty chair next to him. "I figured if anyone in this town knew about them, it would be you two. Don't worry, I've got nothing to say to them," she added when Arne opened his mouth to protest. "They were big guys. You only missed them by about fifteen minutes."

"They're still in town?" Dane asked.

"Yeah, said this is where their trail goes cold. Whatever that means. Personally," she said, leaning in. "I hope they get away." Standing, she moved back toward the kitchen.

"Shit," Arne mumbled. "Do I smuggle them out of here until everything blows over?"

"You saw how good hiding worked for Tani and I. No, I still believe they're safer with us. You live in the middle of nowhere. What are the chances they'll find their way to your house?"

"Mom and Dad's though. Everyone knows where they live. It's not exactly like they're Fort Knox."

"Dad can take care of himself," Dane hissed back. "Mom can too for that matter. But Jinn and Kip might actually be safer at your place."

"What do we do in the meantime? They can't stay hidden forever."

"I know, but we also can't ask around for those guys' personal information in order to have them arrested. They technically haven't done anything we can prove was illegal. It would be a he said/she said thing. It would just throw up red flags."

They both lapsed into silence as their food was delivered. Arne took a bite of his chicken fried steak chewing thoughtfully. Dane was right. If they went to the sheriff's office to file an official complaint, it would be Jinn's word against what could be a powerful man.

He knew how things worked in this area. It was too easy to bait the sheriff with gifts. He already held a grudge against Dane just because he broke up with the man's daughter in high school. Or was it when he decked his son? Either way, the man hated his older brother.

"You're right," he finally admitted. "But I think I need to do some modifications to my house if we're going to stay there."

"A trip to the hardware store it is then," Dane said.

"Yeah, and I'm going to need a favor from Roar."

THAT EVENING, Arne stood stretching his back. Jinn was standing next to him admiring his work. With the help of his brothers, they now had a trap door leading under the house and out the back. He had also installed the cameras that Roar had shown up with after work. They automatically sent an alarm to the house and Arne's phone if someone came down the road.

"We have the reinforced doors on," Dane said, walking over to where Arne was affixing the last camera to a tree. "Shouldn't be able to just kick them in."

"Dinner's ready," Kip said, bounding out of the house. "Roar helped me make it."

"Just a little," he said behind her. He had been working on hooking up the cameras to the computer inside. "You're a quick study."

Kip beamed at him. It looked to Arne that she might have developed a crush on the oldest brother, too.

"I would love to, but I'm sure Tani is wondering where I am," Dane said. "Rain check?"

"Okay, I'll let you off the hook this time," she said with a grin. "But only because it's Tani."

Then his brother did something Arne knew he rarely did. Dane, the grumpy one, leaned over and planted a kiss on the top of Kip's head. With a wave, he climbed into his truck and drove off. Kip stood with a dreamy look in her eyes until Jinn cleared her throat.

"The rest of you wash up," Kip said, waking up from her stupor. "Chicken waits for no man." With a flourish, she walked back into the house.

"Wow," Jinn whispered. "Your brothers bring the drama right out in her. Thank heavens Erik isn't here."

"It's nice to see her come out of her shell," Arne answered.

"You're right; it is."

"Come on, you two," Kip said, sticking her head back outside. "No holding up dinner while you suck face."

"Maybe a little too out of her shell," Jinn mumbled.

But Arne saw the smile on her face as she climbed the steps to the front door.

CHAPTER

TWELVE

"It's not hard, Kip," Jinn said with a sigh. "You open the door and drop under the house."

"But there're spiders under there."

"Since when are you scared of a few spiders?"

"Since finding out there are people who live without having to wake up every morning with bites covering their arms."

Her sister had her on that point. The basement they lived in before had not only spiders, but mice, roaches, and bedbugs most of the time. The week spent in nature was better than the basement. Arne's house was like living in luxury.

"I understand that, but we need to practice just in case someone comes for us."

Reaching down, she pulled on the trapdoor that led under the house. She had purposefully waited until Arne went to work before rousting Kip out of bed. There was no guarantee that he would be around when they came. Slinging her legs inside the opening, she dropped down under the house.

"Now what?" Kip asked, swinging down beside her. Jinn was proud of Kip. Even though she complained, she still had the courage to save herself.

"Arne said to crawl to the back."

On her hands and knees, she worked her way to the back of the house. It was the farthest point of the house from the road. They were less likely to be seen by anyone pulling up outside.

"Once we reach the back, it's a short sprint to where the hill slopes toward the bottoms."

She nodded her head toward the point where the ground disappeared about three hundred feet from their location.

"Alright, here we go." Kip shot out from under the house like a scared rabbit and raced for the edge. Jinn was right on her heels. Kip stopped when she reached the side to look back. "Not too bad. I don't think anyone would see us unless they knew to look."

"That's why Arne wanted the cameras to set off an alarm when someone was at the far edge of the property. If we drop everything and run, we should be away from the house before anyone arrives."

"Makes sense."

"You have to promise me one thing, though," Jinn said, turning to her sister. "No matter what happens, you go immediately. Don't wait for me or Arne. You need to get as far away as you can as quickly as possible. Promise me."

"Jinn—" Kip began to protest.

"Promise me," Jinn snapped.

Kip nodded her head forlornly.

"You run as hard as you can to Papa Ulvmand's house. It's through that bottom and over the far hill," she added, pointing. "Not far at all. Whatever happens, you have to get there. They can protect you. Understand?"

Kip nodded her head with more determination this time.

"Good. Now let's go do it again, just for good measure."

Kip groaned but followed her back to the house.

Jinn didn't make Kip drop under the house just one more time. She made her do it five until it was ingrained in her sister's head. She also taught Kip how to check the cameras on Arne's computer, how to load and fire his gun, and how to fight back if she is grabbed.

They also made a batch of cookies just to even everything out. She didn't want Kip living in complete fear when so much was right with their current circumstances.

"Do you think Arne will like these?" Kip asked, pulling the last of the snickerdoodles out of the oven.

"Have you seen anything Arne doesn't like?" Jinn laughed. "Especially when it comes to food."

They heard a key inserted into the lock on the front door at the same time.

"It's just me," Arne called before opening the door. "Is that snickerdoodle I smell?"

"It is," Kip answered, grinning at Jinn.

"They are possibly my favorite cookies."

"Try one; they're still warm."

Arne slid a cookie off the cooling rack and popped half of it in his mouth. "Mmm, that's amazing," he moaned.

Somehow the sound shot straight through Jinn's body to land in the core of her being. How could he not have had more sex than he could handle if that's the noise he made just having a cookie?

"Everything okay?" he asked, gazing at her.

"Yeah, yep, everything's great," she answered.

He looked at her quizzically, but chose to stuff the rest of the cookie in his mouth instead of questioning her further. Problem was, her body was still buzzing. Never had she felt turned on by a man before. It was new and not wholly unwelcome.

"Why are you home so early?" she asked, trying to ignore the sensations floating through her.

"It's the weekend," he answered, stealing another cookie. "It was suggested I take you to the city to do some shopping. We'll head to Dallas just to be safe. What do you think?"

"I think that sounds amazing, but we don't have money to pay for anything," Jinn said.

She ignored the excited vibrations coming from Kip at the idea of shopping. Her sister had never gone shopping before. Come to think of it, neither had she. Her experience just extended to whatever was on sale at the local discount store.

"Not a problem." He took a credit card from his pocket and waved it at her. "Dad sent me with the company card and strict instructions to get anything you want."

"We can't do that," Jinn said, shaking her head.

"That's fine, but you go explain that to him. I know not to argue with that man when he's set on something." He smiled at her and shoved another piece of cookie in his mouth.

"I guess we're going shopping then."

"Guess so." His eyes sparkled with mirth. If she stood around any longer staring into that cerulean gaze, they might not make it to the city after all. "Pack anything you need for overnight in case we don't make it home until tomorrow."

Jinn turned on her heels and sped to the bedroom. She needed the distance to regain control of herself.

"What has gotten into you?" Kip asked, walking into the bedroom.

Jinn ignored her as she tossed an extra shirt in the small bag.

"Is it just me, or does Arne just keep getting hotter?"

Jinn felt her face flare a deep crimson red.

"Ah-ha, I thought so. You like him, don't you?"

"Shh, keep your voice down," she snapped. "I don't know, I've never felt like this about anyone."

Kip didn't say anything more, but her smile told Jinn she was busted. Was what she was feeling for Arne love or just infatuation? Would she even know the difference? She was too old to have a schoolgirl crush on him. Was he falling for her?

"Ready?" Kip asked, jarring her out of her thoughts.

She nodded and followed her sister out of the room.

By the time they settled into the big truck with the back seat, Arne had showered, changed into clean clothes, and smelled like the stuff of dreams. His hand rested on her thigh as he pulled onto the main road. She felt her face flush at his touch. When had she turned shy?

"Is this okay?" he asked.

She had never been asked permission to be touched before.

"Yes, it's fine."

It was strange to be given control of something so simple. He had yet to try and force himself on her. She had even kissed him first. She laughed softly at the memory.

"What?"

"I was just thinking of kissing you the first time," she answered.

"I have to admit, you did take me by surprise. A good surprise."

They drove through town to another highway and went west. It was the first time she had been to town since they moved in. She took in everything all at once. There was a small fire station, the restaurant where he went to lunch, several small gift shops, and the school Tani taught at and Thyra went to. There was even a store that boasted ice cream. Good thing Kip had fallen asleep before they hit the pavement.

"I like your town," she said.

They passed by a supply store with several old men standing around a truck talking. She turned to watch them as they passed. "It's a lot like the town I came from. When I was a kid, not where I ended up."

"Oh yeah, where was that?" he asked.

"Doesn't matter." She laid her head against the headrest.

It did matter, but she didn't want anything to ruin their day. Especially not what happened to her in that other town.

ARNE FORGOT that doing anything in a small town set you up for the local gossip. It didn't escape the old men standing around the truck in the farm supply parking lot that there was a young woman in his truck. They didn't know who it was, but they did know it wasn't any of his family. Those same men decided to take their conversation to Donna's where two large strangers sat that afternoon having a late lunch.

"Did you see who was in the front seat with Sten's boy?" one asked the others.

"Which boy?"

"The middle one. The younger middle one."

"That boy always has a passel of girls around him. Has since junior high. Mother had to beat them off with a stick."

"He's too friendly for his own good," another piped up.

The strangers at the other table perked up. The conversation wasn't wasted on them. They had been scouring the countryside looking for the two women who had escaped. There were strict orders not to return without them.

"I don't think he's passed by a stray that he didn't take home." The old men chuckled. "What's that boy's name?"

"Arne, I believe. They all have odd names."

"Arne who?" one of the strangers growled at the table of old men.

"Don't believe we've been introduced," one of them said. It was polite speak for fuck off.

"Arne who?" the stranger asked again.

"Ulvamand. Everyone in these parts knows the family," the old farmer said.

The other men shot looks at him, but there was something about the strangers that screamed violence. He wanted nothing to do with getting on their bad side. The strangers stood and left the diner.

"What did you do that for?"

"I wouldn't worry about it," he responded. "Sten can look out for his own."

In the parking lot, one of the strangers pulled out his phone and pressed a number. "Boss? Yeah, we've found them, we think. Seems they're living with some farm family." He paused as he listened to the other end of the line.

"Don't worry. We'll get them back." He paused once again. "Yes, and leave no witnesses. We'll handle it, boss."

"What did he say?" the other stranger asked.

"Get the girls back, bring this Arne guy back to the house for him to teach a lesson, and dispose of anyone who gets in our way."

"Sounds perfect," the other said, cracking his knuckles. They didn't just radiate violence, they thrived on it. "How do we find this guy?"

"We ask nicely."

They grinned at each other.

"We'll follow the old guy home. I don't think he'll hold out too long before telling us everything we want to know."

Sliding into the black SUV with dark windows, they pulled across the street where they could watch the door of Donna's without being discovered. It wasn't long before the old man in question said goodbye to his friends and walked out to his truck.

They followed as he wound his way out of town and pulled through the gate of a small farm on the outskirts. He was allowed to park and move inside his house before they drove through the gate.

The strangers climbed out of their vehicle to assess the home. From the looks of it, they lived alone far enough from their neighbors so no one would hear them scream.

One of the strangers knocked on the door. When the old man answered with a smile on his face, they forced their way inside. It didn't take long for him to understand why they were here, though why they needed directions to the Ulvmand's place was beyond him. Still, he handed over the information freely rather than the strangers following through on the threats to him or his wife.

"You tell anyone we were here, we'll come back. Understand?" The old man nodded his head, a trickle of blood flowing where they pistol-whipped him just to reinforce their point. "You call and warn them, we come back."

"No. No, we won't," his wife assured them.

She was cowering in the corner of the living room holding her husband. Later, she would clean up not just his head but also where blood had dripped onto her carpet.

The strangers left as quickly as they came, slamming the screen door behind them. They laughed, hearing the dead bolt lock before they could clear the porch. Chances were good that door would be kept locked from now on.

CHAPTER

THIRTEEN

The shopping trip to the city passed without incident. Arne suggested they stay the night, but relented when Jinn became nervous. He understood it was hard enough sleeping at his house. A motel might just be too much.

Instead, they drove home, arriving just after midnight. Arne stepped out of the truck to unlock the gate unaware that two strangers were searching the area for him. He pulled the truck through and relocked it on the other side.

"I'll get the bags if you want to drag Kip to bed," he said.

He parked in front of the door and began gathering their bags from the back seat. He chuckled at the grumbling from Kip as her sister pulled her from the truck. He carried the first load of bags into the house and returned for the second load. When he locked the door, Jinn stood in the living room surveying the load on the table.

"I think we got carried away," she said.

"I think you got carried away just enough," he answered.

She smiled and turned to face him. "How do you always know the right thing to say?"

"I'm sure most of my family would disagree."

"I don't care what they say," she said, sliding her arms around his waist. "You're a good man." Pushing up on her toes, she kissed him. "Why do you shiver whenever I touch you?"

"It's a long, complicated story best left to another day."

"Will you tell me someday?"

"I will, but for now I think we could both use some sleep." He ushered her down the hallway in front of him.

When she turned into the bathroom, he continued to the bedroom. He waited for her to finish in the bathroom before brushing his teeth and getting ready for bed. His eyes were just closing when he felt the bed dip.

"Tell me your story," Jinn whispered.

He settled more deeply into the mattress, facing her. She wasn't ready for the whole story; that would take more than one late night. He could tell her a little, though.

"The whole story will take longer than tonight," he said. "I can tell you we don't know why we shiver like we do. Dane always did when he was around Tani. I think it has something to do with fate choosing our mates. I don't remember if Roar did it when he was with his college girlfriend. After she left, he's never bothered with anyone else."

"So you think the universe is trying to tell us we belong together?"

"I don't know about that. It's just a theory anyway."

The bedroom grew silent. He wished he could see Jinn's face to know what she was thinking. It was too dark to see more than just her form under his covers.

"It's a beautiful theory," she finally said. Her hand brushed his jaw.

"Will you tell me what happened before you escaped here?"

"That's also a story for another time," she whispered.

SSHE WOKE up in the cinderblock room with no idea what time it was. There were no windows, nor was there a clock. It took her a few minutes to remember where she was. The evening before came back to her as if it were a horror movie she had watched curled up on the couch. But this wasn't her couch, and there was nowhere to watch a movie.

"Hello?" she said, sitting up on the edge of the cot.

All she heard was her words echoed back at her. She stood and made a trip around the room. The door was securely locked when she tried opening it. The bathroom was barely large enough to hold the small shower, toilet, and cracked sink.

She was just returning to the cot when she heard a key scrape in the lock. The door opened and one of the largest of the henchmen stepped inside.

"Boss wants you cleaned up and brought to him," he grunted.

He threw a pair of the smallest shorts she had ever seen at her. It was accompanied by a white T-shirt and a scratchy towel. No shoes or underwear.

"Get showered."

She waited for him to leave. When he didn't, she walked slowly to the bathroom. There was no door in the room.

He moved into the room for a better view of the bathroom and leaned against the wall with a smirk. Turning her back to him, she slid from her clothes. Stepping into the shower, she tried to wash as quickly as possible. The old towel did nothing to cover her nakedness nor remove much of the water. Still, she held it against her as she pulled on the clothes.

"Let's go," he said, taking a firm grip on her arm.

She was marched up several flights of stairs before reaching a hallway landing. They walked down the hall until they reached a door. With a quick knock, he opened it and shoved her inside. She landed hard just inside the door on her hands and knees. Looking up, her gaze was met by that of the man who had paid her father's debts in exchange for her.

His eyes held hers in a glare of detachment that worried her more than the clenched fist at his side. He was the first man in a long time that she couldn't read. Should she stand defiantly in front of him or cower on the floor? They all wanted something from her; she just had to learn what this particular man wanted.

"Stand her up," he barked as if she were simply a piece of furniture that had fallen over.

The big man, who reminded her of the villain in an old James Bond movie, grabbed her by the arm and yanked her off the floor. Bond villain (or Bond for short) shook her slightly for good measure. "How old are you?"

"Sixteen," she answered.

She was barely fourteen, but she was so used to lying about her age now that it was second nature. He studied her for a few minutes. She tried to meet his steely expression, but her gaze kept sliding to the floor.

"Look, I don't know how much he owes, but I'm sure we can work something out. I'm pretty good at cleaning or even cooking a little." She faded into silence when he just chuckled.

"Get pictures," he barked at Bond. Then he turned to her. "There's nothing to work out. He owes me a lot of money, and you're going to make it back for me."

She opened her mouth to speak again but then closed it. Maybe it was best if she didn't ask too many questions.

"In a month," he said to Bond before turning back to his desk.

She was pulled from the room and deposited back in the basement. She sat on the cot and waited for what was to come next. Only nothing did.

For the next month, she was fed, taken outside for some sun, and brought clean clothes. Each time they took her into the backyard to walk, she studied the fence. She was no closer to figuring out how to escape than she was when she first arrived. Still, there had to be some way to get away from here.

Then, a month later, she was woken up in the afternoon by a key entering the lock to her room. The door opened, and a woman stood just outside. She carried a small box and a stack of clothes in her arms. She stepped solemnly into the room as the door closed behind her.

"Hi, I'm—" Jinn began.

"Take off your things and get in the shower. Wash your hair well, wrap the towel around your waist, and come back in here," the woman said, cutting her off.

Jinn took the towel offered; she was getting used to showering with an audience. The shampoo she was given smelled like cherry blossoms. After shampooing her hair twice, she scrubbed her body with jasmine-smelling soap. Feeling cleaner than she had in a long time, she returned to the cot where the woman waited.

"Lay on the bed and spread your legs."

That was her first introduction to waxing. She was smacked after the second whimper escaped her lips. When they were done, she was sat up while her hair was twisted into an updo. Makeup was applied making her look even older than she was. A sheer slip dress was slid over her head and heels she could barely walk in were strapped to her feet.

"Turn," the woman snapped.

Jinn did her best to turn in a full circle without falling.

"You'll do." The woman rapped on the door once.

It was immediately opened to allow one of the other guards (she thought of this one as Jabba) inside. He fit a collar around Jinn's neck and led her from the room. In the hallway, she was joined by two other women also being led upstairs. She wondered briefly where they had come from. Were there more than just her trapped in this cellar?

"Behave tonight, or I'll beat you bloody when we get back downstairs," Jabba snarled at her. He jerked on the chain connected to her collar, and she almost fell over her shoes as she climbed the stairs.

"Clumsy little bitch," he sneered. He gave another pull on the chain, but she was ready for it this time. They climbed toward what sounded like a raucous party upstairs. Of course, her first job must be bartending.

"Ahh, here they are, gentlemen."

She was led around the room until she arrived at the front next to the other women. There was a tall round platform with steps attached to the back. There was also a smaller stage with a lectern on it. He was standing behind the lectern talking to the room full of men. Jinn looked closely at the audience; there wasn't a single woman save the three of them in the group.

"First up for offer is our beautiful Lotus," he said.

Jinn watched as one of the women was helped onto the tall stage. She stood shaking as she took in the crowd. Numbers were called and the bids grew higher. Were they all just being sold to the next man?

Jinn wasn't sure what the winning bid was, but Lotus was soon helped off the stage and led away. The girl called Apple climbed the steps next. The bidding quickly rose until the gavel was brought down finally. She was led away by the man holding the end of her leash.

"We have saved the sweetest for last," he announced. "Our own little Cherry Blossom to charm her way into your bed."

The men around her laughed, but Jinn couldn't find anything funny in what he said. Was she now named Cherry Blossom? Jabba jerked on her chain, and she was helped up the steps. Standing on the stage, she could see at least three dozen men were watching her. Bidding started; she flinched each time someone held up their card.

"Anyone else? No? Sold for forty-three thousand to you, sir."

Jinn followed where he was looking to find an older, sweaty man with a smug look on his face. Jabba pulled on her neck collar, almost jerking her off the stage. He managed to catch her arm and upright her before she hit the floor.

"Let's go," Jabba said.

He led her out of the room. At the other end of the house, he pulled her into a large bedroom. Taking the chain from her collar, he locked her to a different chain attached to the wall above the headboard. He tossed the key on a table near the door. She couldn't reach it to unlock herself if she tried.

"Do whatever he wants. Make the client happy, and I'll

see to it you have an extra pudding at supper." He laughed all the way out the door.

Jinn took in the bedroom when the door slammed closed. It looked like any other bedroom, except it had furniture in it she had never seen before. The door opened half an hour later. The same old, sweaty man from the auction waltzed inside. Grabbing her ankle, he pulled her down on the bed until the collar had her gasping for breath. Then he began to undress.

Even now, Jinn couldn't bring herself to remember most of what happened that night. The man had sold her virginity to the highest bidder. A man with bad body odor and a kink for choking women.

The next day she was returned to her basement room with bruises covering her neck. She also had a black eye from him hitting her in his fervor to make her scream. She heard later that he had to pay extra for the damage he inflicted on her. Or as Jabba explained it, he broke the merchandise.

JINN PRESSED her body against Arne's sleeping form. Even in sleep, he wrapped his arms around her in a protective cocoon. Sometime in the night, Kip had slid into the bed behind her. She hugged her sister to her. Shaking the lingering memories from her brain, she reveled in the peace that being with Arne brought her.

She knew she would never tell him all the details about living in that house for so long. His lips pressed silently against her forehead. No, there was nothing to be gained by introducing evil into his world.

Arne was everything good in this life. She knew she would do whatever it took to keep him that way. Even if it meant hiding her innermost darkness deep inside. He had enough sunshine for both of them.

FOURTEEN

Arne woke up late the next morning in a bed full of women. Two to be exact. Jinn was smashed as close as she could get to his chest while Kip lay tucked up behind her. They all only took up half of the available space.

It wasn't a bad way to wake up, he decided. The only problem he could see with his current circumstance was the morning wood raging and barely contained.

He eased out from in front of Jinn. Quietly, he walked to the bathroom. He closed the door behind him, leaned against the wall, looked in the mirror, and blew out a long breath.

The picture that greeted him was concerning. His hair stood straight up, he had a shadow covering his jaw, and his face had wrinkles from being pressed against the pillow.

That didn't even begin to describe the tent in his sleep pants. Actually, it had moved past the tent stage right into the peeking out the top stage. If he were a betting man, he would say his balls had reached at least the ultramarine shade of blue. It had been so long since he had felt any relief—not since the women had moved in down the hallway.

He jumped when the bathroom door slid open, and Jinn slid inside the bathroom. He opened his mouth to speak, but she placed a finger over her lips. Closing his mouth again, he waited to see what she was up to. She stood in front of him and took a long gaze down his body and back up. It was almost enough to take care of his current problem.

"Shh," she whispered.

Reaching over, she turned off the overhead light. He could still see their shadows in the mirror from a small night light. Gripping the back of his neck, she pulled him down so she could reach his lips. She pressed them to his for just a moment before her mouth opened. His tongue swept inside. How was it possible to taste so sweet after just waking up? He fought a sudden urge to taste her every-where, every single inch.

She pressed her hand inside his sleep pants and wrapped her hand firmly around his shaft.

"Jinn," he growled in warning. He pushed back up to his full height to slow down the path they were on. Trying to still the hand stroking him, he caught her wrist. His pants were already puddled on the floor at his feet.

"Don't, Arne," she whispered. "Let me take care of you this time."

"There are some things you need to know first."

"I promise we won't go that far. Not yet, anyway."

"Make sure we stick to that," he answered. "Because I know the moment I slide inside you, there's no turning back for me."

She nodded her head, and he slowly released his grip on

her wrist. "There's lube in the cabinet behind you," he added with a nod at the cabinet.

Even in the semi-darkness, he caught the smile on her face when she turned around to grab it. She squirted a generous amount into her hand before gripping him again. This time, he couldn't mask the gasp coming from his lips at the feel.

His mouth crashed back against hers. His body screamed for more of her. Finding the hem of her sleep shirt, he pulled it over her head. Her nipples begged for his hand, his mouth, his teeth. He swallowed her moan as he brushed his thumb over a tight nub. She gripped him tighter as he rocked his hips, her fingers sliding over his hard cock.

"That's it," he groaned, feeling the tingling begin in his spine. "Just like that. Fuck, you're going to ruin me. Harder, babe, harder." He could no longer control the stream of words coming from his mouth.

His eyes closed as she worked him harder. He was so close, barely hanging on at this point. The slightest thing would send him over. Then she reached up and pulled his lips back against hers.

Arne came harder than he could remember. Or at least he thought he did. The fact he didn't pass out doing it was a miracle. One second all he could feel was the stranglehold she had on him, then he was trying to ride out the ringing in his ears. Light burst behind his eyelids as warm liquid coated her hand. Air wheezed in and out of his chest.

His eyes popped open when she stooped to pick up her discarded shirt. It was one of his old college practice shirts, but it looked better on her than it ever did on him. He caught her wrist when she stood. Pulling a towel off the rack next to him, he wiped her hand off. He took the shirt from her hand and tossed it back on the floor.

"We're not done," he rumbled.

"We're not?" she asked.

"Do you want to be done?" He waited for her answer. All he wanted was just a little more of this woman, his woman. "Nothing that will get us into trouble."

She remained mute.

"I promise you'll like it if you trust me."

"I do trust you," she said finally.

"Then let me take care of you." He brushed his lips across hers.

The next time they met, he swept his tongue inside as he pushed her against the counter. He felt the moment her body relaxed into his. His lips traced a path down her neck to her collarbone. Her head fell against the cabinet with a gentle thud as he kissed his way to her breasts.

"Arne," she moaned as he pulled her rosy nipple between his lips.

Her hand threaded through his hair as he worried her nipple into a hard point. He released it with a chuckle when she pulled his hair to the other side. He nipped it with his teeth; she responded by grinding her heat against his thigh.

His strong hands wrapped around her waist lifting her onto the counter. His boxer briefs she now wore as shorts to sleep in joined his T-shirt on the floor. Sinking to his knees, he pressed her thighs apart.

"Let me see how wet you are for me," he said, his gaze burning into hers.

"Arne," she moaned again, but she opened her thighs wider.

He pulled one of her legs over his shoulder. She had no option but to place her hands flat behind her on the counter to maintain her balance. With his gaze still fixed on her, he ran his tongue slowly through her folds.

"Dripping," he growled.

Her head fell back against the cabinet as he began to feast.

"So sweet."

His arm wrapped under her leg and pulled her closer to the edge. His tongue found her clit swollen and hungry. He knew she wouldn't last any longer than he had. Moving down, he pressed inside her entrance. She bucked her hips, grinding against his face.

"That's right, ride my fucking face."

He teased her trying to postpone what he wanted to give her most. It had to be the best she'd ever had. He needed her to come back for more over and over.

"Arne," she begged as her hips rose in the hunt for his tongue.

He took a hungry swipe at her clit. Then he gently sucked it between his lips. He listened to her trying to stifle a cry as she came undone around him. His fingers slid inside her so she could ride her orgasm as far as she wanted.

She slumped back against the cabinet, and he rocked back on his knees. He found her scowling at him.

"What?" he asked. "Are you alright?"

"Yeah," she said, shaking herself as if from a trance. "I was just wondering where you learned to do that. No one else has ever made me come like that." She tilted her head slightly as she watched him. "You know what, don't tell me. I'm going to just pretend I was the first."

"You were definitely the first I've ever been that... enthusiastic about," he said with a grin spreading across his face.

"Yes, you were working very hard. I very much liked the part where you pushed your tongue inside."

"I'll make a note of that." He chuckled.

"We get to do it again?" She hopped off the counter and swept her clothes off the floor. She pulled her T-shirt over her head before turning to him with an eyebrow raised in question.

"As much as you want. I'll even test out a couple of new things."

"Yay!" she said, hopping into her shorts. Her hand was on the doorknob when she paused. "This was good, right? This is what people do in a real relationship?"

"Yes, it was good." He stood and took her face in his hands. "And I don't care what other people do in relationships; we can do whatever you're comfortable with. Okay?"

She nodded. He pressed his lips to hers. When he turned her loose again, she slipped out the door with a smile.

Quickly, he cleaned up and found a new pair of pants to slide on. Sneaking back into his bedroom, he pulled a clean T-shirt from his drawers without Kip so much as moving. He found Jinn in the kitchen mixing a bowl of blueberry muffin mix. The container of fresh blueberries he found at the grocery store stood at her elbow.

"I'm starving," she said, adding them to the mix. "I hope you don't mind me starting breakfast."

"Starving, huh? Can't imagine why." He smirked at her.

"Must be all the fresh air," she answered with a wink.

"Why is everyone up so early?" Kip asked, walking around the corner. The end of her sentence ended in a yawn.

"We would hate to waste my day off sleeping, wouldn't you?" Arne teased.

"Not when you could be teaching me to ride Elmo," she answered. "Please, Arne." She wrapped her arms around his chest from behind.

"Fine," he said. How could he resist the pleading going on behind him?

"Eeek," she exclaimed.

"But only after breakfast, coffee, and at least a little of the morning show."

"Deal." Kip moved from where she clung to him to a stool at the bar. "What are we eating for breakfast then?"

Arne had barely finished his second cup of coffee before Kip was dancing around excitedly in front of him ready to learn to ride. "Let me throw some clothes on, and I'll meet you outside."

He found both Kip and Jinn petting Elmo when he stepped outside. Unhooking the halter from the gate, he stepped into the pen.

"Come here," he said, walking to Elmo. "Some girl thinks she needs to ride you." He slid the halter over Elmo's head. The horse threw his head several times. "I know, I don't like it either, but what can you do?"

He heard Jinn laugh. The sound made his heart skip a beat. She so rarely laughed that each time was a gift. Kip was too busy waiting anxiously at the gate to appreciate his humor.

"Go grab one of the brushes hanging in the shed," he said.

Kip rushed off to find a brush while he led Elmo from the pen. He tied him to a post on the pen.

"You're going to need to brush him well. He likes it and you need to make sure there's no mud or burrs where his tack goes." He ran his hand down Elmo's side, explaining how important it was to check his belly. Kip nodded enthusiastically before diving into grooming the large red horse.

"That should keep her occupied for a little while," Jinn mumbled. "Would you like another cup of coffee?"

"I would love one. Someone wore me out this morning."

"I'm sorry." She looked over at him with big puppy dog eyes.

He laughed and pulled her against his chest. "No you're not," he said.

"I'm really not," she agreed, but her face grew a bright crimson. "But the least I can do is get you another coffee." She wiggled out of his arms and walked back to the house. "Right now, anyway," she threw back over her shoulder as she stalked inside.

Arne would follow her just to find out what else she had in mind, but he had a fourteen-year-old awaiting further instruction.

"Good and clean?"

She nodded.

"Okay, time to learn how to tack him up."

Kip happily followed him to the shed for the rest of the gear. He handed her the heavy saddle while he grabbed the pad. If she wanted the responsibility of riding a horse, she needed to be able to do it all herself. That included carrying his heavy saddle.

"Is this right?" she asked once everything was cinched up.

He pushed off the side of the house to inspect her work. He pulled on the cinch to test that it was tight enough, adjusted the bucking strap in the back, and showed her how to put the bit in Elmo's mouth. Hooking a lunge line onto the bridle, he led Elmo away from the house.

"Put your left foot in the stirrup, and I'll help you up."

He had Kip sitting nervously in the saddle in minutes. "You okay?"

She nodded vigorously.

"We're going to walk in circles for a while until you learn some basics."

He taught her how to move Elmo forward, stop him, and turn him in a different direction. She grinned at him with every new skill she learned. "I think you're ready to go it on your own."

He unhooked the line from Elmo, and she led him in circles around the house. "Look, Jinn. I'm riding!" she squealed.

"You look amazing," Jinn encouraged.

"Can I ride to Thyra's house yet?" Kip asked after half an hour.

"Hmm, I don't know," Jinn said.

"I texted Mom. She said they're at home, so it's fine. Up to you," Arne added.

"Please, Jinn," Kip pleaded. "I'll be careful."

"Okay, I guess," Jinn relented.

"Let me show you where you're going. Tell Mom to text me when you get there." Arne walked around to the back of the house. He stopped at the edge of the hill before the terrain dropped into a valley below. "Down the hill, through the trees on the left, then straight to their house. It will probably take you half an hour."

"Please be careful," Jinn said.

"I will." Without looking back, Kip started down the hill on Elmo. She leaned back slightly in the saddle just like Arne had taught her.

"I don't know about this," Jinn said as Kip reached the bottom. In a few minutes, she would disappear from view.

"She'll be fine. I told Mom she's on her way," Arne reassured her.

They watched as Kip disappeared into the trees. They turned to walk back to the house when an alarm lit up his phone.

"Someone is driving up the road." He watched a black SUV creep by. When it reached the gate, a man jumped out and cut the lock.

"Get down," he hissed, pulling Jinn off the edge of the hill behind some scrub. The thing that they had dreaded most had finally arrived on their doorstep.

FIFTEEN

J inn found herself pulled to the ground behind an outcrop of brush. Arne brought his phone up to check the camera feed. She saw a vehicle pull up outside the door of the house. Bond and Jabba climbed out of the front seat. The air left her lungs in one stuttering breath. Suddenly, she felt light-headed.

"Stay with me, baby," Arne whispered in her ear.

She closed her eyes and let his closeness settle her. She wasn't alone in this fight anymore; he was right here next to her. She opened her eyes again to watch the screen with him. The men disappeared inside their house. They hadn't bothered to lock the front door. Why would they? They weren't more than three hundred feet from it.

"They're here for me," she said. "I know them."

"Just stay down. They should leave when they don't find anyone. Is there anything inside that can identify you?"

"No, I don't think so. We didn't have anything of ours when we left. I hid the hunting gear."

They watched the men exit the house.

"That one I call Bond, and that one is Jabba. I don't know their real names."

"You'll have to fill me in on your name choices later," he whispered.

She held her breath as Jabba slowly began to walk around the house, looking. He said something to Bond, but they were too far away for her to hear.

Arne's hand gently pressed her head to the ground. His finger pressed against his lips as she stared into his face. The men were getting closer. Her foot shifted, and she heard several rocks rattle down the hill.

"I think I heard something back here. I'm going to check," Jabba said. He started stalking them.

"I need you to stay very calm and quiet," Arne whispered so quietly she almost missed it. "I will explain everything later, just don't freak out."

She only had a moment to wonder what he could be talking about before she was no longer lying next to him. Instead, a large tawny-colored wolf had taken his place.

There was a moment when everything in her body told her to panic anyway. Though she couldn't understand why. Somehow she knew there was more to this world than what we could see. A man who could shift into a wolf was not that far outside the realm of possibility. He had, after all, warned her that there were things about him she needed to know first. This was a pretty big thing.

The wolf stood with a snarl. She watched Jabba from behind the bush as he froze in his tracks.

"It's a fucking wolf," he called back to Bond. He ran back toward the house with the wolf on his heels. "Open the passenger door," he screamed.

She watched on Arne's phone as Bond jerked open the car door before running around to dive in the other side.

Interesting that neither man thought about just shooting the wolf.

Jinn stood carefully when Jabba fled toward the house. She crept around the side until she could watch the SUV peel out of the gate with a snarling wolf chasing them. They disappeared in a cloud of dust. The wolf returned to the front of the house and sat on the porch before turning back into Arne.

"Can you grab me some pants?" he asked.

Jinn stepped out cautiously from the side of the house.

"I could smell you is how I knew you were there. We have heightened senses when we shift."

She walked around him into the house. A few minutes later, she emerged holding a pair of sweatpants.

"Thanks," he said, pulling them on. "I'm surprised you didn't run."

"Why?" she asked.

He smirked at her. She knew most women would have run down the hill screaming in horror, but that wasn't her.

"Explain it to me."

"Mom explains it best, but I can give you the abbreviated version," he offered.

She nodded.

"Family legend says that long ago my ancestor fell in love with a sorceress. She put a curse on him so he would return for her. She made him into a wolf since he was a warrior, and wolves mate for life. He had to go back and get her. All men born into our family can shift."

"What about the women?"

"Ahh, so here's the thing about that. Only a true mate can protect a shifter by casting protection spells on amulets we wear." He pulled the cord that held the ones his mother made long ago out so she could study them. "It makes the women more powerful than we are. Without these, havoc reigns."

"And once you find your mate, you're bound for life?"

"We don't know for sure, but none of us are willing to risk it. So, yes, once we sleep together, we're bound for life. I am at least."

"So, if we have sex, we would be forever? We would grow old together?"

"Yes, that's why I told you we needed to wait. If you still want to leave and build a new life for you and Kip somewhere else, I don't want anything to stop you," he said.

She studied the side of his face as he looked out at the pasture. What would it be like to stay here with Arne forever? She envisioned dinners together, laughing over game night, and his hands roaming over her body late at night. She swung around until she straddled his lap. He looked up at her, confusion plain on his face.

"I want to stay here with you," she said. Her hand slid into his pants to squeeze his growing erection. "I want to grow old here." She pressed her lips against his. She wanted him hot and needy inside of her now. She wanted to throw caution to the wind and never look back.

"As much as I'd love to fuck you raw on this porch," he hissed through gritted teeth. "My brother sees this same feed. I don't doubt he'll be here in a minute."

Her hand released him, and she sat back on his thighs. "However, I don't see a problem with making out before he gets here. He could use a little TMI after what I had to deal with when Tani moved in with us."

"TMI?" she asked, moving back against his chest.

"Too much intercourse," he said with a grin before pulling her in for a kiss.

As if on cue, Dane pulled his truck up to the house. He

climbed out of the driver's side and Roar out of the passenger side. Jinn slid off of Arne's lap to sit next to him.

"You look better than I was afraid you would," Dane said. "My phone alarm went off like it was a prison escape. I grabbed Roar and shot over here as fast as we could. What happened?"

"We were paid a visit," Arne answered.

"Was it the same guys?" Dane looked at Jinn.

No further explanation was needed; she knew exactly who he was referring to.

"It was the guards I named Bond and Jabba. They watched over us most of the time. There were two others also: Jaws and Khan," she said.

All three men stared at her like she was crazy.

"That needs more explanation. How about we get y'all back inside where it's warmer, and you can tell us about that," Roar finally said. He pulled Arne off the porch and ushered both of them inside.

Dane jogged around the back of the house to collect Arne's clothes. Jinn pulled the blanket off the back of the couch to wrap Arne in. They both sank onto the couch.

Roar joined them shortly with a tray of coffee. Dane walked through the front door as Roar was handing the mugs around. He tossed Arne's clothes on the table before sinking into one of the lounge chairs.

"So how likely is it that they'll be back?" he asked.

"They'll be back. I don't think he'll let them come back without us," Jinn answered.

"Then you're not safe here."

"What's our alternative?" Arne asked.

"We can hide you until they give up," Roar suggested.

"I don't think they will ever give up," Jinn said.

"You could move in with Mom and Dad temporarily," Dane added.

"I'd rather take my chances here," Arne answered with a scowl. "Last time I did that, it was like being back in high school."

"The only other option is we add reinforcements here," Roar said. "I'll stay with you in the evenings, and Erik can switch with me when he gets home next week after finals."

"We can't ask you to do that again."

"Again?" Jinn asked.

"Yeah," Arne added. "Tani had a stalker who could shift into a bear, but that's a whole other story."

"A bear? How many of you are out there?"

"Honestly? We have no idea. We thought it was just our family until the whole bear surprise. These guys, though, seemed very human."

Both brothers stared at Arne for a full minute like he was crazy before turning back to her.

"Are you okay?" Roar asked. "I know this is a lot to take in."

"I'm fine," she assured him. "It's weird really. There is a part of me that can't quite believe it, then there's a part that isn't surprised somehow. I think my brain already accepted that Arne was special."

She saw Arne grin out of the corner of her eye, and Roar rolled his eyes.

"Please don't give his head any reason to get any bigger," Dane said. "He's unbearable as it is."

"You're just jealous because I'm always the lady's favorite," Arne teased.

"Oh really?" she asked, turning to glare at him.

"No," he said, the grin disappearing. "Just yours hopefully."

"Barf," Roar said, standing. "Dane's going to take me to my car. I have my overnight bag in the trunk. I've learned not to show up here without a bag packed."

"Why are you here?" Arne asked.

"Getting a jump start on the ranch taxes. No rest for the weary." He pulled Dane from the couch and shoved him toward the door. "Lock the door while I'm gone. I'll bring Kip back with me. You should have seen how proud she was to reach the house without falling off or getting lost." He chuckled. "She's a natural rider." He followed Dane to the front door.

"Hold on," Dane said, pausing. "You haven't told us where you came up with the names for those guys."

"They never said names around us, so I had to come up with something," she answered. "Bond reminded me of the bad guy in the early movies."

"Blofeld?" Arne asked.

"Yeah, only I couldn't remember his name, so I used 'Bond villain' for a while. That got shortened to Bond. Jabba is the man who led me upstairs by using a leash he hooked to a collar around my neck."

She heard Arne growl next to her but chose to ignore him. There had been nothing she could do to prevent how Jabba handled her or the others.

"Jaws is huge like that other Bond villain, and Khan yells all the time."

"Huh," Dane said. He glanced at Roar. "Clever. You might want to pick something to watch that's not sci-fi or Bond." The comment was aimed at Arne. He was still glaring at the floor. "Roar should be back in about half an hour. Lock the door and load the guns in the meantime. I'll send him back with some heavier chain and a lock for the gate." He stood with his hand on the doorknob. "Arne!"

"Yeah, I heard you. Half hour, guns, locks."

Dane heaved a heavy sigh before opening the door. Roar followed him out the door. Jinn locked the door behind them and watched out the window as they pulled out the gate. She let the curtains fall closed again.

"How long does it take to load the guns?" she asked.

"Probably two minutes. Most of them stay loaded since I'm not the one with a baby in the house. It will take us longer to pull them out than to load them."

"Perfect. That gives us around…" She paused to calculate the time in her head. "Twenty-eight minutes until Roar and Kip are back. Longer if she fights having to leave like I expect she will."

"Okay?"

"Plenty of time."

"For what?"

She stalked over to him, spread her legs, and slid onto his lap. "For what we started outside." Fisting the band of his sweatpants in both hands, she yanked them down his thighs.

"Hold on, I'm not sure I explained the consequences of doing this," he said, catching the edge of his pants. "You can move on afterward, but I'm trapped. If you leave—"

She interrupted him by slapping the side of his face as hard as she could with her open palm. It stung all the way to her shoulder.

"Oww!"

"Get over it!" she said, then grinned. "I learned that from an old movie too."

He stared at her in surprise before his eyes narrowed. He clamped her arms in his fist and tossed her onto her back on the couch. She hadn't even finished bouncing when he was over her.

"You want to fuck?" he snarled. "Then let's fuck." He pulled her jeans open and ripped them down her legs. Her panties followed quickly behind. "Is this what you want?" he hissed in her ear before sucking her earlobe between his lips.

"Yes," she moaned.

How could this be what she wanted? She had been treated like nothing better than a piece of meat by every man she had ever crossed. They had all tossed her around leaving her bruised and bloody more often than not.

But this wasn't most men; this was Arne. She knew one word would stop him. That she could trust him. It was a heady feeling knowing she had so much power.

"You like it rough." It was more of a statement than a question, but heaven help her, she did. Her shirt was pulled over her head, her bra unhooked and ripped away. "Are you sure?" he asked, his hand tracing its way down her breastbone.

She bucked her hips, rolling him off onto the floor. Following him down, she straddled his prostrate body. "Do you need me to slap you again?" she growled. "Because I can." Her hands trapped his wrist to the floor.

A smile crept over his face. They both knew it would take nothing for him to throw her off of him.

"Do your worst," he hissed. He bent up to sear her with a kiss that left no doubt in her mind that he was all in.

Adjusting her body so it aligned with his, she sank down on him. It was fast and brutal, and they both moaned in response. He threaded his fingers with hers as she sat up. Her hips rolled several times as she hunted for the rhythm she was looking for.

Her head fell back on her shoulders as she rode on top of him. He was thick, filling her entirely. This was the way it was supposed to be. She hadn't had to beg for lube, build up his ego, or convince him to use a condom. As a matter of fact, she doubted he had any condoms. It didn't matter, she had been on contraceptives since before the auction.

"You've played enough," he snarled before rolling her on her back.

He rose on his knees to push the coffee table out of the way before plunging back into her. His lips met her shoulder; then his teeth were nipping the soft flesh. She wrapped her hands around his biceps and hung on as he plowed into her. It was shocking how much she was enjoying the feeling of him pinning her to the carpet.

She might have thought more about it if the tightening sensation from the last time they were together hadn't started to buzz through her system. It began low in her core before spreading up through her stomach to her chest and into her brain. The feeling grew so strong that she thought she'd pass out from the intensity.

Suddenly, every nerve in her body screamed at the same time. She felt herself lose touch with the world as she hurled into her second orgasm ever.

"Fuck, Jinn," Arne said from somewhere above her.

She found her arms holding him in a death grip on top of her. Slowly, she relaxed her muscles as her body tried to return to normal. Her eyes popped open to find him watching her.

"Have I mentioned how gorgeous you are when you come all over me? Stunning really."

Her breath was still coming in short pants, or she would have thanked him.

"FYI, you're stuck with me now."

"Good," she panted. "What do we do now?"

"I'm going to go out on a limb here and suggest more

sex." He checked the watch on his wrist. "We have at least ten minutes."

"I could use a shower. I smell like your horse," she answered.

"Need help?" He wiggled his eyebrows at her.

"What a great idea." She looked around his shoulder at the door. "But we should probably hurry."

"We got this." Standing, he gathered up their clothes in one arm and threw her over his shoulder with the other one. She laughed as they walked to the bathroom. "So how are you enjoying this relationship so far?"

"Pretty sure this is the one I want to keep around."

"Good answer," he said before carrying her into the bathroom.

SIXTEEN

The front door opened, and Kip all but burst into the house followed by Roar. She was rambling on about horses. Roar grunted in agreement at all the appropriate places. Arne had to hide a smile at the scene. He was chopping up vegetables in the kitchen. Somehow, they had managed to have a really good time in the shower but still got dressed before Roar brought Kip home.

"Did you take a shower?" Roar asked, escaping to the kitchen. He left Kip in the living room describing every moment of her ride. Roar turned to take in Jinn then looked back at Arne. "Seems everyone took one."

Arne glared at him for a moment before returning to his chopping. What Jinn and he did was none of his brother's business.

"I'm going to get in the shower myself if you don't need any help," Kip said, walking into the kitchen. She stole a piece of carrot from the cutting board and popped it into her mouth. "I brushed Elmo, and Papa Sten helped me give him some grain before putting him out."

"Thank you," Arne answered. "I think I'm good for now." She spun around and headed for the bathroom.

"You appear to have settled into this life fairly quickly," Roar said.

"What's that supposed to mean?"

"It doesn't mean anything. We're just looking out for you. If you want this life, then you know we'll support you. I just want to make sure this is your choice and not an obligation you've talked yourself into." Roar raised his hands in surrender at Arne's glare. "Watching out for you."

"I appreciate that, but I'm not twelve anymore. I'll let you know if I need advice on my personal life."

"Fair enough. I'm not here to fight." Roar snatched a piece of celery from the bar. "Just know I'm here if you need to talk about something."

"Since when did you turn into Mom?" Arne teased.

"Fuck off."

"That's better." Arne dumped the vegetables into a pot of boiling water. He could feel his brother's gaze on him as he began mixing ingredients for pie crust.

"Hey," Jinn said, sliding onto one of the barstools. "What are you talking about?"

"Roar was pointing out how unsuitable we are together," Arne answered.

"Hold on, I didn't say that," Roar argued.

"He's right, though," she said. "Think about it. A pretty, successful cowboy meets a damaged runaway. That stuff only happens in the movies." She shrugged at his look of consternation aimed at her. "Doesn't change anything, but, yeah, I get it."

Roar began to laugh. "Sweet Jesus, where do we keep finding these brilliant, head-strong women? It's like there's a sign at the gate or something. You'd think we'd eventually get one that doesn't like to throw it back in our faces."

"That'll have to be on you, I guess," Arne answered with a grin on his face.

Roar could have whatever meek woman he wanted. He'd stick with the fiery one he was dealt. He knew Dane felt the same way about Tani. Did any man want a pushover of a woman to order around? Not in this family obviously.

"Not me, I'm a confirmed bachelor at this point," Roar said.

"Just jinxed yourself there, big man." Jinn laughed.

Arne watched his oldest brother out of the corner of his eye. They had speculated for years about Roar's college girlfriend. He had never seemed interested in dating anyone after she left. Dane was convinced they had slept together, which is why Roar hadn't been able to move on from her. Arne and Erik weren't sure, but none of them wanted to risk winding up in the same place.

It was a big reason the remaining brothers had stayed celibate into their twenties. Whether they believed the old fairy tale or not, they weren't taking any chances.

"Afraid that ship has sailed."

"No, I don't believe that," Jinn said. "I think everything happens for a reason. We might not understand it, but it's all part of a master plan. Maybe everything Kip and I went through was just leading us here."

"A cosmic predestination, so to speak, huh?"

Arne turned back to preparing supper as he listened to them talk. Leave it to Jinn to win his brother over bit by bit. She would have Roar agreeing to anything soon. As large and foreboding as he appeared, underneath that Viking exterior lay a man who believed in kindness and loyalty. It was his greatest strength, the one the rest of the siblings relied on.

He was pulling supper out of the oven later when Kip finally wandered out of the bedroom. She slid into the seat next to Roar at the small table in the dining area. Another large haul of books from Thyra was sitting on the coffee table.

His house was slowly looking like a teenager had taken over. It was an odd feeling to realize he liked it. He barely had room for his toothbrush in the bathroom around the hairdryer, face cleanser, and the rest of their stuff. He didn't mind that either.

"I was thinking of sleeping arrangements," he said during a lull in the conversation. "Why don't you and Kip move into my bedroom, and I'll share with Roar? That way he doesn't have to hang off the end of the couch."

Jinn's gaze flicked to his. He didn't want to sleep with anyone but her either, but what could he do?

"I don't mind the couch," Roar answered.

"I know, but this makes more sense."

After supper was cleaned up, and they sat through a movie of Kip's choosing, they headed to bed. Arne lay awake listening to the freight train that was Roar in the other bed. He fought the urge to sneak down the hallway and climb in next to Jinn. It seemed like a rocky start to a relationship. Was it what Dane felt when he first got together with Tani? Of course, he at least had her sharing his bed.

He sat up when the door slowly eased open. A hand motioned for him to follow, so that's what he did. That same hand wrapped in the front of his T-shirt and pulled him into the bathroom. The door clicked closed quietly behind them. He was pushed up against the wall next to the towel bar. This was becoming a not unwelcome habit.

"You know the problem with good sex?" Jinn whispered in his ear.

"It doesn't last long enough?"

"I was going to say you just can't get enough. Did you want it to last longer?"

"Well, yes. All we've had time for are a couple of quickies. I would like to find some privacy to take it slower and stretch out the orgasms. You should be coming more than once."

"Really?" she squeaked.

"Really." He chuckled. "At least twice if not more. And a lot more kissing is needed, to every part of your body."

"I like the sound of that."

"Problem is, we have a house full of people all the time. I don't think it's going to end anytime soon either."

"Then we have to take what time we do have," she said before sinking to her knees.

She slid his shorts down his legs to his ankles. He gritted his teeth to stifle a moan when she gripped his length in her small hand. Then her tongue darted from between her lush lips for a taste.

"Jinn," he moaned before he could stop it.

"Don't wake Kip," she hissed. "Or Roar either for that matter."

Her lips sucked the tip of his hard cock before her tongue went to work. It swirled around the head several times before she pulled him all the way to the back of her throat. She swallowed, and he thought he would pass out from the pleasure.

His hips buck involuntarily, his hand pressed against her head. She bobbed it up and down several times, which would have been enough for him, but then she hummed. Vibrations shot from his cock through his whole body.

"Fuck, Jinn. I'm going to come."

He expected her to back away. Instead, she dug her nails into his ass and doubled her efforts. He heard the wet noises as she fought not to gag every time he reached the back of her throat. Hot tears streamed down her cheeks that he tried to catch with his free hand.

Her tongue was everywhere. It slid up the sensitive underside tracing the vein that roped down his cock. Then it was flicking the soft skin just under the head before twirling around the slit. It was more than he could handle. Without warning, he pressed as far into her throat as she could take. Hot cum slid down her throat as she worked to swallow him. When he found his way back to reality finally, he pulled her up to her feet.

"Are you okay?" he asked.

She licked the corner of her mouth and smiled.

"You taste just like I thought you would. Strong, rugged, sexy." He pulled her against his chest. "I should get back before Kip wakes up and comes looking for me."

"You don't want me to reciprocate?"

"Tomorrow. Maybe we'll find those couple of hours to be alone."

"Hours? That sounds intimidating."

"Not intimidating, just exhausting. In a good way." She smiled up at him before bending to pull his shorts up. "You know, I think I'm going to like this relationship sex."

"Yeah," he said with a grin. "Relationship sex is awesome."

～

Arne awoke the next morning with a smile on his face. He was certain it had remained there all night. He rolled over and shut off his alarm. Roar growled at the early hour. He was the only one of them with a schedule that started later in the day.

Arne grabbed his clothes and headed to the bathroom. His smile grew when he closed the door. If they kept sneaking in here to have sex, he was going to need to expand the room. Maybe bump out the side for a soaker tub.

"Hey," Jinn said quietly, slipping into the bathroom. "What's on the agenda for today?"

"Feeding. I feed every Monday, Wednesday, and Friday. This afternoon, after I'm done, I need to ride a fence line. I guess the neighbor called Dad again this weekend to complain about our cows in his pasture. I thought Kip might want to ride out with me."

"Ooh, she'll love that. Okay, I'd better go wake her so we're ready. I know we can't stay here by ourselves anymore." She gave him a quick kiss before slipping back out through the door.

By the time he walked into the kitchen, Roar was pushing buttons on the coffee maker.

"Want some breakfast?" Arne asked. He pulled a box of frozen sausage biscuits out of the freezer.

"Thanks, but I think I'll get something at Donna's. Do you have a travel mug?" Arne pulled one out of a cabinet and placed it on the counter. Roar made a double cup of coffee, pouring each one into the mug. "Okay, I'm heading out. Are you good until this evening?"

"Yeah, I've got it. We're heading out in a couple of minutes too." He watched his brother walk out the door. Popping a couple of biscuits in the microwave, he opened the security app on his phone. Roar was just unlocking the front gate. No one else seemed to be lurking around outside.

He didn't know if that was a good thing or not. He'd just as soon get this problem solved so they could go on with their lives. He could take the fight to them, except Jinn didn't even know their first names. It was impossible to find them without even basic information.

"Are these mine?" Kip asked, walking into the kitchen just as the microwave timer went off.

"Absolutely," he answered. He found another plate for more biscuits. Grocery shopping was going to be a common occurrence now he supposed.

"Thank you," Jinn said as she took the plate out of his hands. He turned back to the microwave. "What does Mrs. Ulvmand have in store for you today?"

"We're working on a math workbook Tani brought. I think we're also doing some science thing, but I'm not sure what," Kip answered. She sat down with the second plate of biscuits. "She said she'll have me up to grade level by the time I'm enrolled in school."

"Really?" Jinn said.

"Mom taught school before we all came along," Arne explained, sitting down at the table with his third try at breakfast. "I think after Dane, it was just too hard to keep teaching. It was too expensive with childcare. She still tutored half the county, though. Sloughing off homework was almost a capital offense in my household growing up."

"She's good at explaining everything when I get confused," Kip added. "Do you think I can play softball like Thyra when I go to school?"

"I don't know why not," he answered. "We'll keep working on your game so you'll be ready."

"Hey, do you think Roar and Dane would get mad if I call them Uncle?" she asked.

"I think they'd love to be Uncle Roar and Uncle Dane, even Uncle Erik."

"No, he's too delicious."

"Lord, don't let him hear you say that." Arne laughed. "His head is too big as it is."

"I'll just think of him as another brother, like you."

"Technically, they'd all be your brothers."

"Huh," she said with a shrug. "I hadn't thought of that."

Arne couldn't help the feeling that spread through his body. It was a feeling of belonging and family. Kip had created their family just now sitting innocently at the table. It was perfect.

He caught Jinn smiling at him. Did she feel the same? He hoped so because he was falling for them both. One as another little sister, the other as his perfect mate. Nothing could hurt them as long as they had each other. Or that's what he hoped anyway.

SEVENTEEN

The strangers pulled into a gate drive that looked like it hadn't been used in a while. Bond shut off the engine and climbed out of the driver's side. He met Jabba at the back of the SUV. They had brought their semi-automatic rifles this time. Even if the wolf surprised them, they had a way to deal with him.

"What's the plan?" Jabba asked as he checked his ammunition.

"Straight forward," Bond answered. "We'll approach from the back, bust in, take Jinn, and kill anyone who gets in the way."

"What about the sister?"

"Boss said he doesn't care what happens to her. He just wants to teach Jinn a lesson."

With their guns at their sides, they climbed the gate into the pasture. It was an easy fifteen-minute hike before they saw the back of the mobile home on the horizon. Bond gave a signal indicating there would be no talking going forward. Jabba had his instructions anyway. He had to cut the feed to the cameras and alarm before Bond broke down the door.

They approached the house slowly, sticking to the shadows as much as possible. When they reached the side, Jabba removed his wire cutters from his pocket. Bond nodded at him and he went to work. He found the wires quickly that connected the security system to power. Bond kicked in the door as soon as the cameras were down.

"I don't think anyone is here." Bond said after stepping back outside.

"They're always home by now."

"Well, they're not tonight. Let's toss the place, then head out. It'll send a message that we can get her whenever we like."

"If she's even here," Jabba pointed out.

So far, they hadn't seen any trace of the women. Rumors were all they had to go on. That, and the assurances of an old man.

"Let's see if we can find out."

They returned inside the home. Bond began trashing the living area. He knocked pictures off the walls, broke anything he could get his hands on, and dug through every drawer.

Jabba watched for a moment before moving to the bedrooms with a shrug. The first room looked like two men were sharing it. There was a set of twin beds with clothes thrown on top of them. He held up one of the hoodies, taking note of the size. These weren't small men sharing this room. He tossed everything on the floor, smashed the lamp on the bedside table, and helped himself to some loose change on the dresser.

The next bedroom looked more promising. Jabba looked around to the sound of Bond breaking dishes in the kitchen.

There was a row of strange metal art sitting on the dresser. He picked one up to study it before hurling it at the wall. Ignoring the rest, he began upending the dresser drawers. There were still men's clothes everywhere.

The nightstand boasted an impressive array of men's magazines, lube, and a handheld video game console. He was on his way out of the bedroom when his gaze caught on something hanging in the closet. Throwing the door open, he found a small row of women's clothes. There were shirts, pants, and even one skirt. Bras and panties were neatly folded on the floor below.

"They're here!" he shouted down the hallway. Bond stuck his head in the room. "This has to be theirs."

Jabba moved back to the nightstand where a stack of books took up most of the surface. He picked up the first one and read the title. "Anna Karenina. Stupid fucking name for a book." He tore pages from it before tossing it on the floor.

"I read that in school," Bond said. "You want to check the bathroom while I finish up here?"

With a nod, Jabba walked into the bathroom. The vanity looked like it had been commandeered by a couple of women. Hair products, face cream, and even some makeup sat at the back of the counter. He raked it all off onto the floor. For an added statement, he threw all four toothbrushes into the toilet and broke the mirror with the hairdryer.

"Okay, let's go finish fucking up the cameras, then we're out of here," Bond said from the hallway.

Jabba took one last look around before following Bond outside.

"Just rip out whatever you find."

They spent the next ten minutes busting up cameras. It

was only pure luck that they heard the wolf before he reached them.

"IF YOU OPEN that oven door even one more time, I'm going to smack you," Freja scowled.

Arne let his hand fall where it was poised to open the oven to check the casserole one more time. He had never understood how she just set a timer and ignored it. Weirdly, she rarely burned anything this way.

Roar had a late meeting at work, so he wouldn't arrive until later. His mother had been quick to insist they stay for supper while they waited for him to make it. Dane had stayed also, and Tani met him with the baby. He was currently playing in Dane's arms while he leaned against the kitchen counter.

"You know Arne, Mom. Can't leave well enough alone," Dane teased.

"What's that supposed to mean?" Arne asked. He was just tired enough from today that he might be itching for a fight. Dane was always good for brawls. Even if it was just verbal.

"Get your panties out of their wad," Dane answered. "You'd think a man getting it on the regular would be in better humor."

"Arne Ulvmand," his mother said, turning to glare at him.

Dane grinned from behind her. Arne made a mental note to deck him later when their mother wasn't around. Jackass.

"Is there something you need to share? I'll need to start her training if that's the case."

Sex was definitely not something he wanted to discuss with his mother.

"And you, Dane Ulvmand," she said, turning on his brother. "Stop ratting your little brother out like y'all are still children."

Arne smirked at Dane. At least they were both in trouble this time. Where was Roar when they needed him? Surely he could take some of the heat off them. He always had in the past.

"Yes, ma'am," they answered in unison.

"When is this damn thing going to be done?" Arne asked, turning back to the oven. "I'm starving."

"Here," Freja said. She handed him a large bowl with salad in it. "Put this on the table."

He took the bowl and carried it out of the kitchen. Jinn smiled at him when he walked into the dining area. She was setting the table while visiting with Tani. They waited for him to walk away before continuing their conversation. He could only guess what that was about. At least Kip and Thyra were upstairs, no doubt talking about books.

With a sigh, he moved through the house until he found his father sitting in his office.

"Get kicked out of the kitchen?" Sten asked.

"Fucking Dane," he answered.

"How many times have I heard that over the years?" Sten closed the screen on his laptop. "You know he takes great pleasure in baiting you, right? Every time, you take the bait."

"Yeah, well, it's one of my many toxic traits."

His father laughed. "Or it's Dane's superpower." He chuckled for a few more minutes before sobering up. "How's everything going at your house?"

"It's...complicated."

"I would imagine. They've been through a lot, but they seem to be resilient. Are you being careful?"

"Define careful."

"I thought so," Sten mumbled. "Well, that will be your mother's problem now. Come on, let's see if dinner's ready. She chased me out of the kitchen an hour ago."

They walked together to the dining room.

"Looks like you've outdone yourself again, sweetheart." He kissed Freja on the cheek.

They had just tucked into supper when Arne's phone alerted him. Pulling it out of his front pocket, he checked the message.

"Huh," he said, opening the camera app on his phone.

"What's wrong?" Dane asked.

"I don't know. It says there's no power to the security system. The whole thing is down."

"Do you think the electricity is out?" Thyra asked.

"I don't know. I guess I should go check." He pushed his chair back from the table. His phone rang as he stood. "Hello?"

It was a neighbor telling him he thought he saw someone near his house when he drove by.

"There's a big, black SUV parked in the gate down from the Green's. It looked like your door was open," the man said.

"Thanks, I'm just on my way there now." He hung up the phone. "I think the two men from the other day are at the house. Perry saw a black SUV parked down the road."

"Let's go," Dane said, pushing to his feet.

"There's no way we'll get there in time to stop them," Arne pointed out.

"There is if we go cross country."

"Stay here," Arne said, turning to Jinn. "I'll be back. Call

Roar," he added, addressing his sister, "Make sure he doesn't pull into an ambush. Let's go."

He jogged through the house and out the door with both Dane and Jinn at his heels.

"Please be careful," Jinn said.

His hands embraced her face. He pulled her to him for a kiss. "I will," he assured her, then the man she knew was gone. In his place, the tawny wolf ran out the gate toward the fields beyond. There was a large white wolf next to him.

It was a short trip as the crow flies. If forced to take the road, it takes much longer to reach his house. He left his mate standing at the door watching him leave. His brother panted next to him as they made up as much ground as possible. It was the only way he knew to reach the house in time. They slowed as they crept up the slope the house sat on.

Two men were beating something on the ground with the butt of a gun. The wolf stopped to watch. He recognized the men; they were the ones who had come for his mate. His paws crunched softly as he crept through the side yard. The white wolf circled around the other side of the house. It would be better if they could flank them.

"There's that son of a bitch," the one said, swinging his gun up.

The wolf only had a moment to dodge behind the house before a searing pain ripped through his shoulder. It would have to be dealt with later, he needed to chase the intruders from his home right now. Growling came from the other side of the house as the white wolf charged at them.

The wolf shook off the blood running down his front leg to join his brother in the attack. Another shot rang out, but he knew his brother was fast enough to escape. He felt the hair rise on his hackles as he charged forward, growling at the men. They hadn't waited to fight. Instead, both men ran for the road. He debated chasing them down, but they were shooting back at the house as they ran.

He hunted for the white wolf, finding him tucked behind one of the trees. Bullets bounced off the tree as he hunkered behind it. The wolf ran past the house howling to distract the men so his brother could retreat. They took a few more wild shots at him before the sound of gunfire died out. He trotted back to the house to find the white wolf now standing on the porch.

"Jesus, Arne," he heard as he shifted back. Dane, in all his glory, stood on the front porch staring through the broken door.

Arne joined him, pushing the door the rest of the way open. Stepping inside, he took in the destruction. His kitchen looked like a tornado had struck it. The rest of the house didn't look much better.

He found a pair of sweatpants on the floor in the bedroom and tossed them to Dane. Pulling on a second pair, he surveyed what was left of his bedroom. They had gone so far as to slit the mattress with a knife.

"Did they take anything?" Dane asked from the door.

"Who knows in this mess."

"Why would they show up and just destroy everything?"

"I have no idea."

"Hey!" they heard Roar shout from the living area.

"Back here," Dane answered.

"They really did a number on this place," Roar said, reaching the bedroom. "I'm just glad you weren't here when they showed up. Have you called the sheriff?"

"Why?" Dane asked.

He had gotten crossways with the sheriff in high school. They still couldn't stand each other.

"You need to file a report. At the very least, you'll need one for the insurance company," Roar answered.

"They'll never feel safe here now," Arne mumbled.

"Hey, don't. We've got this; we'll make sure they're safe," Roar said. "We managed to protect Tani, we've got Jinn and Kip, too. Call the sheriff."

"I'll head back to the house and let everyone know what happened," Dane added. "Plan on staying there tonight. I'll be back to get y'all in a little while."

Roar handed him the keys to his car. He was gone before Arne finished his phone call to the sheriff's office.

"Let's gather up the women's stuff," Roar said. "No reason to confuse the law. They'll need it anyway. Oh, come on!" he shouted, walking into the bathroom. "I just bought that toothbrush."

Arne laughed when he joined Roar in the bathroom. Then they got to work emptying what was left of the house from any trace of Jinn and Kip.

EIGHTEEN

Jinn stretched in the bed, dreading having to leave the warm cocoon of soft blankets. She and Kip had stayed at Freja's while the men dealt with Arne's house. She knew there was still a lot of work to be done to clean everything up, but he didn't feel comfortable with either of them there today.

Freja had regaled them with the whole story of how they became wolves. Jinn thought the best part of the tale was how powerful the sorceress was.

The body in the bed behind her yawned loudly and stretched. Arne had slid into her bed sometime after she had retired for the night. She was shown into his childhood room which was now transformed into a guest room. The bed was large, the blankets soft. It hadn't taken long before she was asleep.

Kip had accepted the invitation to share Thyra's room for the night. When Jinn checked on her, she was happily curled up in the extra twin bed next to a stack of books.

"Why are you awake so early?" Arne growled behind her.

His voice was rough from sleep, and the sound shot right through her body to rest between her legs. The very place he used last night to wake her back up. He had been right. Slow sex was the best, even if neither one of them had gotten much sleep. She wiggled back against him only to find him already hard and wanting.

"What are you doing today?" she whispered.

"I think I'll start by doing you," he answered.

His hand slid into the back of her shorts and pulled them down her legs. She had insisted they put clothes back on last night just in case Kip snuck into the room. With her shorts tossed to the floor, he settled back behind her. He pulled the blankets back up to her chin.

She rested her head on his arm while his other one snaked around her body. Strong fingers slid through her heat to play with her clit. He was getting better at driving her crazy each time. Her hips began to rock against his hand, begging for more. He spread the slickness of her need down her thigh before pulling her leg over his hip. In one hard thrust, he was fully seated inside her.

"Arne," she gasped.

This was the first time she had woken up with a man, much less had one insist on morning sex. Arne was turning out to be not just insatiable, but full of surprises. He rocked his hips against her buttocks. The friction was delicious even though he couldn't get that deep in that position. He held on to her hip with his hand. She slid her hand between her legs this time. Her fingers found where they connected and simply enjoyed feeling where they joined.

"You're going to make me come too soon doing that," he moaned.

Her hand shifted to her clit. She worked at a feverish pace to guarantee she was with him when he came. The tides of ecstasy begin to build in her chest. It spread through her mind and shot through her body as she found her release.

"Fuck," he groaned as he joined her.

She had never experienced anything so perfect.

"You're everything," he whispered when he regained his breath. He still had her pinned down as he gently rocked against her.

"Arne?" she asked. She pushed out from under him and rolled over. "What did the sheriff say last night?"

His fingers traced a lazy line down her jaw as he contemplated her. What was he trying to hide?

"Please don't start trying to hide things from me. Last time a man hid something from me, I was sold to clear a debt."

"I won't," he assured her. His gaze landed on hers. "It's hard not to hide things that I think might hurt you."

"Only lies can hurt me. Anything you say in truth will only make me stronger."

He nodded like he understood. She wondered if he really did. He was such a good man that he could never understand how it felt to be used without your permission. Keeping her in the dark about what was happening would just be another way to abuse her.

"They took a statement, pictures, that sort of thing. The house was pretty torn up. Dane and I gathered up everything that belonged to you or Kip and brought it here. I don't want any record of where you are. They were smashing the cameras when we showed up. Roar helped me clean up what we could."

"Do you think the sheriff will be able to find them?"

"I doubt it. People get broken into all the time. They'll just chalk it up to drugs and move on."

"So what do we do now?"

"I'm not sure yet, but we'll figure it out. You'll both be safe here until then."

They were interrupted by a soft knock.

"Yeah," Arne said loud enough to be heard through the door.

They were both surprised when the door opened, and Sten stuck his head in.

"Your mother wants both of you to come down for breakfast," he said.

"Why?" Arne asked.

"Just do it," Sten growled back. He closed the door and stomped down the hallway.

"Great," Arne said, climbing from the bed. "Can't wait to see what I'm in trouble for this time. I love my parents, but staying with them is like being fifteen again. I was always in trouble for something."

"Maybe your mom just made something special for breakfast, and she doesn't want it to go to waste."

He smirked at her.

"What? It could happen."

He grabbed her ankle and pulled her to the edge of the bed. "Keep dreaming, baby."

She knew it was silly, but every time he called her by a pet name her heart fluttered. He tossed her a pair of sleep pants. She pulled them up her legs and added a robe. She then sat back on the bed to watch him pull on his jeans. The view of his strong legs, muscled torso, and cocky grin never grew old.

They reached the kitchen to find his parents sitting at the table. Roar had joined them and was sipping on a large cup of coffee. On the table was a large coffee cake that smelled heavenly. Without a word, Freja cut a large piece.

Jinn laughed at the scowl on Arne's face when the first piece was slid in front of her.

"Mom," he whined. "I thought I was your favorite."

"Favorite dumbass maybe," Roar mumbled.

"Roar," Freja warned.

Jinn wondered if all brothers acted like these four did. Did they all tease, banter, and threaten? She hadn't seen them throw punches yet, but Arne had told her stories about the fist fights of their youth. They hadn't hesitated to help, though, when Arne's house had been ransacked. It seemed she still had a lot to figure out about being part of a family.

"If y'all are done, we need to figure out what to do going forward," Sten said before the squabble could escalate. "I assume the sheriff was of little help last night."

"Couldn't find his ass with both hands," Roar grumbled.

"Dude," Arne said, looking appalled. "Who pissed in your cereal?"

"Who's pissing on breakfast?" Dane asked, walking into the kitchen.

"I have absolutely no qualms about banging your heads together to see if I can rattle some sense out," Sten said.

All three brothers laughed. Jinn felt her shoulders relax from where they had worked their way up to her ears. None of their sparring ever seemed to contain any real heat.

"Now try to pay attention. What are the chances these men will just move on?"

They turned to look at Jinn.

"I don't think very high," she answered. "He won't let them return until they've accomplished whatever he gave them to do. It's not too late for us to go into hiding somewhere else."

"Yeah, I think it is," Freja said, looking over at Arne.

He simply nodded his head.

"But what would happen if we laid a trail to lure them away?"

"I don't think we could sustain that for very long. They'd just come back eventually," Roar answered. "The problem is they're just part of a bigger issue. It's not enough to just shut these two down, more will follow."

"So what do we do?" Arne asked.

"We have to find that house where Jinn and Kip were kept and get the Oklahoma Bureau of Investigation involved," Dane said. "You said there were other women there from time to time?"

Jinn nodded. She had seen quite a few over the years.

"Then we wait for them to show up again or find them in town and follow them back."

"I don't know how we'd do that. We don't even have their actual names."

"It's a small town; I'm sure we can ask around."

"But I don't want it getting back to Jabba and Bond who was trying to find them. That would tip them off to Jinn's location for sure."

"I don't know," Sten piped up. "They broke into your house and trashed it. Seems only natural that you'd ask around town. See if anyone has heard anything. I'd start at Donna's around lunch. I can see what I can find out."

"Okay, I guess," Arne answered. "What are we supposed to do while you're poking around town?"

"How about work," Dane said. "You remember what that is, right?"

"Dick."

"Ass."

"Hey!" Sten snarled. He shoved his chair back and stood. "Y'all both can get to work."

"I should get going too," Roar said. "See you tonight."

"You'll be alright?" Arne asked.

Jinn nodded, and he bent to kiss her cheek. She turned in her chair to watch the brothers leave the house. Their laughter could be heard even after the door closed behind them. Sten left for his office leaving her alone with Freja.

"Are they always this much when they're together?" she asked.

"Wait until Christmas when they're all home," Freja answered. "It's all just show. I think it's how they figured out how to interact as adults with each other."

"Mr. Ulvmand doesn't seem to like it."

"Don't let that man fool you. He often joins right in. He just likes to maintain a sense of propriety around us. Bless his heart." Freja laughed. "How do you find living with Arne?"

"He's amazing," she said before thinking about it.

"Good. I'm glad you think that. He has always been the most easygoing of my kids. I think being right in the middle of his siblings taught him to roll with the punches. I would hate to see him hurt."

Jinn understood what Freja was saying. Problem was, she couldn't agree to it. She knew that no one could be guaranteed not to get hurt in this life. There was no doubt in her mind that she would do everything she could to prevent Arne from ever feeling that kind of pain. The world didn't work on promises, however. All she could do was fight for them. The rest was up to fate.

"Well, anyway, we have a big day ahead of us," Freja continued. "It's time I introduce you to the shed."

Jinn felt a shiver rack through her body. Anything that sounded like a basement room couldn't be good.

"Don't worry. I promise you're going to like it. It's where you'll find your real power. I assume you and Arne are sleeping together."

Jinn felt her whole body flame red. She wasn't sure why; it wasn't like they weren't adults. In the past, she wouldn't have batted an eye at the question, but she didn't want Freja thinking any less of her than she probably already did. She stared at her hands clutched in front of her on the table.

"I'll take that as a yes. Sorry to be intrusive, but it won't work if he hasn't already chosen you as his mate," Freja added. "Thyra has the day off from school, and Tani is taking a personal day so they can be here. Kip is welcome to join us too. We should have almost everything we need."

Jinn listened to Freja talk as they ate breakfast. Nothing she said put her at ease. It was still a shed only now some preparations had to be made.

Then it struck her, she was being brought into the fold. She was becoming one of them. A woman who could cast spells to protect the man she loved. It hit her all at once. She loved him. Maybe she had all along, but now she understood what it meant.

"If I get to protect Arne for once, then I'm ready," she assured Freja. "It's about time I got to turn the tables."

CHAPTER

NINETEEN

The shed wasn't at all what Jinn expected. She followed Freja outside and down a path to a wooden structure that looked ready to fall apart in the first strong wind. Then the door was opened.

Jinn found herself walking into every historical fantasy reader's dream. There were jars full of herbs lining one wall, old vintage rugs covering the floor, and a worktable with various measuring devices sitting on it.

"I'm not late, am I?"

Jinn was still staring at the little building in awe when she heard Tani. She walked inside the shed carrying Aksel on one hip. Pulling out a tub of toys, she sat him on one of the carpets to play.

"Of course not," Freja assured her. "We just got here ourselves. Thyra should be down soon. You know how much she likes this."

"What do you want me to do?"

"How about starting the coffee? I know I could use a second cup."

"I'm on it."

Tani turned to a small sink that Jinn had missed on her short tour. The coffee pot was rinsed well before Tani assembled the machine. A second cup of coffee didn't sound like a bad idea. Especially if this is where she became a human sacrifice.

"Hey, guys," Thyra said, stumbling into the room. Kip followed happily behind her. "We're here; we're ready." She stopped to yawn. "Ahh, coffee."

"Anyway, if everyone's here, I guess we should start," Freja said. She pulled a large book out from under the workbench and set it on top.

"Each generation of women in this family is tasked with passing on the skills of the sorceress to the next. She taught her daughters and daughters-in-law how to cast spells to protect the family. Today, we're going to teach you the same ancient methods she used."

Jinn listened with rapt attention. The story of the sorceress that Freja told her the night before had captured her imagination. It had been an interesting discussion explaining to Kip why Arne dissolved into a wolf, but she had accepted it without much questioning. Today, Jinn noticed that she looked excited to learn more about the family. The family that was quickly becoming theirs.

"The first thing we do before we start is to find our center. You have to open your mind to the possibilities and shut down everything else that might be plaguing it. What do you do to find your peace?" Freja asked.

Jinn stared at her blankly. She had no idea how she should find peace. It had never been required of her before. "Anything come to mind?" She began to panic.

"I don't know," she said softly.

"I didn't either when I first started. Sten's mother would drink something hot and meditate. Or that's what she claimed anyway; I think sometimes she just took a short nap."

"I say a short prayer asking that my mind be focused," Tani added, trying to help. "Think of what connects you to the world."

"How about if I read you something?" Kip suggested. "You always seem to relax when I read to you."

"That's a great idea, Kip," Freja added.

"Yes, that might work," Jinn said.

"How about you girls go pick something out while we start hunting for Jinn's charm?" Freja suggested.

"We'll be back." Thyra tugged Kip out the door. "Don't do anything cool without us," she called from the yard.

"I assume you've noticed the charms that hang around Arne's neck?"

Jinn nodded.

"You need to find what speaks to you to charm. It can be anything. I used silver beads, Tani had stones, just about anything works as long as it's special."

Jinn didn't have to think about it very long. The thing Arne treasured most, after his family, were the pieces of art scattered around his house made from bits of scrap metal. She could find some small pieces of it and have Dane grind it down so it wasn't likely to cut Arne as he moved around.

"I know what I need. Do you think Dane will help me?" she asked Tani.

"Of course he will. I'm sure he's in the shop. I'll help you if you'll watch the baby?" she asked, turning to Freja.

They were waved off as Freja sat on the floor to play blocks with Aksel. They found Dane bent over a piece of equipment in the shop. "Hey, sugar. Jinn needs to dig through your metal scrap pile."

"Don't tell me Arne has infected you with his art hobby," he answered.

"Sort of. I've been working on a piece for a while now. He showed me how to solder the pieces together. It seems like the perfect thing to make charms out of," Jinn said.

"It's out back." He led them to the scrap area containing a multitude of different-sized pieces of metal. "Knock yourself out." He returned to the shop.

Jinn found an old bucket she climbed onto look inside the old trailer at the pieces of metal tossed away after finishing a project. Most of the pieces were too thick for her needs. She pushed it aside, as well as the wire, to dig for what she had in mind. Finally, she chose several smaller pieces and took them back to Dane.

"Can you help me file off the rough edges?" she asked. "I want them smooth and round. About the size of a dime."

"Give me a few minutes," Dane said, taking the metal pieces to the grinder. He threw on a pair of safety glasses and turned the machine on.

Sparks flew as he worked to smooth the edges. In minutes, she had a dozen small disks.

"Can we drill a hole in the middle so they'll string on a piece of leather?"

Dane took her to the drill press sitting near the workbench. After teaching her how to use it, he left her to drill the holes herself. Something about the effort she spent drilling the holes perfectly in the middle made her feel like she truly was part of Arne's life. With a feeling of pride, she followed Tani back to the shed, charms in hand.

"That was fast," Freja said when they returned to the shed.

Aksel was sitting on her lap giggling at the bubbles she blew out the door.

"Are these okay?" she asked.

"They look perfect. Ah, here come the girls."

Thyra and Kip returned carrying a small hardbound book. "Did you find something?"

"We picked out a sonnet," Kip announced.

"That sounds perfect." Freja sat Aksel back on the carpet with his toys. She rose and held out her hands. "Let's join hands and focus on Kip's voice." She closed her eyes, so Jinn did the same.

Kip flipped the book open and began to read. Jinn didn't think she had ever heard it before, but Kip was all in so she let her continue. She wasn't positive that she was any closer to finding her center when her sister ended than she was before. She wasn't sure she even knew what that felt like.

"Okay, thank you, Kip. Now we move on to mixing." Freja dragged the large book on the table to her and flipped through the pages.

Jinn found that every page was written in funny letters.

"It's old Danish. None of us can read it, we rely on the translations in the margins." She finally found what she was looking for. "We'll start with a protection spell."

"I'll get the ingredients," Thyra said, turning toward the back of the shed.

"I'll help you," Tani added, following her.

"Kip, can you take the sticks out to the fire ring and make a symbol that looks like this?" Freja pointed to a rune in the margins of the book.

Kip studied it for a moment before walking outside with an armload of sticks.

"Now to assemble the bags," Freja continued. She pulled out a handful of small burlap bags from a box under the table. "You need to use a bag that burns easily made from natural ingredients. We found these work the best."

She handed the bag to Jinn. "You need a small scoop of Danish soil."

Tani set a large jar of soil on the table.

"We have an uncle in Denmark who keeps us in supply. I can just imagine him living with a giant pit in his back-yard because of all the dirt we need."

"Will it work with any other dirt?" Jinn asked.

"We've tried, but it's never been successful. You can always toy around later with different elements. It's best to work on a travel or money spell when experimenting. I'm not sure how to try a new protection charm without risking injury to one of the men."

"I understand. I won't try anything without your guidance."

"Now, you have to use the correct herbs for the spell you're weaving. Protection takes a whole bunch of them. You just need a sprinkle of each in the bag." She explained each herb and its properties as Jinn added them.

There was fragrant peppermint, sweet cinnamon, and tangy garlic to start. Several of the herbs Jinn had never heard of, but she dutifully listened to their descriptions.

"Here's the tricky part," Freja said. "You place your charm inside and then you need something from Arne. It might be spit or hair or even sweat—whatever you think will work."

"I'll have to find him," Jinn said. She wasn't sure what he had planned for the day. He could be at the back of the ranch feeding his cows.

"I told him to stay close. He should be working around here somewhere."

Jinn nodded then left with the sack to find Arne. She already knew he wasn't helping Dane in the equip-ment shop. She walked to the feed room. He was inside lifting mineral bags and setting them on another pile of bags.

Taking a second to watch the muscles in his shoulders bunch under his shirt, she thought about what she would need. She had to admit, though, that it was hard to focus with his sleeves rolled up. His forearms rippled with exertion as he added another sack to the pile.

"Hey," she said.

He stood abruptly and turned to find her. It made her heart thump when a bright smile broke out on his face. He tossed the sack on the pile and crossed to her. She let herself be pulled into his embrace.

"You're a sight for sore eyes," he said. "What are you up to? Has Mom driven you crazy yet?"

"Your mother is amazing," she answered. "She sent me to get something from you."

"Ahh, the old spit in the bag trick."

"She said I just had to see what spoke to me." She took a step back and studied him from head to toe. "I'm thinking a couple of drops of blood."

"Really? That seems excessive."

She held out her hand, and he reluctantly put his in it. He fished his pocket knife out with his free hand.

"Remember, there are several potions you have to do. Don't take it all this first go."

With a smirk, she pricked his finger with the end of the knife. Blood dripped into the bag. When she thought she had plenty, she slipped his finger into her mouth to stop the bleeding.

"Damn, save that for home," he teased.

"Don't worry, I fully intend to," she answered.

"Jesus, now I have to finish cleaning with a hard-on."

"Sorry, but I have other things to do right now." With a

flick of her hair, she walked to the door. She turned around to find him still watching her with a grin. "I'm sure I'll be back shortly."

"I hope so."

Jinn was still grinning when she reached the shed. She had never met someone like Arne before. How was it possible to still be friends with someone you had sex with? That certainly wasn't her experience in the past. Of course, no one was paying for her either. If she was going to be bonded forever to anyone, she had picked the best person out there.

"We were getting worried Arne had spirited you off somewhere," Freja said when Jinn found her standing next to a fire ring. Inside the ring were the sticks in the form of a symbol. "It's the rune used for protection. You'll repeat the verse in the book as best as you can, then throw the bag in the middle of the rune. If everything goes to plan, it will catch on fire and etch the rune into the metal."

"Is this what I'm supposed to say?" Jinn asked.

"I've been practicing it forever, and I still can't get it right," Thyra said.

"You just have to do the best you can. It doesn't seem to matter if it's right," Freja added.

"I used my native language," Tani agreed. "Still worked."

"Okay. If you can hold the book, I'll give it a try."

Jinn stood near the fire ring. Everyone else, minus the sleeping Aksel, joined her. She closed her eyes tight, focusing on what she held in her hand. It had to work. She couldn't risk Arne growing disgruntled with her and sending them away. Taking a deep breath, she opened her eyes and recited the words.

"Heill sé þú ok í hugum góðum! Þórr þik þiggi, Óðinn þik eigi."

With both hands, she hurled the bag at the rune. It felt like slow motion as the bag hit the sticks. They shook for a moment before bursting into flames. The flames turned into a fireball as it reached toward the sky. The force threw them to the ground. She had just sat up when she saw the fire die as quickly as it began.

"What happened?" Dane yelled, running from the equipment barn with Arne on his heels. "Is everyone okay?" he asked, reaching Tani.

He helped her up before turning to his mom. Freja pointed to the trees that shaded them.

"Fuck," he yelled, running for the house.

Sten arrived just as he was pulling the garden hose over.

"What is going on out here?" Sten asked. He helped Dane put the tree branches that had caught on fire, out. "Is everyone alright? Mother."

"I think we're all fine." Arne had helped Freja to her feet. "That was a potent one. We might have a real-life sorceress in the family finally."

"That was insane," Thyra agreed. "Leave it to Arne to find someone that powerful."

"Maybe it was just an accident." Jinn felt her head spinning. Not from being knocked on the ground but more from the words coming at her. She was powerful? Since when?

"Look at the charm." Thyra dug through the ash until she found it. The fire had not just etched the rune in the metal it had turned the small disk silver. "I'm almost scared to touch it. You're going to be invincible, Arne."

He squatted in the dirt next to his sister. Carefully, he pulled the charm from the ashes. Holding it up, he studied it carefully.

"I'd say that's one down," he said, handing it to Freja.

"I'd say you're right," she agreed. "Put this on a cord for now. We'll move on to the next one."

"How about we move the ring away from the house a little farther?" Sten suggested.

The men helped, and soon they had a new fire ring a safe distance from both the house and shed. They went back to work while Freja led the women into the shed.

"That was exciting. We usually include charms for courage, peace, and to bind us together. What do you want to try next?" Freja asked.

"I'm a little scared to try anymore at this point," Jinn said.

"Don't be. You'll learn to control your power. We honestly haven't seen anyone do that ever. Well, I haven't, maybe back in Denmark years ago." Freja flipped through the book. "I say we attempt courage."

Thyra and Tani happily started pulling herbs from the back wall. Kip jogged off to build a stick rune in the new fire ring. Freja handed Jinn a new bag, and they began the process all over again.

This time, she tried him spitting in the bag. The fireball was just as impressive. This time, though, they stood well back when she hurled the bag at the runes. She also managed not to catch the trees on fire again.

TWENTY

Arne followed Jinn up the stairs of his parents' house. She was dragging a little more than usual. It had been a long day for both of them. He had stuck around the house until told he could leave after lunch.

Grabbing Kip, they had tacked up two horses and headed out to see if they could find where the cattle were getting out this time. It was a never-ending process.

He knew Jinn had had an equally exhausting day. His mother had raved about how gifted Jinn was all through lunch. She had managed to create a fireball that could be seen for a mile every time she cast a spell.

His father had finally just left the hose hooked up and lying next to the fire ring. They only caught the pasture on fire one other time, but it was quickly extinguished.

"So do you like them?" she asked when they reached their temporary room. Her eyebrows were creased in the middle in concern. It melted his heart into a puddle instantly.

"Of course. I love them," he said. "They're the best gift I've ever received. They're stunning, just like their creator."

Her brows evened out as a smile crept on her face. That was better. He much preferred her happy. He pulled the four charms out from under his shirt to show her as if she hadn't seen them before.

"I love them. Not as much as I love you, but close."

"You love me?"

"Absolutely. Did you doubt that?"

She shrugged, but he could still see the smile on her lips. "How do you know?" she asked.

"It's just a feeling deep inside that grows bigger every day." He began removing his dirty clothes in anticipation of a shower. "I love my family of course, but this is different. It runs hot through my blood and sinks deep in the marrow of my bones."

"It makes every nerve light up like there's electricity flowing through them," she added. She began to remove her clothes also.

"Exactly," he agreed. "As if I need you to breathe."

"Or the world is a darker place when you're not there." She took his hand and pulled him into the bathroom. "I think I'm beginning to understand why the sorceress cast the spell on the warrior. She needed him too much to let him go."

She turned the water on in the shower. He followed her inside. Wrapping his hands around her buttocks, he lifted her to his waist.

"I think I now understand why he went back to find her." His lips found hers under the cascade of warm water. "He couldn't live without her." He lowered her until she sheathed him with her warmth. The time for talking was over; his blood boiled in his veins for a different reason.

Pressing her back against the shower wall, he thrust hard inside her. She gasped with each movement. He nipped at her lips, neck, and shoulder until she moaned his name. Her nails dug into his back as he pinned her with his body. His rhythm became brutal as he pushed them both toward something that promised to be almost spiritual in intensity.

"Arne," Jinn begged as he pushed her up the wall.

"You'd better fucking come for me," he growled.

Then she was. He marveled at how beautiful she was with her eyes closed in concentration and her head back. If he lived to be a hundred, he would never see anything better. She slumped onto his shoulder as he spilled his seed into her. He managed to stay on his feet without dropping her as he let the sensation of being with the woman he loved pull him away from the world.

"I love you," she whispered as they tried to regain their breath.

He stood in the shower simply holding her locked in their cocoon. She placed gentle kisses on his jaw, then his shoulder, and finally on the charms hanging around his neck.

"It's why I know they work," he said. "Only two women can enchant my charms. My true mate or my mother. Her time is done with me, I'm yours now."

Slowly, he set her back on her feet. He washed her long hair, soaped her body, and massaged her shoulders. Anything to take care of her.

"Are you ready for bed?"

"I am. Protecting you is exhausting." She turned off the water and stepped out of the shower.

"Probably harder than most," he agreed. He handed her a fluffy towel. "What do you think about helping me clean up the house tomorrow? Roar was working on getting at least one camera reinstalled down the road. He said he'd do a better job at hiding it this time."

"I don't think Kip should go, but I don't know if I can stop her. She's very stubborn."

"Hmm, I wonder where she gets that from," he said, moving back into the bedroom. "Erik should be home tomorrow. I'd like to move back when we can. I don't like the idea of those men showing up here."

"If anything ever happened to your mother, I don't know what I would do." Jinn crawled into bed next to Arne. She wore one of his old, soft flannel shirts. It hung to her knees, so it was as snuggly as she was.

"She's pretty tough. I wouldn't worry too much about her. She can hold her own," he said with a yawn. "Tomorrow then after I do a few things around here."

He waited for her to respond until he heard a soft snore. Yeah, they could deal with it tomorrow. He drifted off holding her close in his arms.

~

"Wow, they did a number on this place," Erik said, standing in the living room of Arne's house.

Roar and Dane had helped him secure the front door where it was kicked open, but the rest of the house looked pretty much the same.

"I can't believe they did this. This is all my fault," Jinn whispered.

"Hey, listen, this isn't your fault any more than it's mine. But we're in this together now. We'll deal with it," Arne said.

"I wonder if I can cast a spell on them," Jinn mumbled.

"Yeah, I heard I missed all the excitement. I guess it's true what they say about being a day late and a dollar short." Erik walked into the kitchen to start picking up pieces of what were Arne's dishes. He snapped open one of the large trash bags they brought.

"Mom said she has natural ability," Arne said proudly. He was on his knees in the living room throwing what was left of his game console in a box.

"That's cool. Hey, is insurance covering this?" Erik held up one of the kitchen cabinet doors that had been ripped off its hinges.

"They said they are. Everything was documented."

"That's something at least."

"I guess." Arne froze in the middle of assessing the destroyed couch. "Is that crying?"

Without waiting for Erik to answer, he walked down the hallway. He found Jinn sweeping up the remains of the broken bathroom mirror as tears rolled down her cheeks.

"Hey, hey. What's going on?" He took her broom and set it aside. Pulling her into his arms, he held her close.

"I'm just so pissed," she hissed. "Did they think this was going to intimidate me? They can fuck right off."

"There's my girl," he said, holding her at arm's length so he could peruse her face. He would swear he could see the fire burning behind her eyes. "So what do you want to do about it?"

"I want to burn them to the ground," she snarled. "I don't know how, but they're going down." She angrily swiped at her tears. "Between your family of wolves and my superhuman spell-weaving ability, we're bound to be able to come up with something."

Snatching up her broom, she swept up the glass like it

had personally offended her. Arne had to jump out of the room or risk having his shins bruised.

"That's what I'll do. When we're done here, I'll go get the potion book. Then we move back in and dare them to show up again."

"Damn, bro. You've got a live one there," Erik quipped as he walked to the first bedroom. "Where do y'all keep finding these livewires?"

"That's exactly what Roar said."

"Great minds and all."

"This one tried to shoot me with a bolt," Arne answered.

"Classic." Erik laughed.

"Are y'all just going to stand around flapping your gums, or are y'all going to get to work?" she barked.

"I chose work, sorceress," Erik called from the other room.

Arne just shook his head and moved back to the front of the house. The kitchen still wasn't in great shape, but Erik had done most of the sorting. He just had to carry any unsalvageable cabinet doors to the dump trailer out front.

His microwave had to go too. They had ripped it from the wall and thrown it into the living room. At least the coffee maker still seemed to be in one piece.

"Now this is just a crying shame," Erik said, appearing in the doorway to the kitchen holding one of the shredded Playboys. "This was a good one too. Criminal." He shook his head before adding it to the garbage sack. "Most of the rest are in the same shape."

"Just chunk them all. I have the real thing now," Arne said.

"End of an era. What about the comforter that's soaked in lube? At least I hope that's what that is."

"Throw it, we'll buy new." He paused cleaning to listen to Jinn cussing as things hit the trash can.

"Dude, I'm sort of scared to go back by the bathroom door," Erik said. "She's on a mission. I think she's planning on turning them into toads or something."

"Pretty sure she's not that powerful."

"Don't be so sure. The first sorceress turned us into wolves." Arne shrugged. Erik did have a point. Though that was all just conjecture. Hopefully.

"I need help getting what's left of the mirror off the wall," she said. They both jumped. Erik widened his eyes at Arne.

"I'll go," Arne said. He followed her into the bathroom. All she needed was for him to hold the mirror while she finished taking the brackets off. Fortunately, it wasn't glued in place. "I think you have Erik worried."

"Why?"

"You've been in here mumbling about what you're going to do when you catch Jabba and Bond."

"Well, he needs to decide if he's a friend or foe." Arne worried for a moment until he saw her smirk. "If he's good I won't turn him into a toad too."

"Do you know how sexy you are when you threaten destruction like that?" Carefully, he carried the mirror to the front door. She pulled the door open for him so he could toss it into the trailer. "Absolutely diabolically luscious."

"Stay around, you might even get to glimpse total villainous lasciviousness."

"Mmm, you really know how to turn a man on." She laughed as he pulled her to him for a kiss.

"Okay, do I need to throw a bucket of ice water on you two?" Erik asked.

With a sigh, they parted and returned to their jobs. Jinn

went to finish the bathroom while Arne headed to the kitchen. They both ignored Erik on the way by.

"That's fine," he said. "I see how it is. Little brother is just good for some heavy lifting."

"We've been telling you that for years," Arne answered.

He moved into the small room behind the kitchen that served as the laundry room. Blessedly, the room didn't look like they had touched it. The washer was probably too heavy to be heaved into the living room. He went to find Erik in the main bedroom.

"I think I have all the clothes separated. I put back anything clean and tossed the rest in the laundry basket. They pulled all the drawers out, but none of them were torn up. You'll want to vacuum well."

"I'll get on that then."

He pulled the vacuum out of the hall closet. After reminding Erik to keep an eye on the camera feed, he began on the carpet in the bedroom. The whole house was full of broken glass. His brother worked in front of him trying to clear the largest pieces. Arne wondered what the men would have done if they hadn't been alerted. Would his house even still be standing?

"It's probably as good as we're going to get it," he said finally. He had vacuumed every inch of the floor until he reached the front door. "I'll see if Roar will pick me up some new bedding before he comes back down tomorrow. So one more night at Mom and Dad's?"

"Yeah, I think that's best," Jinn agreed. "Tomorrow we take our house back. Without Kip though. I don't know if I want her in the line of fire. She might have other ideas though."

"If so, I'll be here, and we can see if Roar will stay during the holidays too," Erik offered. "They can try to take it again, but good luck. Ooh, we should get a flag to fly upside down. It'll show we're at war."

"You're an idiot," Arne said. He playfully smacked Erik in the back of the head.

"Still have more game than you," Erik mumbled.

"I'm sorry, who's getting it on the regular now?" Arne fired back.

"Oh Lord, I think it's time for me to get back to the land of women and spells." Jinn rolled her eyes.

"Lead on, sorceress," Erik teased. She threw her nose in the air and led them out of the house like a queen.

TWENTY-ONE

Kip clutched Jinn's hand as they walked into the house behind Arne. She understood her sister's fear, even though Kip had insisted that she return with them. It helped that Roar and Erik were staying the night, though where they were all going to sleep was a bafflement. Arne unlocked the front door and paused before throwing it open. She suspected, even knowing what awaited him inside, he still braced for it.

"Wow," Kip whispered when they stepped into the living room.

She was the only one of them that hadn't seen the destruction the men had done to the house. At least, it wasn't as bad as it had originally been. Arne had gone to the city that morning and picked up a microwave, mirror, and new dishes. The cabinet doors were scheduled to be replaced later in the week, and there was a new couch on the way.

"Are you sure you want to stay?" Jinn asked her sister. "Mrs. Ulvmand said you could stay with them as long as you want. No one would fault you for going back."

"No," Kip said, pulling her shoulders back in defiance. "They're not scaring us out of our home."

"Besides," Erik assured her. "I'll be sleeping right here in the living room and nobody gets past me."

"We'll be right down the hall if you need anything. Anything at all," Roar added.

"Do you remember the plan if we need to escape?" Jinn asked.

"Through the trapdoor, hide until the danger is over," Kip repeated what Jinn had drilled into her.

"One of us will always come to find you," Roar said. "You stay hidden until you hear or see us." Kip nodded.

"How about we have some ice cream and relax before bed," Arne suggested. "Erik, why don't you hook up the new console and teach Kip a couple of games? I'll get the ice cream."

Kip happily flitted after Erik as Arne walked into the kitchen. Roar made himself as comfortable on the couch as possible no doubt to offer up words of advice to Erik.

"So what do we do if they come back?" Jinn asked quietly in the kitchen. She started pulling ice cream out of the freezer while Arne stacked five of the new bowls on the counter.

"I'm not really sure," he answered. "Dane brought a stash of guns over this morning. I'm hoping it doesn't come to that. With any luck, we'll have enough warning to alert the sheriff." He paused digging the scoop out of the drawer to turn to her.

"Whatever happens, you and Kip run. That's the one thing I need you to do. Okay?"

"I know," she answered. "I told Kip not to wait for me, just run. I'm so sorry, Arne."

"Hey." He set the scoop down and cupped her face in his

hands. "You don't have anything to be sorry for. You didn't pick this fight, they did. Now my brothers and I will end it." He pressed his lips to hers.

"You're supposed to be getting ice cream," Erik yelled from the living room. "Try to focus."

Jinn stepped back and laughed. Arne just shook his head. The longer she was around his family, the more she fell in love with them.

"Shut up and hook up the console," Arne yelled back. "I'm coming to whip your ass at MarioKart."

"Good grief. How old are you?" Roar grumbled.

"Old enough to kick your ass too," Arne said, handing him a bowl.

Erik took his bowl and handed one to Kip before they both settled back down on the floor in front of the new television. Arne chose his chair to sink into. Jinn was debating if she could straddle the giant rip in the cushion next to Roar when Arne pulled her down on his lap.

"So what is MarioKart?" Kip asked.

"Only the best game ever invented."

"Debatable," Roar mumbled.

Erik slid the game into the console and began to demonstrate how to play. Jinn listened as she worked on her ice cream. Sitting on Arne's lap felt like the most natural thing in the world. How did life come to this? Everything felt so normal. No one seemed to think there was anything unusual about her snuggled up in the chair with him. She liked the relationship thing.

She jumped when Arne's phone buzzed in his pocket. She watched as all three men checked their messages.

"Thyra's on her way," Erik said before returning to the game.

"Hey, bitches," she said a few minutes later when Erik

opened the door. "Mom sent cookies. I decided it wouldn't be a proper slumber party without me. Hey, y'all have ice cream." She set a plate of cookies on the table and walked to the kitchen. "I figured I'd just sleep with you in Arne's bed."

"Sounds good," Jinn agreed. "There's plenty of room."

"What are you doing?" Arne grumbled in her ear. "This place is busting at the seams with people."

"I know. Isn't it great?" she answered.

Thyra returned with a bowl of ice cream and a blanket she threw over the split in the couch cushion. Flopping down, she swung her feet up until they pressed against Roar's thigh. He tried to swat them away, but she persisted until he finally gave up. Jinn just smiled at the interaction. Her forever home just kept getting better and better.

"What am I doing wrong?" Kip whined when her kart spun off the side.

"Let me have the controller, and I'll show you," Roar said.

She handed it to him.

"You have to watch Erik; he cheats."

"I do not," Erik argued.

The game started again. Erik began maneuvering in front of the television blocking Roar's view.

"See?" Roar said.

He swayed on the couch until, with a growl, he tackled Erik to the floor. When his brother was finally lying prone with Roar sitting on his back, the game continued.

"No fair," Erik complained.

Kip joined Roar on Erik's back so she could watch how he was racing. He tried to shove Roar's kart off the side.

"See, you have to dodge him. Remember, he's been playing this a long time."

"Arne," Erik pleaded.

"Nope. You brought this on yourself." Jinn grinned at him as she snuggled even tighter against his chest. Yep, this life was going to be alright.

~

"WHAT DO YOU THINK?" Jabba asked Bond as they watched the house from just beyond the latest camera's view.

"I think there are too many of them right now. I'm pretty sure that was a gun bag the big guy hauled inside, and they have the added advantage of fortification," Bond answered.

"We would have the element of surprise."

"We don't know how they've fortified the house. There are at least three men inside who are well-armed. We need to catch her alone with just the fucker who's been harboring them. They'll let down their guard eventually. That's when we attack."

"Yeah, but how long will that take?"

"As long as it takes. Do you want to go back empty-handed?"

"No," Jabba acquiesced. He leaned into the back seat of the SUV and dug a bag of chips out of a sack. "It just seems like a lot of effort for one whore," he added between bites.

"I'll let you tell him that." Bond sneered at Jabba.

It seemed he was always eating something. How the man stayed in any kind of shape was beyond him.

"We should have installed some cameras of our own when we were inside."

"I can't believe they moved back in." Jabba had moved on to a candy bar. "Rumor is he's already replaced a lot of what we destroyed."

"I will give him this; he's a determined bastard."

"Or too thick to know any better."

"I don't think he's stupid," Bond disagreed. "Seems like he's daring us to come back. Have you seen any sign of those fucking wolves?"

"No, but they could be inside."

"Huh," Bond grunted. "There's something odd about all of this. Who keeps wolves? I understand pit bulls in this area, but wolves seem over the top."

"I don't know, but next time they go down first. I'm not chancing getting mauled by one of them. I bet if we can catch that white one, his pelt is worth a nice chunk of change."

"Maybe. We could always train them to fight."

"Nobody's going to let you into a fight with a wolf. No, their pelts are more valuable," Jabba argued.

"Fine. We'll skin the wolves, catch the whore and her boyfriend, and haul them back. We can split the money for the pelts."

Jabba dug around in the sack until he pulled out one of the sandwiches they bought at a local sub shop. They sat in silence while he chewed.

Bond fantasized about smashing his head repeatedly on the dashboard just to remind him to chew with his damn mouth closed. The thought of having to sit for hours in the SUV with Jaws though was worse than suffering Jabba's smacking.

"What time is it?" Jabba asked, spraying half-eaten breadcrumbs everywhere.

"It's only ten. We'll wait another hour, and if they're all still in there, try again tomorrow. Hand me the other sandwich."

Bond unwrapped the other sub and took a bite. It was

better than he had expected it to be. At least that podunk town was good for something. They had been forced to lay low when an older man started asking around about them. The last thing they needed was to get crossways with the locals.

So far, the old man they roughed up had remained silent as instructed. But then, they had made sure he understood the consequences of flapping his gums around town about what had happened to them.

"Did the lights just go out?" Jabba asked.

Bond, taking the binoculars from Jabba's beefy hands, checked the house. He was right; the lights in the front room had shut off. He searched what he could see of the rest of the house. There was no way to tell about the back bedroom, but there was a faint glow from the bedroom off the hallway.

"Who goes to bed this early?"

"They're farmers, remember."

"Man, I always thought that was just a myth. Why would anyone want a job that means you're in bed by ten?"

"I guess if you have to get up early, you would."

"Fuck that. I like my job. Stay up late, get up late."

"Eat well, drink even better, and all the pussy you can handle," Bond finished for him with a grin.

"Yeah, I bet Tony disagrees after the beating those whores gave him."

"Serves him right. You never let your guard down around them. Idiot."

"Idiot," Jabba echoed. "Are we still staying until eleven? 'Cause I'm starting to run out of something to eat."

Bond shoved the rest of his sandwich at him.

"Thanks. I don't care what they say, you're alright." With a laugh, Jabba took a large bite.

"I guess we can go." Bond chose to ignore the jab this time. "We'll just have to be patient. We'll have our chance soon."

"They say patience is a virtue."

"Who wants to be virtuous?" Both men laughed as Bond started the SUV.

"Hey," Arne whispered, stepping into the hallway.

"Hey," Jinn answered.

"I was just making sure the house was locked up."

"Same. Kip and Thyra are both lying in your bed with a book."

"Roar is in bed, and Erik is finishing in the bathroom. He's sleeping on a pallet in the living room with a loaded shotgun next to him. You might not want to scare him in the middle of the night."

"Duly noted."

They stood for a moment in the middle of the hallway staring at each other. Then Arne pulled her against him cupping her face in his hands. He kissed her long and deep. She sighed when he pulled away. Her eyes fluttered open to find him watching her.

"I'm sorry that the house seems to be bursting at the seams with my family," he said.

"I think it's wonderful. To go from just Kip and me to an entire family is more than I could have ever hoped for. You're a lucky man, Arne Ulvmand."

"Don't I know it," he agreed. "I found you."

"Oops, sorry. Private moment," Erik said, stepping out of the bathroom. He quickly walked to the living room.

Jinn laughed watching him skitter away.

"Private moments are hard to come by in a large family," Arne said.

"I can see that, but I'll take it." She didn't tell him that privacy wasn't even thought about when you had guards watching you shower. "Arne, do you think we'll survive this?"

"Absolutely. We stay together, watch each other's backs, and fight. I promise it will all work out."

"I hope so," she whispered. "I've grown used to having you around."

"Just try to get rid of me," he teased.

Before she could answer, he pulled her into another one of his toe-curling, panty-melting, soul-lifting kisses. Get rid of him? That was a laugh. She couldn't walk away from him if she tried.

"Never," she breathed.

There was a brief smile, then his lips were back on hers, and she silently promised to fight anyway she had to to keep that promise.

TWENTY-TWO

Arne hadn't realized how exhausting having a house full of people could be. Roar had headed home the next day, as had Thyra. Erik, however, had moved into the spare bedroom with him. He sat on the edge of the small twin bed watching his brother snore like there was no tomorrow. Erik was stretched out on his bed with his legs hanging off the end.

It was time for work, which meant Arne had to wake everyone to get ready. Might as well start with the freight train. He scratched his chin as he thought about how Dane used to wake him up. Slowly, he leaned forward until he could reach Erik. He raised his arm and then let it drop with his palm, smacking Erik in the stomach.

"What the hell?" his brother sputtered.

Now Arne understood why Dane did that. It was instant gratification to watch Erik stumble out of the bed.

"Dude, what is wrong with you?"

"Get dressed, I've got to be at work soon. I'm going to wake the rest of the house." Arne left Erik muttering at him and walked down the hallway. He eased the door open to his bedroom. Jinn, of course, was already dressed. She was trying to wake up Kip. "I'll start some breakfast," he said.

"Let me help," she answered. "Kip, get up." She followed him out the door. "It's getting harder and harder to wake her up. She keeps arguing that she should be on Christmas break like Thyra."

"I wish I could leave all of you here to sleep in. I think everyone could use a break."

"Not your fault."

They fell into a companionable silence as they worked in the kitchen to make breakfast. Arne would almost swear they had been cooking together for years instead of just weeks.

Everything about their relationship seemed easy. Except sleeping in separate rooms. He was ready for that to come to an end. It was torture to finally find his perfect partner only to have to return to celibacy.

An occasional quickie in the bathroom or the front seat of his feed truck didn't count either. He was ready to fall asleep with her in his arms every night and wake up to her every morning.

"You're a dick," Erik said, flopping down on one of the barstools.

"Get over it. You're not hurt," Arne answered.

"Arne," Erik whined. "You're the nice brother, remember? I expect that from Dane, not you."

"Such a baby," Arne said, rolling his eyes. He noticed Jinn was still quietly working on breakfast. It occurred to him that she never got involved when he sparred with his brothers. "Jinn?"

She pulled the bacon from the griddle and turned to face him.

"Does it bother you when we start squabbling?"

She simply shrugged her shoulders.

"You know we're just teasing each other, right?" Erik asked. "We'd never do anything to hurt one another. Not on purpose anyway."

"We can do better," Arne added. "I know the men in your life have always been too much. Now, we're too much. I promise we won't argue around you anymore."

"No," she finally said. "I don't want you changing your relationship with your brothers for me. I'm learning that men can be together without one fighting to control the others.

"Growing up, my father was always slapping my mother around when she did something he didn't like. The rules changed all the time, usually without her knowing it.

"The men at the big house were much the same. It was nothing to be at the receiving end of a fist just for saying the wrong thing."

"That will never happen here," Arne said, pulling her into his chest. His long arms wrapped around her.

"That's not what I heard. Kip told me y'all came out slugging from the beginning." Erik teased.

Arne knew he was trying to lighten the mood. It worked when Jinn laughed against his chest.

"He's got you there," she said.

Kip soon joined them, and the conversation turned to her continuing argument on sleeping in. Erik agreed with every word she said while Jinn took her turn rolling her eyes. They loaded into the truck and drove to headquarters. He knew Jinn was anxious to work on more spells under Freja's supervision. Kip disappeared into the house to curl up on the couch until Thyra woke.

"Hey," Dane called to them from the equipment barn. "Can Erik help me this morning?"

"Yeah, I don't have anything for him to do," Arne answered.

"Or we could ask Erik since he's standing right here," Erik said.

"Would his grace join me in lending his mighty body," Dane teased.

"I would be happy to, my liege." Erik bowed and followed Dane into the barn.

"Idiots," Arne mumbled.

He rolled up the overhead door of the feed barn. He didn't have time to deal with them. He had an entire ranch worth of cattle to feed before he was allowed to move on for the day. Pulling the truck out of the barn, he pulled under the bins to fill the feeder. In his mind, he mapped out the best routes around the ranch to take. Just one more example of the exciting life of a cowboy.

He worked his way slowly around the ranch. There were several new calves this time. He made a mental note to bring Jinn out to see them later. It was almost noon when he finished and returned to the feed barn. After lunch, he would put hay out to the handful of pastures that needed it. Jinn met him as he was pulling down the roll-up door.

"Hey, I need to run back to the house. I forgot to grab my notes on the new spells I want to try."

She had been spending her evenings studying different properties of the herbs used in charms. There was almost a whole notebook full of notes sitting on the coffee table.

"Kip asked if she could ride with us to get a couple of books to trade out. I've already told your mom that we'll just grab a sandwich there for lunch."

"Yeah, that's no problem. Grab Kip, and I'll meet you at the truck."

She walked back to the house. He found Dane and Erik still working on a hay baler.

"Hey, we're running to the house for a few minutes."

"I can go with you," Erik said. He began to hunt for a shop rag to wipe his greasy hands on.

"Don't worry about it. We'll just be a minute."

Erik shrugged and went back to work. Arne walked to the truck where Jinn was waiting with Kip in tow.

"So, notes, books, sandwich. Is that right?"

"I thought I might heat some soup too," Jinn answered.

They drove the twenty minutes around to the other side of the ranch. Pulling up to the house, he let them inside before walking to his small horse barn. It was cold, so he might as well feed Elmo a little early to help maintain his body heat. He was in the barn scooping feed into a bucket when he felt someone behind him.

"I'm on my way," he said, thinking it was Jinn.

He only had a second to register his mistake before the butt of a shotgun crashed down on his nose. He reached for something to throw at the man standing over him when the butt slammed into the side of his head. His last thoughts were of Jinn and Kip alone in the house, before he slid into blackness.

Kip left Jinn in the kitchen finishing lunch preparations to hunt for the books she needed to return. Thyra had checked out a handful of mysteries for her from the local library. She had discovered she liked mysteries the best, especially the ones that took place in the British countryside. One day, she'd go over there just to see all of her favorite book settings. She might even be old enough to enjoy a pint by then.

All four books were placed carefully on Arne's dresser. She had a stack of returns, one of the books to be read and one that she had read but was still thinking about. Thyra had informed her that she could only keep a book from the library for two weeks before it needed to be returned. It seemed like an odd rule for books you get to read for free, but she was careful to return them before they were due.

She swept the books one by one off the dresser and added them to a large book bag. It was one of her most treasured possessions. The side of the bag had a purple dragon wrapped around a stack of books. Tani had brought it to her after one of her trips to the city. Kip had decided she would keep it forever, even after it was in tatters. When she had all the books inside, she headed out of the bedroom.

"Hands," Jinn yelled from the dining area.

Kip made a turn into the only bathroom in the house. She was always being reminded by her sister to wash her hands. Arne never seemed to care how clean her hands were. He argued that if you use utensils, it shouldn't really matter. Jinn had rolled her eyes, but Kip knew he was arguing on her behalf.

She turned off the water and was just drying her hands when she heard a splintering crash. It sounded like something had slammed into their house. She stepped into the hallway and froze. At the door, Jinn was wrestling with Jabba.

"Go," Jinn screamed at her.

Without thinking, she dropped her books and ran into the spare bedroom. She heard more shouting from the living room as she sprinted for the closet.

Pulling the trap door open, she slid under the house

right as she heard footsteps coming down the hall. She wondered if she should wait for Jinn. But Jinn had given her clear instructions about not waiting, so she slid the door closed.

With her belly on the ground, she crawled to the edge of the house. It would have been nice if Jinn hadn't insisted she leave her boots by the front door when they got home. Jinn had also insisted she change her wet socks. She had been in the barn brushing horses when Jinn got her to come home. It wasn't her fault that her boots were muddy and her socks wet.

"Jinn," she whispered before clamping her lips shut.

Her sister had warned her to stay quiet and get as far as she could. She crawled until she reached the small door in the siding Arne had installed. Slowly, she pushed it open just enough to wiggle through. She listened for a second before sliding outside.

Now she had the sprint to where the hill sloped down. She counted to three then sprinted like she was in the Olympics.

Reaching the edge, she slid on her hip off the side. She lay on her stomach and peered carefully over the edge. There was just enough of a view of the front of the house to watch as the men threw a limp Arne in the back and shoved Jinn inside behind him. She thought they both looked bound at the hands and ankles.

It took everything she had to wait for the SUV to leave, but she knew her best chance was to grab Elmo and go for help.

Slowly, she crept to the front of the house. Her bare feet already felt like they had stepped on a field of glass. The SUV was nowhere in sight. Running into the house, she searched for Arne's phone. Neither she nor Jinn owned one, and the house didn't have a landline.

She didn't even think about her extra shoes in the closet or the coat by the back door. She ran outside to Elmo's pen. He was upset but came to her when she opened the gate.

"Elmo, I really, really need your help."

He stood while she slid the bridle over his head.

"We're not going to take the time to put your saddle on. Besides, I don't think I can stand to walk much farther."

She led him from the pen to the porch. Climbing up the wooden stairs, she leaped onto his back. He tossed his head when she landed on her stomach but waited patiently while she righted herself.

"I need you to be very good and get us to the house as fast as you can. I'm going to sit here and hold on."

She pointed Elmo toward Sten's house and tightened her legs. Hunkering down, she grabbed two handfuls of his mane. She could survive this. It was the only way the Ulvmands would know what happened. If Jinn could be brave enough to escape that house with her in tow, then she could be brave enough to get help.

She squeezed her legs harder, and Elmo sped up.

Arne had taught her about the different gaits a horse has. He said that a walk was smooth but slow, a trot was bumpy, but you could ride a long way, and a canter was somewhere between the two in comfort but covered a lot of ground. A gallop, though, well she wasn't that brave.

She let Elmo slide down the hill before pushing him forward. He broke into a canter as she clung to his neck.

Crossing the flat bottoms was no problem, but they soon came to the river. Last time, she carefully let him pick his way across through the water. This time, they hit it at a canter.

Elmo stepped into the cold water and jumped toward the far bank. Kip managed to hold on long enough to reach the far bank before falling off.

Her head hit the ground, but the blow didn't knock her out. Standing, she brushed the mud off as best she could and climbed up the bank. Tears started to build in the back of her eyes, but she quickly wiped them away. This wasn't the time to break down; that could come after her family was home. Besides, she was already half frozen without adding to it.

Elmo stood on the top of the bank as if waiting on her. She supposed it wasn't his fault she fell off. Next time, she'd figure out how to ride it out.

She looked around until she found an old stump she could stand on. Her feet screamed in agony as she balanced on the splintering post, but Elmo stood patiently until she made it back on. He only gave her a moment to settle before they were off again.

This time, she didn't need to convince him to hurry. It seemed he already knew too much time had passed.

TWENTY-THREE

Kip wasn't sure how she made it to headquarters. Somehow, she managed to stay on Elmo the rest of the way until she reined him in in the middle of the driveway. He spun looking around as she fought to hold him still.

"Kip?" Dane, the first person to step outside, asked. "Kip, what happened?"

Quickly, he moved to catch Elmo's reins. The horse's body shone with sweat as he tossed his head. "Easy, boy. Easy."

"Arne," Kip managed to get out. Between the pain in her feet and her adrenaline wearing off, it was all she could get out in one breath. "Jinn. They're gone."

"Dad," Dane bellowed. Elmo was startled, but he held on tight to the horse. "Dad."

"What is it?" Sten asked, pushing out the back door of the house. Freja followed right behind. "Kip, what happened?" He rushed through the gate when he realized she was hurt.

"Thyra, take the horse," Sten barked as both Erik and Thyra walked out of the shop.

She rushed to hold Elmo's head. Gently they slid Kip off Elmo's back into Dane's arms. He carried her to the bed of his truck and sat her on it. "Tell me exactly what happened."

"I'm not totally sure," she answered. She gritted her teeth as Freja examined her swollen feet. "I was in the hallway with my books when they broke the door down."

"The men who broke in the other day?" Dane asked.

"Yes," she said with a nod. "I slid through the trapdoor just like Jinn said. All I could see was the men loading them into the SUV." She paused for a moment before adding quietly, "Arne didn't look good. It looked like he was unconscious."

There was a collective gasp, and then Sten was giving orders.

"Mother, call the sheriff. Then, when Thyra is done with Elmo, you drive to Arne's and wait for them. Stay in the truck until they get there," he said.

Freja ran into the house but returned moments later with a blanket to wrap around Kip.

"This will help," she said.

Without waiting for an answer, Freja disappeared back inside. Kip didn't know much about the sheriff she had to call, but she hoped he could help. Didn't most of her mysteries end with the law arresting the bad guy?

"I'll see if Tani will come take Kip to the hospital so someone can look at her feet," Dane added. "Erik, you're with us after you carry Kip inside."

"No," Kip argued. She slid off the tailgate onto her feet. Jabs of pain radiated through her. "I'm going with you. I think I know how to find the house. That has to be where they're going. You'll also need me to show you how to get inside and where to find them."

Sten considered her a moment before nodding. Erik swept her off her feet into his arms and walked quickly to the truck.

"I still need to let Tani know what's happening," Dane said, sliding the truck into gear. "Mom can pick her up on the way to Arne's. Aksel went with his grandpa to visit some of her family. She's catching up on some of her school stuff for next semester at the house." He pressed a number on his phone and cupped it against his ear as he tore down the road.

"How do you think you can find them?" Erik asked. "Do you remember something?"

"The first night after we left, we walked through this nice neighborhood for a little while. Then we crossed to the other side of the town where there was a sign for a small engine repair place. If we can find that sign, I think I can retrace our steps," she said.

"What was the name? I can look it up on my phone when we get to town and have service again."

"I'm trying to remember. There was a D." She sat staring at the ceiling. If she could just remember. "It was a name. Dan, Dave? No." Her eyes slid closed as she hunted through her memories. She didn't have to focus on getting away when they fled. That was Jinn's job. So, she got to look around more and take better note of their surroundings.

"Donnie. That's it. Donnie's Small Engine Repair."

"I'm on it." Erik checked his phone. "Well, I'm on it in about half an hour when we reach town."

"We're swinging by to pick up Roar. He's meeting us in front of his house," Sten added. He looked at Dane, who was still speaking on the phone. Dane nodded he had heard. "How are you doing, sweetheart?"

"My feet sting," she answered.

"I'm sure they do. They're pretty cut up on the bottom. There's probably some aspirin in here somewhere."

Sten dug through the glove compartment until he found a small bottle of ibuprofen. There was a half-drunk bottle of water in the door pocket. She took the pills and the water gratefully. Anything to help her feet.

Half an hour later, Dane slid the truck to a stop at the stop sign in the middle of town. Kip stared out the window trying to take it all in. When they went to the city shopping, she had fallen asleep before she saw it. This was her first glance at what was going to be her hometown. For the rest of her life, when people asked where she was from, this was where she'd tell them. It was the first place where she felt at home.

"Shit," Erik mumbled as his fingers flew over his phone. "I'm not having any luck finding anywhere nearby named Donnie's Small Engine Repair. Found a ton of other ones. Who knew there were so many repair shops around here?" She was sure he was talking to himself, but she listened closely anyway.

"Maybe social media." He began clicking away on his phone again.

Kip doubted, if she ever got a phone, that she would be half as good at using it as Erik was.

"Any luck?" Sten asked.

They had turned the corner into town and were flying down the road to Roar.

"Do you still have any friends from high school around here?"

"Yeah," Erik said, acting slightly insulted.

Kip grinned; these men were always being insulted by each other.

"Call some of them and see if they've ever heard of it," Sten continued. "I'll text Roar to start with his group. Maybe between the three of us, we'll come up with something."

Both men turned back to their phones. She looked out her window. Houses and cows and everything in between flew by.

Roar was pacing back and forth in his front yard when Dane squealed up to the curb. In a few huge strides, Roar was sliding into the truck next to her. She was now sandwiched between the two giant brothers. She didn't think it was a bad place to be. Nowhere else felt as safe as being in the middle of her new family.

"I think I found it," he said, waving his phone in the air. "A friend from work said he took his fishing boat to a place with that name. It's on the other side of the interstate toward the lake."

She remembered Jinn mentioning a lake once.

"It's like an hour from here."

"Damn, that's some impressive miles you made," Erik said.

"We could only travel at night. I think we would have gotten farther if we were traveling down a road in the daylight," she answered. "Jinn didn't want to take any chances. We only spent one night in your shack when Arne found us. Or more like Jinn found him. On accident." She looked at Erik. "She didn't mean to shoot at him."

"Probably did him some good," Sten said with a laugh. Nothing about his laugh sounded natural to Kip. She knew he was just as worried about Arne and Jinn as she was. "Crazy kid," he mumbled.

"We'll get them back, Dad," Dane said.

"You're right," Sten agreed. "We will. We just have to find them first."

"What do we do when we do find them?" Erik asked.

"That's where we're going to need Kip's memory. What can you tell us about the house?"

"There's a tall fence with spikes on top around it," she began. "There's nowhere to hide and usually the doors are locked. Guards patrol the house outside. Inside it's just the trusted four who watch the women. You have to find the basement, which is the first door from the back entrance.

"Jinn said there are two stories on top. I guess the top floor is nothing but bedrooms. She didn't talk much about those rooms. I don't know anything about them."

"Piece of cake," Dane said, cutting his eyes at Sten.

Kip thought she caught his dry sarcasm tempered with worry.

"When we ran, there was a party in the front rooms of the house which kept everyone distracted. It was why Jinn said we had to go that night. I hit Khan over the head when Jinn lured him into our room. It was the one night she thought we could make it past the fence. She was right."

"Must have been terrifying," Roar said. He patted her on the leg.

She was glad she had him as a big brother now. He was the kind, authoritarian brother. She had them all figured out at this point. Dane was grumpy but a pushover. Arne was the charming goofball, and Erik took life in stride. It was a good blend.

"I did what Jinn said. It was probably worse for her." She watched out the windshield as they passed under a large highway.

"I don't think it's that far from here." Roar searched out the window for several more miles. "Here it is."

Dane pulled into the parking lot and threw the truck in park. They all turned to her. There wasn't much more they could do until she figured out where to go from here. Leaning over the front seat, she searched the surroundings.

"We walked along the edge of the road just inside those trees to the tattoo place," she said.

Dane put the truck back in gear, and they drove to the next landmark.

"From here, we need to go behind that row of houses for a couple of blocks."

Dane eased around the corner onto the dirt trail behind the houses. They bumped along until she said to stop.

"Through those trees to the road that Jinn said goes to the lake."

Their journey continued the same way for the next hour. Dane would drive a few minutes and then they would wait while she slowly pieced their trip together. A couple of times they had to double back so she could try again. The only person who ever seemed to get irritated that she had gone down the wrong path was her.

"It's okay. Take your time," Sten had said to her time and time again. "You can do this."

She just wished she had as much confidence in her as he did. Finally, she found the entrance to the housing development where the big house was. They wound through the houses until she pointed out the fence that surrounded the house. Dane pulled down the street and parked under a tree.

"The back door is over there," she pointed out. "You can get over the fence back there. I don't know if the door will be unlocked. It was when Jinn and I left, but today could be different."

"I think we need a distraction," Sten said. He had been studying the house through a set of binoculars that happened to also be in the glove compartment. "We need to draw the guards to the front." He checked his watch. "It should be getting dark in half an hour. We'll go then. Everybody should be busy dealing with what's happening in the front of the house. You can sneak around back while they're not paying attention."

"How will we create a distraction?" Erik asked.

"Leave that to me. I'll get in position. When you hear me, count to sixty before moving. Kip, you stay in the truck. If something happens, you slide the truck into gear and leave."

"I don't know how to drive," she protested.

She could probably figure it out, but she didn't like the idea of leaving anyone behind. Again. Dane ignored her argument and walked her through how to drive the truck. All she had to do was get far enough to get help. Erik also explained how to dial the emergency number on his phone. He handed it over to her so she could practice using it before he left.

"Okay, I'm gone." Sten slipped out of the front door. He laid his shirt and jeans on the front seat. "Damn, it's cold out here."

Then he was gone, and Kip watched a tan wolf trotting through the woods in front of them. It was easy to forget that this was a family of beasts and sorceresses. It was what made her family unique. A few minutes later they heard a howl from near the front gates.

"Stay in the truck with the doors locked," Roar

reminded her. "Whatever happens, stay inside. First sign of trouble, you're out of here."

She nodded.

"Promise us."

"I promise," she said with her fingers crossed behind her back.

She had done that once and watched the two people she loved most in this world taken from her; she didn't know if she could do it twice.

She watched as they climbed from the truck. Dane pulled two rifles from under the backseat. He handed one to Roar.

"Please," she whispered.

She wasn't sure exactly what she was asking for. To bring her sister back, to save the man her sister loved more than anything, to come back alive? She guessed all of these.

"We will," Erik assured her.

She handed him the blanket that was wrapped around her shoulders.

"You're going to get cold without it."

"You'll need it for the spikes on top of the fence. I'll be fine."

They closed the doors and she scrambled into the front seat. She watched as they skirted around the edges of the properties until they were near the fence. It was a marvel to watch how easily they climbed over it. Being tall was a definite advantage when it came to breaking and entering. They hunkered down next to the bushes by the fence.

She waved at them madly even though she knew she was too far away for them to see in the twilight. Her focus swung over to the other side of the house where the guards were trying to find the wolf. The guards had come as far as the front gate obviously to prevent venturing into his hunting ground.

"Eat them all," she whispered to the wolf.

When she swung back around to watch the back of the house, they were already gone. How they made it through the back door, she had no idea. Now, all that was left was to wait.

TWENTY-FOUR

Arne moaned when he heard his name. It seemed every time he managed to regain consciousness they beat him unconscious again. His nose throbbed where he was hit with the gun, one eye would no longer open from swelling, and he was certain he had a broken rib or two.

Still, the voice didn't sound like one of the guards. It called to him again, and this time he managed to open his good eye.

Dane's face swam in front of him. He must be hallucinating. The last thing he remembered was being knocked out in the tack room at his house. There was a vague memory of coming to in the back of an SUV next to Jinn. Jinn! His head shot up as he tried to stand. He had to find her.

"Slow down." Strong hands pressed him back into the chair. "We're still trying to get you unbound."

It was then that he realized it wasn't just the one brother; it was all three. He tried to peer behind him without twisting too much. A glance of red hair told him Roar was working on his restraints. He felt the ties fall from his wrist. Dane caught him as he slumped forward. Then his ankles were cut free.

"I doubt he has much feeling in either his hands or his feet," Roar said. "Give him a minute to regain some of it."

"We only have a minute," Dane replied. "Any idea where Jinn is?"

"Kip said there were bedrooms on the second floor. I say we check there next," Roar answered.

"I can find her," Arne mumbled.

"What?" Dane leaned closer to him. He cocked his ear close to Arne's mouth.

"I can find her," he repeated. "I have a binding charm. It should lead me to her."

"You can barely move. We need to get you to a hospital."

"Not without her," he said louder.

His brother nodded. He understood what it meant to no longer care for your own safety. That the only thing worth risking your life for was the woman you loved.

"Okay," Dane answered simply. "How?"

Arne took a second longer to gather his courage then he shifted into the only thing that could track his mate; a large tawny wolf. He sniffed around the edges of the room while his brothers watched. They would go where he led them without question. They were warriors just like him. He caught the faint scent of jasmine floating in the air.

He stalked into the hallway and up the stairs. Nothing seemed to be moving through the house when he got to the first floor. Stepping into the hallway, he sniffed the air again. Something was drawing him closer to her.

The charms around his neck began to sing a song only

he could hear. His brothers were behind him when one of the guards stepped out into the hall.

The wolf didn't hesitate. The man drew a gun from his side as the wolf's jaws closed around his throat. He fell to the floor with the wolf still on top of him. After a few gurgling breaths, he lay still, a gaping gash at his throat.

The wolf stepped past him to a stairwell. The stranger was forgotten as he raced up the steps. She called to him even stronger up here.

His brothers followed behind him to the second floor. They spread out to check behind the closed doors that lined the hallway. Her heartbeat grew stronger in his ears as they worked their way through the rooms.

Then he began to hear voices coming from behind one of the doors. He led them to the last door on the right and waited. Roar stepped forward and tried the door. They weren't prepared for what they found.

Jinn was sitting, bloody and bruised, in a chair next to a large mahogany desk. An older man sat looking over some papers. He was better looking than the wolf had imagined with his graying hair and powerful build. He sneered at them as he held a gun to her head.

"I wondered how long it would take the rest of you to find her," the man said. "You know she's too valuable to me just to let her go. It's hard to find a whore this popular with the clients. They come back time after time just to fuck her."

The wolf snarled at the man.

"Call off your dog, or I'll put a bullet in her lovely head." He pressed the barrel against her head.

"All we want is Jinn, then we'll go," Roar tried. "We're not looking for trouble."

"Are you sure?" he asked. "You have your dog distract

my men, which is more their fault than yours. Then you break into my house and try to take my little whore? And you think I'm just going to hand her to you and wish her luck?" He laughed. "How about I have my men kill you all and keep her to boot? After all, she is my property."

The wolf was poised to launch himself at the man, but something in her eyes told him to wait. While the man was pressing the barrel of the gun against her head, he had failed to notice her bound hand dip into her pocket. He tried to understand what she wanted him to do. His lips raised in a snarl, but she shook her head just enough for him to catch.

The man had become distracted listening to Roar trying to plead for her release. In one swift motion, Jinn withdrew her hand from her pocket and threw something in his face.

A strange chant began to resonate through the room. It took the wolf a few minutes before he realized it was coming from her. The language sounded vaguely familiar as if he had heard it long ago.

The gun the man was holding fell to the floor with a clatter. Still, the chanting continued. The wolf glanced at his brothers who watched her as if they too were trapped in her trance. Except, his brothers stayed on their feet while the man dropped to his knees. The chanting grew louder. A trickle of blood ran from her nose, but her voice never wavered.

"No," the man said, rocking back and forth on his knees. "Please no. Stay away."

The wolf wondered who he was talking to. So far, none of them had dared to step much farther than right inside the office door. Then the man let out a piercing scream. Falling on the floor, he began to thrash. His arms flailed in front of him as if trying to fight off something.

"Jinn," Roar said quietly. "We need to go before the guards return." Stooping down, he picked up the man's gun. "Take my hand." He stood and held his hand out to her. "Arne's hurt. We need to go."

The words finally seemed to penetrate the fog that had descended over her. The chanting stopped abruptly as she turned to look at him. Her gaze traced over the brothers before finally resting on the wolf. A sob broke from her lips as she crashed to her knees in front of it.

Roar gently pried her hands from the wolf's fur and helped her back to her feet. Cradling her against his side, he nodded for Dane to lead them out.

Erik took Roar's gun so he could help Jinn down the stairs. The wolf began to limp. He had done what he had to to rescue his mate, but now his injuries were starting to catch up with him. Dane scooped him up in his arms. He was no longer the wolf stalking through the halls. He was once again just Arne, very naked and very much in pain.

"How are we going to get back over the fence?" Erik whispered as they stood at the back door.

"Wait here," Jinn said, pulling away from Roar. Before he could catch her, she sprinted through the house. When she returned, she was carrying a pair of pants and a set of keys. "I found these in one of the bedrooms." She helped Arne into the pants when Dane stood him up. "I hid the set of keys I took from Khan when Kip bashed him on the head. There's a side gate if we can get to it."

Roar nodded and opened the back door. There still didn't seem to be an alarm set. They eased outside and then followed Jinn as she crept around the side of the house. Just past a swimming pool was another gate into the woods.

"There's no place to hide," Dane pointed out. He still

cradled Arne as he struggled to keep up. "There are cameras everywhere."

"We're just going to have to make a run for it," Roar said. "If we have to split up in the woods, just try and make it back to the truck. Jinn, stay with me. Dane, do you have Arne?"

Dane nodded.

"Erik, you're covering our flank." Erik checked his gun. "Ready?" He looked at all of them.

"Let's go," Arne groaned.

Roar grabbed Jinn's hand and ran toward the gate. Dane, with Arne in tow, followed behind. Erik brought up the rear keeping an eye out behind them. They almost made it to the gate when they heard a shout.

"Stop," one of the guards at the front gate bellowed.

It took Jinn several tries to find the right key. Finally, one twisted, and it was open. They ran through as the guards sprinted across the lawn at them.

"Split up," Roar said. He pulled Jinn through the trees back toward town.

Erik followed for a minute before dropping to a knee with his gun raised. Arne lost sight of them as Dane lugged him deeper into the undergrowth. As desperately as he wanted to follow Jinn, he knew her best chance was with his brothers. They would protect her like she was theirs, and in a way, she was.

"Sit," Dane hissed, dropping him unceremoniously on the ground with his back to a tree. They crouched in the brush while Dane scouted the area around them. The sound of boots stomping toward them made him sigh in relief. Better they be followed than Jinn. If anyone had to die today, let it be him. He just hoped Dane would be spared.

The sound of boots stopped briefly. Then there was a scream.

"Let's go." Dane jerked him off the ground.

They both started moving again through the woods.

"Dad's still out there."

The screaming stopped just as quickly as it began.

"He's been creating a diversion. Now, I guess he's picking off the guards."

Dane continued to pull him through the trees until they could no longer hear anyone following. With more care this time, he lowered Arne back to the ground with his back against a tree. Dane walked a radius around them until he was satisfied they were safe. Then he slid down next to Arne.

"I'll wait a little then call Roar. I don't think you should keep moving," Dane said. "I think I can hear your ribs rubbing around inside your chest every time we move." He rose on his knees to check Arne's eyes.

Arne swatted at him just like he did when he had a concussion.

"Hold still, jackass. I'm trying to assess you."

"Who died and made you the family doctor?" Arne wheezed.

It was hard to pick on someone when you felt ready to pass out at any moment. Still, he couldn't just let the opportunity pass him by.

"If you don't shut up and let me look at you, I'm going to find a stethoscope to strangle you with."

"Dick."

"Asshole."

Arne started to laugh. The pain in his side turned it into a racking cough which hurt even more. When he was able to catch his breath, he found Dane staring back at him with concern. He remembered looking at his brother the exact same way not that long ago.

"Thank you," Arne said between shallow pants.

"For what?"

"For coming. For saving us."

"Don't ever thank me for just doing what brothers do. I love you; I will always come for you. It's nothing less than what you did for Tani and me."

"Yeah, but still."

"Shut up." Dane scowled at him.

Arne was just too tired to keep arguing. He felt his one good eye start to close. He was so very tired.

"Hey, no. You don't get to check out on me now." He pulled out his phone. The last thing Arne heard was Dane talking to someone on the phone. "I don't care if you have to call in the fucking cavalry, get the medics here now."

TWENTY-FIVE

Kip stared through the binoculars at the house for what seemed like hours. It was probably not that long she reasoned, but still. Roar had left her clear instructions that she was to wait for them as long as she could. If any trouble arose, she was to drive away.

That was never going to happen. She had read several military war books; they said no one was ever left behind. As far as she was concerned, this was war.

There was some comfort in being able to hear a wolf howl in the woods from time to time. At least someone was still alive and free. How long did Roar expect her to wait before doing something?

She wasn't a child anymore. There had to be more she could do. Picking up Erik's phone, she debated her choices. Her feet were killing her, so following them inside was out of the question.

She remembered something about Arne's mom calling the sheriff to meet her at the house. So if the sheriff was supposed to deal with all the crime in the area wouldn't they be the logical people to help now? Her hands shook as she pressed the number into Erik's phone that had been drilled into her head.

"9-1-1. What's your emergency?" the voice on the other end said.

"Hi. My name is Kipling Pierce, and this is going to sound strange." By the time she ended the call, she had told her story at least three different times to as many people. They had all assured her they would come to her aid shortly. She wasn't the one that needed aid, she had corrected, but please hurry.

"Erik?" Freja barked into her ear when she made her next call.

"It's me, Kip," she answered. "They went inside. I didn't know how to help so I called the sheriff. They said they're on their way."

"That's a very smart thing to do, Kip," Freja answered. "Can you tell me where you are?"

"No, but they said they can track Erik's phone to find me."

"Are you safe? If I walk you through how to send me your location from his phone, can you do it?"

She found herself nodding her head before she realized she couldn't be seen. "Yes," she whispered. She listened intently as she was talked through how to share her location.

"Stay in the truck with the doors locked. I'm on my way."

Kip nodded again as Freja disconnected the call. Now all she had to do was sit and wait. Again.

It wasn't but a few minutes later when she saw Roar step outside. Behind him was Jinn. Kip fought the urge to jump from the truck and run to her sister. The only thing that stopped her was the thought of how mad Roar would be if she left the truck. That and the fence she'd have to scale.

She watched Dane half carry Arne out behind them. Finally, Erik followed on the heels of his brothers. She sighed in relief to see them all still alive.

Instead of running to the fence, however, they moved around the side of the house where she lost track of them again. She didn't understand where they were going. They had to get out and fast. She counted slowly in her head to fifteen, but they still didn't appear. If only the sheriff would get here, he would know what she should do.

She sat in the front seat of the truck alone. A few minutes ago, one of the guards must have spotted them because he ran toward the side yard. She offered up a small prayer to every god she had ever read about to keep them safe. With any luck, at least one of them was listening.

Then, as if in a dream, she spotted a line of vehicles rolling slowly toward her. Most of the SUVs had lights on the top. They must be the sheriff coming to help her.

Throwing caution to the wind, she unlocked the truck door and slid to the ground. She almost collapsed to her knees when the cuts in her feet sent searing pain through her, but she managed to stay upright. Holding Erik's phone over her head, she started waving at the vehicles.

"Kipling Pierce?" a man in uniform asked as he pulled up next to her.

She was spellbound when the other cars pulled to the side so a large black tank-looking truck could pull up.

"Miss Pierce?"

Her gaze swung from the tank to the man now standing next to her.

"Yes," she said, galvanized into action. "It's that house. They just came out and disappeared into the woods."

"How many women do you think are being held inside?" another man asked. He was just in a regular-looking suit.

"I don't know, but Jinn said there are others. We weren't the only ones inside."

The two men exchanged glances before turning to the rest of the crowd. That's what Kip thought it looked like, a crowd here to rescue her family. They began shouting orders as officers hurried to do their bidding. The big, black tank crashed through the gate and men in armor followed them inside. It was all very exciting.

"Ma'am," a man said, walking over to her. He introduced himself and explained that he was a medic and needed to make sure she was okay.

"It's just my feet," she said. "They got a little cut up trying to escape when the men broke in."

"Can you make it to the ambulance?"

She tried, but after wincing one too many times, he called for someone to help. They picked her up and deposited her on a stretcher in the back of the ambulance.

She didn't protest since she still had a clear line of sight of the house. Men in black had now broken down the door and were swarming inside. Several guards were led out with their hands on their heads.

"What's that?" she asked.

Something loud was thumping over their heads.

"It's a helicopter. They're picking up someone farther down the block," he answered.

"I need to go." She tried to stand, but he pushed her back on the gurney carefully. "You don't understand, my sister."

Her words ended with a sob. Was Jinn hurt somewhere out in the woods? She shoved him as hard as she could. This time, he fell against the wall. Making it to the back, she threw herself out the door.

"Slow down, Calamity Jane," a big, deep voice said as a large man caught her in his arms. "Your sister is right here."

Roar swung her into his arms before her feet hit the ground. He carried her to the edge of the road where Jinn was looking for her.

"Kip!" she screamed.

Then they were in each other's arms. Roar still held her around the waist to save her feet, but her arms were firmly clinging to Jinn. They cried for a full minute before anyone could pry them apart.

"I thought something happened to you," Kip sobbed. "I called in the cavalry." She heard Roar chuckle behind her. "Did I do okay?"

"You did amazing," Jinn sobbed back.

"I told you we'd get her back," Roar said softly. "You're our family now. You already had the cavalry here."

"Yay, group hug," Erik teased, wrapping his arms around them.

Their sobs quickly turned into happy uncertain laughter.

"I need to bandage her feet," the medic said.

"Have they found my brothers yet?" Roar asked, still holding Kip in his arms.

"The helicopter is taking the one that's injured straight to the city."

"I need to be there," Jinn said, looking around wildly.

"We're to take you to the hospital," an officer instructed, stepping forward. "They want us to stay with you until OBI has a chance to ask you some questions."

"Erik, stay with Kip. Find Dane and get to the hospital

as soon as you can," Roar ordered. He transferred Kip into Erik's hands.

"No, I want to go with Jinn," she pleaded.

"We'll be there shortly, but your feet need attention," he answered. "I'll find out what's happening while they work on you. We can't leave Dad and Dane here."

"Your mom is on the way too. I called her," Jinn said sheepishly.

Had she done the right thing bringing all these people here? But Erik turned his thousand-watt smile on her, and she knew she had.

"Miss Pierce?" The man in the suit climbed into the back of the ambulance.

Erik sat next to her on the stretcher with his arms crossed. He no longer had the smile on his face but a scowl instead. It warmed her heart even more to know he was there watching over her.

"I'm Agent Riggs. I want to take a formal statement later, but if you can answer a couple of questions now, I'd appreciate it."

"Okay."

"Reports say three women are being held in the basement. Is this where you and your sister were?" He opened a notepad and waited for her answer.

"Yes. I never saw the other women, but Jinn said she saw different ones over the years."

"Years?" he asked. His eyebrows raised in surprise. "We've suspected that he was trafficking women for years but have never been able to catch him. We didn't know he kept anyone, though."

"Well, Jinn was thirteen, I think, when she left, and she's like twenty now," Kip pointed out. "So, years."

"Why has it been so hard to catch him?" Erik asked.

"He's a sitting federal judge. Between the power that brings and a tightly guarded clientele list, we've never been able to infiltrate. Without some evidence, no one is going to sign off on a search warrant. Trust me, I've tried. Miss Pierce's call about a kidnapping in progress gave us exactly what we needed." He smiled at her. "One last thing for now."

"Yes?"

"They're taking him out on a stretcher. He seems to be in the throes of a mental hallucination. Do you know of or have you seen any drugs in his possession?"

"Jinn kept me as far away from him as possible. I guess you'd have to ask her," she answered.

"Okay." He flipped his notebook closed. "I'll be by the hospital later to visit with your sister." He stepped out of the ambulance and turned around. "Thank you, Miss Pierce. We couldn't have shut him down without your help." He walked off to a group of men standing around the hood of a cruiser.

"How's it feel to be the hero?" Erik asked, bumping her with his shoulder.

"All I did was make a phone call. Not exactly hero material."

"Are you kidding? You saved us and brought down a major trafficking ring all at the same time. If that's not a hero, I don't know what one is."

"Listen to your brother," the medic added. "Sometimes just making a phone call takes a lot of guts."

"Oh, we're not really related," she began.

"She must have hit her head," Erik told the medic. "Of course we're related. She's my little sister. Come on, we should head to the hospital." He picked her up and carried her to the truck.

"What about Dane and your dad?" she asked.

He set her inside, then climbed in the driver's side. Slowly, he navigated through the police cars.

"Dane went in the helicopter with Arne, and Mom said she'd come get Dad. You know, since the whole no pants thing," he said.

"But his pants are in the back seat."

"You're just the gift that keeps on giving."

They pulled over. He disappeared into the brush with a pair of pants while she texted Freja on his phone. This was definitely not the most conventional family. But that's what made it so perfect for her. Neither she nor Jinn would want conventional anyway.

Erik drove them to the city while his dad finished dressing in the back seat. He had been dripping with sweat when he emerged from the trees with Erik.

She managed to scrounge up some paper towels from behind the seat for him. He sat with his head resting against the headrest. His eyes were closed when they reached the hospital. She hadn't realized how much it took to keep the guards occupied until then. He was the real hero, she decided.

"There she is," Roar announced, meeting them at the emergency room door.

Erik carefully placed her in the wheelchair a nurse brought over. "The doctor wants to check your feet to make sure there's nothing left under the skin."

"But I want to see Arne and Jinn," she protested.

They rolled her into one of the triage cubicles and set her on the bed.

"Please, Roar."

He grabbed the curtain and pulled it aside. Lying in the next bed with her sister sitting on the end was Arne. Even as rough as he looked, she had never seen anything more beautiful.

"Hey, sweetheart," he mumbled between swollen lips.

"Don't ever disappear on me again," she chided. She eased off the bed and slowly slid to his side. Leaning down, she wrapped an arm around his chest. "You're too important to us."

"You couldn't get rid of me even if you wanted to," he slurred. Gently, he ran his hand over her head. "Who would eat all of my ice cream?"

She laughed, but she could already feel the tears starting again.

"Enough reunion," Dane growled. "Back in your bed." He swept her up and deposited her back on her bed.

She looked at the growing group of people around her. Thyra entered the room and beelined straight for her. They clung to each other as the doctor dug on her feet.

The tears threatened once again as she was struck by the realization that these people weren't just here for Arne. They were here for Jinn and her also. They would never have to do life alone again, and that made everything they had ever gone through worth it.

TWENTY-SIX

"Have you ever seen so many?" Kip asked as they stood in the living room at Arne's parents' house.

Jinn gazed over at her sister. Her eyes were the size of saucers. She couldn't blame her for being over-whelmed; there was a tremendous stack of brightly wrapped packages sitting in front of Freja's heavily adorned Christmas tree.

"Never," she said in agreement.

As a matter of fact, she couldn't remember receiving anything for Christmas since their mother left them. She had done her best to earn enough reward points in school to get her sister something from the "model student" shop when they were small.

Every Christmas, she would sneak the trinket into the house and wrap it in newspaper. If she were lucky, there was an old magazine she could piece together to make the present colorful.

"Do you think there are any for me?" Kip asked.

Jinn knew there were at least two. She had finally

gotten to go on a shopping trip with Freja while Arne was recovering at home. It felt amazing to be able to move around the shops without looking over her shoulder, but it was also overwhelming.

Both she and Kip gave statements to the nice man in a suit. Agent Riggs had shown up at the hospital as they were settling Arne in his room. She had begun by telling him from the abduction on. By the time several days had passed, he knew most of her life story.

He assured her that they had arrested not just the man who had held her captive for so long, but all of the guards. She knew that they were still uncovering clients, buyers, and many others who were connected. It gave her an over-whelming peace of mind when he reassured her none of them would see the light of day for a very long time.

"Maybe I'll get some school clothes," Kip said.

She was beginning school after the break. Agent Riggs had pulled a few strings to help Jinn get custody of her younger sister. Freja helped her apply for a birth certificate and everything else they needed for school. Tani had set up a round of testing at the house to help determine what grade Kip needed to enter. So far, she had scored amazingly well on them.

"Maybe," Jinn answered.

She already knew there were a lot of presents under the tree just for Kip. Thyra kept adding clothing to her mom's basket as they hunted through the different stores. The back of Freja's SUV looked like they were opening their own clothing store by the time they returned from their trip.

"What are you hoping for?"

"Nothing. I've got everything I could ever want." She smiled as Arne came through the door.

He still had to be careful of his ribs, but he was healing

nicely. His arm draped over her shoulders as he joined them in front of the tree.

"Are you trying to peek at how much coal you're getting for Christmas this year for being bad?" he teased.

"Oh. Is that what we get?" Kip asked solemnly.

"Sweetheart, if that's what we got, I would be able to run my own steam train by now." He chuckled. "No, I'm sure there are a couple of pairs of socks for you in there somewhere."

"Are you warning them about Mom's affinity for socks?" Erik asked, flopping down on the couch.

"You can never have too many socks," Roar added as he joined Erik.

"I like socks," Kip said. Jinn knew she would agree to almost anything at this point.

She was just so excited about having a real Christmas. They even had stockings hanging over the mantle like the rest of the family; with their names on the top.

"When does Christmas start?"

"We have to wait for everyone to get here first," Erik answered. "Then Mom sets out this huge spread on the table. You fill your plate and sit anywhere you want. She had out both fondue pots earlier. I'm hoping for lots of stuff melted on other stuff."

"Then what?" Kip squeezed between Roar and Erik on the couch.

Jinn had to stop the laugh that tried to bubble up inside. It was good to see her sister so enraptured by something so normal as celebrating Christmas. How had she survived being sold, locked in a basement, escaping, and rescuing them without so much as any obvious emotional scars? Jinn hoped it stayed that way.

"Then we open most of the presents while eating more

and drinking mulled cider. Tomorrow, Santa will come, and we start all over again."

"But Santa's not real," she argued.

"Hey," Roar said. "In this house, if you stop believing in Santa, then he stops coming. I'm not willing to take that chance, are you?"

"No," she said, shaking her head. "Definitely not."

"You know," Arne said with a smile at Jinn. "Nothing says we can't start now. I think I just heard Dane pull up. What do you think, Kip? Want a slightly early Christmas present?"

She didn't have to answer; the way she bounced on the couch in excitement was answer enough.

"Okay then. Let's head outside."

"My present is outside?" she whispered.

"Yeah. Mom said no to bringing it in the house." He rose from the armchair and motioned for Kip to lead them outside. When they stepped into the yard, Dane and his family were just getting out of their car.

"We haven't missed it yet, have we?" Tani asked. She settled Aksel on her hip and joined them.

"No, we planned on waiting for you," Jinn answered.

"Where is it?" Kip was getting more excited by the moment.

Arne took her hand and led her slowly to the middle of the driveway.

"Close your eyes," he instructed.

Jinn watched as Thyra came out of the barn with Kip's present.

"Okay, you can open them."

Kip opened her eyes. A small stunned squeal broke from her lips.

"She's all yours. Go see what you think."

Slowly she walked toward the small paint horse. Her hand shook as she reached out to run it down her downy nose.

"Jinn?" she asked, looking back over your shoulder.

"Don't ask me. Arne was the one who insisted you needed your own horse," she answered. "I was good with just getting socks."

The only argument she had when Arne suggested the horse was to respond that it was too generous. He had ignored her and bought the beautiful mare anyway.

She also knew that sitting behind most of the other presents under the tree was a saddle, bridle, saddle pad, and brushes. His brothers had chipped in for those.

Kip crept a little closer until she could throw her arms around the horse and hug its neck with all her might. Jinn snuck a look at Arne to find the grin on his face was as big as the one on her sister.

"Her name is Tuska," he said. "It means warrior in Choctaw."

Kip released the mare to fly into his arms. He grunted from the painful impact but squeezed her tight anyway.

"Merry Christmas, Kip. I'm so glad you came into our lives. Especially my life."

"Ahh, group hug," Erik teased.

Jinn noticed that his brothers were a little more careful in how they squeezed into the embrace. She suspected that they had all had the joy of broken ribs at some point in the past.

"Can I get on? Just for a few minutes?" Kip begged.

"Go ahead," Roar answered. "We'll stay out here with you until supper is ready. But you'd better not eat all the fondue before we get back inside." He scowled at Arne.

"Don't worry, we'll call you well before," Jinn assured

him. She slid her arm around Arne's waist as they walked back to the house. "That was some gift you got her."

"You think?"

She nodded her head.

"Then wait until you see yours."

ARNE SAT STUDYING the old worn-looking house. How could this be where she lived before being sold to a debt collector? Erik sat on the driver's side next to him. He was the only one of his brothers he trusted not to try and talk him out of what he was about to do. His ribs still ached, but he couldn't put off tying up the last loose end anymore.

Christmas had been one to remember. It seemed all of his family had decided to go overboard this year. Jinn got more clothes, gift cards, perfume, and art supplies than she could manage. She had also said yes to the diamond ring he presented. Kip had become the best-outfitted horse rider, high school freshman, and book devourer in the entire county.

"Are you sure you want to do this?" Erik asked once again.

"I'm sure," he said. "Go around the block and pick me up in fifteen minutes."

The Oklahoma Bureau of Investigation had done an amazing job at closing down the trafficking ring and arresting as many of the participants as possible. He had heard that the other women were either returned to their families or relocated to a safe home. Jinn and Kip had told their stories to countless people and still had to testify in court later in the year.

There was only one person who hadn't had to answer

for selling underage girls. That was whose house he sat staring at now. He pushed open his door and slid out.

Erik put the truck into gear and drove off down the road as Arne walked across the potholed-strewn road. He would be back in exactly fifteen minutes. The brothers believed in having each other's backs, even if they didn't necessarily agree with their decisions.

The front yard was overgrown with weeds and what once was a charming garden gate now hung from one hinge. He left it propped open rather than fight to close it. The paint had peeled from almost everything years ago making the house look older than it was. There was apparently nothing that mattered much to this man.

He stopped at the door and knocked. Screens and curtains were covering the front windows so he couldn't see who was inside. This was the only time he wanted to have to be here; he never wanted to return.

He had chosen to come now because it was the quiet period between Christmas and New Year when no one was home. The neighbors were gone, returning gifts they couldn't afford, no doubt.

He had almost given up hope anyone was home until he heard rustling inside.

"What?" asked the man that jerked open the wood door.

He looked almost as bad as the house. His jeans were covered with so many years of grease that it was hard to tell they were once blue. He had an old button-up work shirt that had holes at both elbows and lunch down the front. The slippers he wore had to be at least as old as he was.

"Mr. Pierce?" Arne asked.

"Yeah, what do you want?" the man snapped. "I ain't buying no new roof or listening to why you love Jesus."

"No, I wouldn't expect you would. I've come to talk to you about your daughter, Jinn."

"What's she done this time?"

"So I do have the right house?"

"She ain't my problem. I haven't seen her in years. What's that little bitch done to you?"

"See, that's just it. She did nothing more than agree to marry me. She's not who I have the problem with," Arne answered.

If his fortitude to do what he needed had been wavering, hearing Jinn referred to as a bitch strengthened his resolve. He was just glad she wasn't here to witness it. Grabbing the rusted screen door, he jerked it open. The lock now swung to and fro from the doorjamb.

"You're who I have a problem with." He could already hear the snarl in his voice.

"I don't see how I'm involved in any of this. She was never worth the dollar it took to feed her." He grunted and tried to close the door in Arne's face.

Arne threw his hand out and held the door open. His ribs protested the strain, but he ignored them. "That's where you're wrong. But then, I guess no one ever taught you how much better your daughters are than their father. It's a lesson well worth learning."

"And you think you're the man to teach me that, huh? Fuck off." He pressed harder against the door.

Arne shoved it with all of his might and flung the man back across the room. He landed in the middle of a pile of empty beer cans on his ass.

"Maybe we should have a chat about that." Arne peeled his shirt over his head and tossed it on the porch. "I say it's never too late to learn from our mistakes." He kicked off his boots and shimmied his jeans down his legs.

There was no room left for humanity in what he had to teach. Retribution was best left between the man who sold his daughters to the highest bidder and the wolf sworn to protect them. They were all that mattered to him.

With a snarl, he slunk into the house. This would be one lesson that no one would come away from unchanged. But at least the wolf still had redemption waiting at home for him. The man just had hell to look forward to.

EPILOGUE

Roar sat staring at his computer monitor in his office. Things had quieted down since Arne and Jinn's small wedding in the spring. She still had to testify in court about what had happened to her, but that was several months out. The task force given the duty to track down everyone involved with the trafficking ring was still rounding up people.

Summer had descended on his area of the country with a vengeance. The fall term started soon, and the campus was gearing back up. Not that it affected him really, he just kept the books. Actually, he was in charge of the book-keeping department.

The end-of-summer activities were in full swing around campus. So far, he had walked into the administration building every morning for the last week to the sound of cheerleading chants. He assumed it was a last-minute high school camp based on how young they looked. Wasn't that a sign of getting old when the students just looked younger and younger every year?

He let out a deep sigh. As if the heat and chants weren't bad enough, his accounts payable person had decided to move across the country for her husband's new job leaving him high and dry. So far, he hadn't been that impressed with the applicants to replace her. She had set too high a precedent with her timely reports and uncluttered work environment.

She had been the exact opposite of the person in charge of the athletic department's budgets. Roar had a regent's meeting soon, and he needed that report.

He sighed again pushing himself to his feet. He would have to walk across campus and sit in the athletic office until the report was produced. There had already been too many ignored emails sent.

"Roar." He was greeted by one of the professors when he stepped outside. "Where are you headed?"

"Athletics."

"I'm going to the theatre building. I'll walk with you. How was your summer?"

"Same as always."

He knew that most of the professors spent the summer on vacation, writing, or teaching summer classes. He spent it doing the same thing he did during the school year. The only concession this year to his schedule was the week off he took for Arne's wedding. He spent most of spring break working on his mother's yard so it would be wedding-worthy.

"The wife and I spent a glorious two weeks on a cruise to the Caribbean. I've even got the tan to prove it."

He held out an arm to show Roar his tan. It was impressive, but you could also get that dark doing just about anything outside locally. His two younger brothers always looked like different people by the end of summer. Working outside also guaranteed they were much thinner. The heat made it impossible to eat much and survive.

"Sounds nice," he answered.

"Oh, it was. You should go sometime."

The idea of going on a cruise by himself didn't appeal to Roar in the least. Although a week of lying by a pool and drinking fruity drinks all alone wasn't without its merits.

"I'll give it some thought."

"Good for you. Well, this is where I leave you."

Roar had spent the entire short trip across campus trying to remember his name. There were so many professors it was hard to keep up with all of them. None of them did he socialize after work with. The only socializing he did nowadays was with his family. He should really get out more often.

"See you around." Was his name Phil or Bill? It was something along those lines.

"Take care, Roar."

He walked the rest of the way in silence. Except for the chanting. Do those girls ever go inside? That question was soon answered when he opened the door to the basketball arena.

The gym was filled with girls in short skirts standing on each other's shoulders. Impossibly, the sound was much louder inside. Ignoring them, he walked down the long corridor to the offices.

"Good morning, Jean."

She looked up at him with an eyebrow raised. She had been the athletic secretary when he was hired to the payroll team right out of college. If rumors were true, she had been here since before Oklahoma was a state.

"Is Jack in?"

"Yeah, go on back."

"Thank you." He walked down another hallway until he reached Jack's office.

Without bothering to knock, he shoved the door open. Jack almost jumped out of his seat. Good, he should be surprised. If he was doing his job, Roar would never have had to walk across campus in the heat to growl at him.

"Roar, I was just bringing the paperwork to you."

"Sure you were," Roar growled.

"I promise. I'm printing it out right now."

Roar slumped in one of the chairs in front of the desk to wait. He wasn't leaving without something. Either that budget or Jack's head, it didn't matter which. Luckily for Jack, the printer sprang to life and shot out the paperwork Roar was waiting on.

"Sorry about that."

Roar took the papers and left without saying goodbye. "Have a good week," he said to Jean as he walked by.

"Same at you," she answered.

He walked back across campus in blessed silence this time. Well, except for the chanting. Did they ever take a break?

He stepped back inside the administration building and sighed in relief. At least the buildings were air-conditioned. Taking the steps two at a time, he climbed back up to the second floor.

Except for the library, the administration building was considered the nicest on campus. It boasted central air conditioning, large offices, and east-facing windows in most of the offices. His office was inside a large pod of desks housing the accounting team.

Financial aid, the dean of students, the provost, and several more offices he rarely entered were on the same floor. He had started at one of the cubicles in the pod before slowly rising through the ranks to a position that demanded its own office. He liked the privacy it afforded.

He glanced in the provost's office on his way down the hallway. It was just supposed to be a passing glance. Something people do all day without realizing it.

However, what he saw standing near the administrative assistant's desk stopped him cold in his tracks. It had to be an apparition. He shook his head to rid himself of the vision, except it was still there when he glanced back.

Something drew him to the door. He needed to be sure what he saw was real before checking himself in for an evaluation. But the moment those soft golden eyes landed on him, he knew it wasn't just his imagination playing tricks on him. They widened briefly when they met his.

"It *is* you," he snarled.

"I take it you know each other?" Dean Kerr asked.

He turned to motion Roar into the room.

"We did," he rumbled.

Without a backward glance, he marched down the hallway and into his office. His assistant opened his mouth to ask something but quickly closed it again. He was smart enough to see Roar wasn't in the mood for questions. He slammed the door to his office and threw himself into his chair.

What was she doing here? More importantly, why was she talking to the person in charge of hiring new staff for the college? It had been close to ten years since he saw her last. She was just as beautiful as he remembered. Maybe more so. But that didn't make up for everything she had put him through.

Kenna O'Neill had been his college girlfriend for three years. Right up until she left him and never looked back.

He had tried to find her; going so far as contacting her

family once a week for almost a year. All they would ever tell him was she was doing fine. So she had moved on and was doing great without him.

He wished he could have said the same. He had been so in love with her that they had slept together. That was what solidified his doom. He hadn't been able to look at another woman since.

He didn't know if he believed the stories his mother told about his long-dead ancestor and the curse surrounding him. He couldn't discount them either. All he knew was she had broken his heart and now she was back. Pouting like a teenager wouldn't do any good though. If she was going to work somewhere on campus, he would meet her again at some point. He needed to bury the hatchet once and for all.

Hunting through the records on his computer, he finally found her. She was a new professor of history. He knew exactly where her office would be located, in the building next to his. He stood and smoothed the wrinkles from his dress shirt. There was no time like the present to take a tortured walk down memory lane.

"I'll be back in a few minutes," he told his assistant.

No one even looked up from their computers as he walked out of the office. He found her office on the third floor of the humanities building.

Taking a deep breath, he stepped inside. She was unpacking a box of stuff on the desk. He took a moment to appreciate the long legs stretching out from the bottom of her skirt and the tight ass he remembered holding in his hands.

"I came to apologize. I had no right to be rude," he said.

She jumped at the sound of his voice and spun around. Her eyes lit up for just a moment before she smoothed her features back to something more professional.

"You have every right to be rude," she answered. "I'm sure it was a shock seeing me after all these years."

"Still, that's no excuse for bad manners."

He couldn't keep his eyes from wandering down the length of her body. His early assessment had been right. She was even more gorgeous now.

"You look good."

"So do you." He wondered if she was just being polite.

The last time she saw him, he was at the top of his game as a catcher on the college baseball team. He still kept in shape, but not to that level.

"So, why are you here?" he asked.

Of the almost three thousand colleges in the country, it made no sense that she would wind up at his. Where had she come from? Where had she been for the last ten years was a better question.

"I'm the new early American history professor."

"I know that. But why here, why now?"

She lowered her gaze to the floor. Looking back up at him she opened her mouth as if to say something, but closed it before she did.

"You know what, never mind. It's none of my business."

He stomped out of her office but only made it as far as the end of the hallway. He couldn't just stomp off. They were adults now and should be able to talk about this. He waited a few minutes before gathering his courage and returning to her office.

"Kenna?"

She jumped again. He needed to give more warning.

"Sorry." His eyes searched her room trying to decide what to say. "Kenna, I—" Nothing more came out. Everything he had wanted to say to her for years had simply disappeared from his brain. Lashing out just wasn't his thing.

Before he could come up with anything reasonable to say though, she grabbed the front of his shirt and pulled him into her office. The door slammed closed, and he found himself pushed back against her desk. He sat down when she climbed up to straddle his lap.

"Tell me to stop," she whispered.

Their mouths crashed together, and his tongue got reacquainted with her taste. It had been so long since he had had her in his arms. He wanted, more than anything at that moment, to learn how she felt when she came all over again. His large hands pressed her against his hardening erection.

"Push me away," she pleaded when they parted for air.

He knew he was powerless to do what she asked. He still loved her, no matter how hard he had tried not to.

"You know I could never do that," he growled.

Her lips pressed back against his, and he was once again lost to her forever.

THANK you for reading Arne and Jinn's story. If you enjoyed it, please leave a review wherever you read books.

To learn more about my books, join my newsletter: https://bit.ly/3sBOegA

Watch for Roar's story in the continuing saga of the Ulvmand family and Sköll Ranch. What happens when the one woman that he can't forget arrives back in town with a surprise in tow?

Watch for the third book in the Sköll Ranch Shifter series coming soon!

ORIGIN STORY

In the days before the Vikings, before Gorm the Old unified the country, before Harald Bluetooth brought Christianity to the Scandinavians, there was the time of the Drott.

During peacetime, the people were governed by a leader who saw to their needs. But in times of strife, the people would choose a warrior called the Drott. It was his job to lead the chieftain's soldiers into battle. His council was made up of an elder warrior, a younger warrior, and the captain of the chiefly vessel who in turn controlled the chieftain's soldiers.

It was during one of these conflicts, perhaps a dispute with another tribe over trading with the Romans, that a fight broke out. The people elected a battle-proven man to be the Drott as tensions rose between the two tribes.

He quickly set about calling in his warrior council. It included a young man who was working on one of the farms left by his father. His father had died under the Drott in the last skirmish, proving himself a man of great courage. He passed onto Valhalla in battle. The current Drott surmised that courage that great would be passed down to his sons.

Leaving the farm to his younger brother to tend, the young warrior picked up his crude knives and homemade shield to answer the call. He was given a group of men to lead south on a frontal assault. The elder warrior's men would flank from the north.

After three days of walking, they finally found themselves ambushed in a pass between two rock faces. The scouts sent earlier failed to report back making it impossible to know where the enemy was.

His men fought bravely. But knowing they had no chance to overcome the enemy, he called for retreat. If he could get his men reformed in safety, they could find another way to attack.

He watched as his men disappeared into the hills before narrowly fleeing from a barrage of arrows himself. He ran from his pursuers for hours until he stopped beside a waterfall to rest.

The young man squatted down on his hands and knees, scooping water out of the pool made by the surrounding rocks to get a drink. When he was finally full, he rocked back on his heels, listening for the approach of an enemy. He had made it this far unscathed. He didn't want to be snuck up on while resting.

Hearing nothing, he sat back against a tree by the water's edge to rest before trying to find his men. As he fought the fatigue that threatened to claim him, he suddenly saw an apparition appear from behind the waterfall.

Peering cautiously from behind the curtain of water was a young woman. Even from a distance, the man could tell she was beautiful with long golden hair. As she approached, he slowly rose from his perch near the tree. He stepped out into the light and raised his hands to his side when she looked up in fear.

"Don't be afraid. I won't hurt you," he said. He took a step toward her, expecting her to run. Instead, she stared him down, daring him to come closer. "I have become separated from my men. Have you seen anyone pass this way earlier?"

She remained glaring at him in stony silence.

"I just need to rest then I'll be on my way." He would get no information from this woman.

Without warning, she suddenly lunged at him, pressing her hand over his mouth. She took his hand and pulled him toward the waterfall. He barely managed to get his shield on the way.

She pulled him behind the waterfall. Rushing to a small fire just inside a cave, she kicked dirt on the flames, dousing any light that had existed. She led him deeper into the dark cave as if she could see without light.

Taking his shield, she shoved it aside and pushed him after it. He found his back flat against a piece of rock. He was wedged into a small cutout in the cave.

Opening his mouth to protest, he quickly found her hand covering it again. Her body flattened against his. He could feel her breath, warm against his neck. She began to whisper something in a language he couldn't understand.

Soon, he could hear the voices of men searching inside the cave. They had found the opening behind the waterfall. They were looking for him and his men.

Offering a quick prayer to the gods, he wrapped his arms around the woman. He moved her slightly so they wouldn't be able to see her around him. If he was to be caught, he could at least try to spare her. He eased one of his knives out and prepared himself to die an honorable death.

Her whispering grew louder as the men moved with their torches closer to the crevice where they hid. He should try to silence her murmurings, but he knew they were not well hidden enough not to be discovered.

He prepared to jump out at the man who walked up to their hiding spot. But an odd thing happened. It was as if the men could not see them. Even the man who stood staring at them, his knife ready.

The beautiful woman slid her arms around him, holding him in place as she continued to murmur at his back. The men filed back out of the cave to continue their pursuit.

They stood together in the dark as they listened to the sounds of the men grow fainter until they faded into the distance. The warrior spun around tripping over a rock. He landed on his backside in the dark cave.

"What are you?" he whispered into the darkness. "Where did you come from?"

His heart pounded as he stared into the blackness. Softly, he felt a hand brush up his chest as if trying to calm him. She gently helped him off the ground and pulled him to the front of the cave.

Turning him loose, she began busying herself rebuilding the fire. He watched her in amazement for several minutes.

"I'll go get more wood," he said, walking out from under the water.

Gathering up the dry wood he could find near the waterfall, the warrior noticed a rabbit emerge from a hole to get a drink. His stomach rumbled. He tried to remember seeing any food in the cave.

Leaving the pile of wood, he crept close to the opening of the warren to wait in the undergrowth. He speared the rabbit with one of his knives when it returned.

He was proud of his speed. He was fast enough to add what he could to her food stores. He turned around to collect his pile of sticks. The woman was standing at the edge of the waterfall, watching him.

Holding the rabbit in the air, he smiled back at her. She held up a basket containing hazelnuts, raspberries, and wild apples with a laugh. Tonight, they would have full bellies to sleep on.

They returned to the cave behind the waterfall. The warrior laid against the wall watching the woman slowly turn the spit he had constructed to cook the rabbit on. The reflection of the fire made her pale skin glow and turned her fair hair into gold. He watched her in silence. His curiosity finally overwhelmed him.

"Is this where you live?" he asked, trying to learn something more about her.

She shook her head sadly.

"Is your home far?"

She shook her head again, motioning to the east and then showing him two fingers.

"It's two days to the east?"

When she nodded again, he sat silently in thought until the rabbit was ready.

"Why did you leave your home?" he asked between bites.

She looked at him with sadness before patting his chest.

"Raiders took your home? What about your family?"

A tear stole its way down her cheek making him want to kill whoever hurt her.

"I'm sorry."

She shrugged.

"I have to find my men soon. We are at war with another tribe. I was to lead my men against them."

She watched him closely as he explained what had happened to bring him to her cave. He told her he would leave at first light to search for his men. She became agitated, motioning to him wildly.

"I don't understand what you're trying to tell me."

Picking up one of the sticks of kindling, she drew in the dirt on the cave floor.

The warrior paid close attention as she showed him a story of other warriors hunting for him. It would be too dangerous to leave until they went back through. He would then be behind them and could easily kill them as he gathered his men.

"I must stay two more nights to let them get ahead of me. You will protect me until then?"

She nodded vigorously.

"How will a woman protect me from the enemy?"

With a scowl, she began to whisper something before pointing at the fire. He scooted back quickly as it exploded in flames almost to the ceiling.

"You're a sorceress," he said, his eyes wide.

Sorceresses were to be feared. They could ruin crops, kill stock, and inflict horrible plagues. He should kill her before she could curse him.

But when she smiled, he knew he could no more kill her than he could defeat the other army single-handed. Her eyes turned soft as she eased toward him. She ran her hand up his chest again like she did earlier in the dark.

"Why would you help me?" he asked.

She grabbed the stick again using it to explain how a vision came to her telling her about a young warrior who was to lose his way. The vision told her she must protect him until he could return to his men. The battle he would win would bring great honor to his tribe and change the course of the world.

"How am I to believe you won't slit my throat in my sleep?"

She grabbed the knife he used for her portion of rabbit and handed it back to him. He laughed at her enthusiasm.

"I guess I will have to trust you then."

She gave him a brilliant smile before pulling two grass mats out from behind one of the large stones.

"You must have had time to plan." Rolling his mat out near the fire, he settled onto it. He fell asleep almost instantly.

When he woke the next morning, he felt more rested than he had in weeks. He sent a small prayer to the gods asking that his men had found shelter.

Sitting up, he had a rough-hewn mug pressed into his hands. He took a sip. It was mulled wine made out of the nuts and berries she had been gathering.

"Is there a stream nearby? I can catch us fish for tonight."

The woman nodded, handing him a pot that contained a gruel she had cooked. Sitting next to him, they took turns eating the breakfast until it was gone.

She gathered her basket and motioned for him to follow her outside. He followed her through the trees until they came to a stream teaming with trout.

He used one of his knives to make a rough spear. Taking off his tunic and shoes, the warrior climbed into the icy stream to patiently wait for a fish.

The woman, having finished her scavenging, sat on a rock overlooking the stream to watch him. He stood perfectly still for fifteen minutes. He stabbed at the water bringing a fish out. She cheered when he held it over his head in triumph. He tossed it on the bank to her. She jumped off her perch to add it to her basket.

When he speared the second fish, he tossed his spear on the bank. He took out another knife as he waded toward her on the bank. He sat down next to her. She was wiggling her toes in the cold water.

He cleaned the fish before trading her for the first one. Quickly cleaning the second fish, he handed it to her. He lay back in the grass on the bank. Setting her basket aside, she flopped next to him and stared up at the clouds.

He must have fallen asleep for a moment. He was woken when he felt soft lips brush over his. Opening his eyes, he looked up at two laughing pools of cerulean blue.

She jumped up quickly and ran toward the trees with a laugh. He raced to slide back into his clothes before chasing after her through the trees. Catching up to her at the edge of the pool by her cave, she put an arm up to stop him. He waited until she nodded it was safe to return.

That night, they once again filled their bellies. He helped her grind the hazelnuts into flour using a large flat rock. She made a flat type of bread they shared with the fish he cooked on the spit.

After dinner, he built up the fire as he told her stories about life where he was from. She sat with her knees pulled up to her chest in rapt attention as he explained how he had been chosen to serve as a warrior.

As he fell asleep that night, he felt her drag her mat next to him. He pulled her against him before falling into a deep slumber. He woke the next morning as refreshed as the day before.

A part of him felt sad knowing this would be the last

day he would see the woman. Tomorrow he must return to battle. Sitting up, he again found her ready with his breakfast.

They spent their last day shoring up her food supply. He taught her how to trap rabbits and spear fish; though that simply had them both shivering from a fall in the stream.

He made sure the wood supply inside the cave was stocked and sharpened one of his knives to leave behind for her. She only rushed him into the cave to hide once when the other warriors crossed through on their way back to the battle.

By afternoon, he had decided he could use a bath before leaving again. He slipped off his clothes and waded into the pool. It was cold but had benefited from a series of warm days, unlike the stream. He was floating with his eyes closed when he heard a splash on the other side of the pool. He watched as the woman swam toward him.

She wrapped her arms around his neck and pressed her naked breasts against him. He was pulled into a chaste kiss. It wasn't enough. He wanted to taste her more than he had ever wanted anything.

He moaned when she opened her mouth to him letting him taste his fill. It only took him a moment to grow impossibly hard as he devoured her mouth at the edge of the clear pool. He hesitated only a minute before sliding inside of the most beautiful woman he had ever seen.

She gasped as he thrusted into her. She moaned at his release, her muscles clamping down on him. He held her to him as he stood in the water whispering how beautiful she was.

He finally softened, and they swam back to the other side. Dressing in silence, he followed her into the cave to help begin their dinner. Soon it would be dark, and he would have to rest for tomorrow.

They ate a small pig he caught out hunting. She prepared more bread. They drank wine she made out of what she could find. He helped her clean up before they retired for the night. She laid out the mats together. Then she waited for him.

He slid her tunic over her head. Naked, he laid her down on his fur cloak covering their mats. He kneeled between her legs as she looked up at him. Lowering himself, he entered her slowly.

He closed his eyes as she wrapped her legs around his hips, pulling him deeper. They made love until they both fell asleep from exhaustion wrapped in each other's arms.

The next morning he woke up from a strange dream. He had been a great wolf pursuing his enemies through the forest. Shaking himself awake, he looked around in confusion.

He was lying completely nude outside the cave in the grass. There was a string with pieces of smooth stone on it around his neck. Taking a closer look, he saw they had strange drawings on them. The woman watched him from behind a boulder.

"What have you done to me?" he growled.

She ducked back behind the rock. Standing, he swayed for a moment feeling dizzy. It passed quickly as she fled. He chased her. Wrestling her to the ground, he straddled her hips.

"Tell me what you've done." He felt himself losing control as he snarled down at her.

She struggled against him until she freed a hand. Calmly she ran it down his chest as she began to whisper.

Something about the motion made him feel calmer. He

rolled off her. She reached for a stick, grunting at him to pay attention as she drew in the dirt.

He struggled to make sense of her story. She had cast a spell on him to make him into one of the greatest warriors this land would ever know. He had been given the ability to turn into a wolf. He could now flank his enemies in silence. The wolf would have greater strength, faster reflexes, and would be able to see in the dark.

She had also enchanted four stones he must always wear. One was for protection from harm. The next was to help him control his new power. The third was for courage. She wouldn't tell him what the fourth stone held but that it would guarantee his safe return to her.

When she finished her story, he stood silently. Without looking back, he walked into the cave to dress. She chased after him begging him with her actions to look at her.

Gathering up his things, he shook her off and walked out of the cave. Behind him, she sank to her knees.

He was cursed to a life as a creature roaming the earth. How could she let him into her body then do something so abominable? Climbing back through the trees, he vowed to forget her.

It didn't take the young warrior long to learn the benefits of turning into a wolf at will. As long as he stripped his clothes off first so he didn't destroy them, it was easy to shift.

He soon found his men hiding throughout the forest and amassed them back into an army. Though scared at first, his men learned quickly to accept the white wolf that slipped through the forest in silence picking off their enemy.

When they reached the battlefield, they found the other force starting to sag after days of continuous fighting.

Rallying around their leader, the men flanked the enemy, quickly overpowering them.

The men received a hero's welcome home that lasted five days. The large party included plenty of food, drink, and conquered women to be passed around.

But try as he might, the young warrior could not get the beautiful sorceress out of his head. He continued to wear the amulets she had enchanted, fearing that taking them off would cause him great harm.

After five days, the chieftain called his warriors forward, bestowing on them large grants of the conquered land. He divided the pillaged valuables among them.

The young warrior was now a wealthy man. Returning to his farm, he announced his brother would be in charge of the farming on his new holdings. Within six months of returning home, he made a good marriage for his brother. He threw them a wedding feast that was talked about for years after. The warrior, however, could not find any interest in the eligible young maidens.

Finally, after a year, he chose five of his best manservants and went in search of the waterfall. They spent weeks hunting for it. As he was giving up hope, one of his men stumbled into a clearing with a pool being fed by a waterfall. Reporting back to his master, the servant led the warrior to the spot.

Climbing through the trees, he stepped out at the edge of the pool. Looking around, he noticed it looked much the same as when he left.

Motioning for his men to wait for him, he entered the cave. He held out his hand near the fire ring and felt the warmth coming off of it. She was here somewhere. He remembered well how she had hidden him when the enemy was near.

He had one of his servants bring him a torch. Walking deeper inside, he began to look for the crevice they hid in. Finally finding the small slit in the rock, he saw nothing unusual. He heard the barest whisper coming from the rocks.

"Wife," he said. "I've come to take you home." He watched carefully as the rock turned into a shimmer then into the beautiful woman he now knew he couldn't live without. His eyes traveled down to the small bundle she had firmly wrapped against her breast. He pulled her into an embrace, careful to not crush the baby between them.

She kissed him. He had come back for her. She knew he would come for both her and their son if she was patient. Without another word, he helped her out of the cave and onto his steed. Sitting proudly, with their son secured against her, she looked down into the glacial eyes of the man she knew could not live without her.

For when she cast a spell turning him into one of the greatest leaders his tribe would ever know, she also turned herself into the female he would need by his side. Much like the wolf chooses his mate for life, so would each generation of men from their family line, starting with her warrior.

Also by A Samson

<u>The Sköll Ranch Shifter Series</u>

Sten

Dane

<u>The Inhuman Protector Series</u>

Intangible

Invincible

Combustible

Justifiable

Inevitable

Writing as Avery Samson

<u>The Sideswiped Series</u>

Hers to Take

Hers to Keep

Hers to Win

Hers to Tame

Hers to Crave

Hers to Forget

Hers Always

<u>The New England Romance Series</u>

Nothing Ventured

Best Laid Schemes

In For a Penny

Actions Speak Louder

<u>The Dansboro Crossing Series</u>

Overdue

Upshot

Brazen

Acknowledgments

I know I keep thanking the same people over and over in every book, but when you find a good team, you stick with them.

First, thank you to every reader, ARC reader, blogger, and influencer who chose to pick up Arne and give it a try. I hope he didn't disappoint.

Thanks also to the crew at My Brother's Editor for helping me weed through the grammar and story holes to give you the best book possible. This is going on year five with Ellie and I hope we get at least another five.

Thanks to Emma Jane Photography for capturing Arne in all his glory for the cover. And thanks to Rachel for using that photo to create the perfect cover.

Finally, as always, thanks to my family for continuing to encourage me to tell my stories. Couldn't do it without them. Love you all.

About the Author

Avery Samson grew up on a ranch outside of a small west Texas town. Since she could remember, she's had her face stuck in a book. High School graduation found her leaving ranch life for the big city.

After living all over the state of Texas, she now finds herself back on one of the family ranches near Dallas with her husband surrounded by cattle. A lot of them. They're everywhere! When not traveling or reading, she spends her time writing.

Avery would love for you to follow her. She's everywhere (just like those damn cows.)

Join my newsletter for all the latest news.
averysamsonbooks.com/newsletter

Visit my website for my current book list.
averysamsonbooks.com

Join my reader group.
https://www.facebook.com/groups/216191437248096

Like me on Facebook.
https://www.facebook.com/averysamsonauthor

Follow me on Instagram.
https://www.instagram.com/averysamson91/

Watch my videos on TikTok.
https://www.tiktok.com/@averysamson91

Check out my Pinterest page.
https://www.pinterest.com/averysamson91/